META**WARS**

FIGHT FOR THE FUTURE

JEFF NORTON

ORCHARD

To Sidonie. For believing in me

1

The race was on.

Jonah Delacroix pushed the wheels under his feet hard into the ground, propelling himself forward and breaking away from the pack. Tonight's race, under the cover of darkness and in full violation of national curfew, brought over a hundred racers from across south London to compete in a vicious roller derby. The prize was cold, hard meta-dollars. Enough cash to keep Jonah and his mum fed and sheltered for at least six months. He needed to win.

Jonah was smaller than the other racers and he would be cut down and torn up if he stayed in the pack. He charged ahead to put a safe distance between him and the twenty lead skaters he'd been keeping pace with. Jonah felt his blades eating up the road. His posture, his balance and his rhythm were perfect. The mouldering warehouses that lined this disused service road flashed by with breath-taking speed. It almost felt like flying.

Almost.

It was the closest Jonah could get in the real world. When he raced, when he felt the wind whip back his hair, he could almost believe he wasn't here at all, in the failed state of Britain that supposedly used to be Great, but back in the Metasphere, back in the virtual world that felt so much more real to him than this course, this night, this race.

'Focus,' he whispered to himself. He knew that if he thought too much, let his mind wander, he might hit a pothole and fall.

He had skated this race three times before, and twice he had come close to winning. But not close enough. Jonah had been practising each night for two months. He knew every bend, every turn, every bump and pothole on this course. He knew where every fallen lamppost and overstuffed recycling machine was that would get in his way.

He spotted the bus stop, the halfway mark, and had to force himself not to laugh at its quaintness.

He could win, this time. He had to win. He had cashed in nearly all of his meta-dollars to enter the race, but the pot was well worth it. Enough to pay for food and even rent on the upper deck for half a year, if he and his mum ate carefully. It would be their first lucky break in years.

Jonah trailed behind only four competitors, but he was keeping pace with them, doing better than he'd ever performed before. But then, as he tried to overtake one of the bigger racers, he saw something sparkling on his leather jacket. Razor wire!

The razor-clad racer swiped furiously at Jonah with

his right arm. Jonah crisscrossed his legs and pulled himself into a tuck. The deadly arm swung over his head and Jonah pushed all of his power down into his left blade to escape.

I cannot lose tonight.

He sprinted hard, out of the reach of the razor wire.

Up ahead, he spotted the tall, faded sign of a shuttered DIY warehouse that marked the final stretch. Jonah had a clear but distant memory of visiting that building with his dad. He remembered standing on a pushcart, hovering over the shiny floor as his dad pushed him down the main aisle, rows of toilets and tools whooshing by. It had felt like flying.

When Jonah reached the sign, sun-bleached and cracked, he took encouragement from its slogan: *DIY: Get To It!*

He pushed his aching legs harder and faster than ever before. One more burst of speed and he could actually win. He made a perfect lunge turn, and stalked the three leaders, gaining on them.

For the first time in a long time, Jonah felt hopeful.

Get to it!

Oblivious to the roller race that was about to speed past, two figures skulked outside the boarded-up DIY warehouse.

Sam, the smaller and younger of the two, a seventeen-year-old girl with short-cut red hair, didn't know what

'DIY' meant, but took comfort in the encouragement that the faded sign gave her. *Get To It!* She was about to. Even if *it* was illegal and very dangerous.

Wearing a fitted black jumpsuit and a charcoal backpack, Sam blended into the darkness as she kept watch over the empty stretch of road.

A few steps behind Sam, an older man worked at the warehouse door with a crowbar. An old-fashioned tool for an old-fashioned job. The man had greying hair, a straggly beard and intense eyes. He wore black coveralls like Sam's. He was called Axel, but to Sam he had another name. To her, Axel was 'Dad'.

With a splintering of wood, the door flew open. Axel motioned to Sam to follow him through it. She pulled a torch from one of her many pouches, snapped it on.

As she stepped into the dark warehouse, she felt a chill settling on her shoulders.

Great, angular shapes towered before Sam, rows and rows of them. In the light of her torch beam, she could see their dull grey surfaces. Mainframe computers. Server racks. They were old, decades old, but still working. They hummed and clicked almost smugly to themselves.

Sam hadn't imagined the drop in temperature. A cold draught played about her neck from an air-conditioning vent in the wall. Despite this, the air in the warehouse was thick with dust, and her nose itched uncontrollably.

In a far corner of the ceiling, she could see a red

pinpoint of light. She took Axel by the arm, directing his gaze towards it. He nodded. 'Motion detectors,' he muttered, 'and they've already sensed us. Nothing we didn't expect.'

'All the same,' said Sam, 'we should get to it.' She shrugged the pack from her back and fumbled with its straps.

'No need to rush, kiddo,' said Axel. 'The police will be across town, chasing after Bradbury's distraction. They'll never get bikes here before we're done.'

'You hope,' said Sam, 'but what if they didn't fall for the distraction? What if they left a patrol in this area?'

Sometimes, she felt like she was the grown-up and Axel the teenager, like she had to look after him when it should have been the other way round. Her father was all impulse and no thought, and in Sam's eyes this was a dangerous thing, especially in their line of work. She had to admit, though, that his instincts were usually good.

She produced the first of the explosives from her pack, handed them to him. They were plastique, off-white in colour, the size and shape of house bricks. Axel began to place them around the warehouse, as Sam unwound the detonator cord.

Her hands were trembling. She willed them to stop. There was nothing to be afraid of – as long as she kept her cool. Anyway, it was too late to back out now, even if she had wanted to.

Sam and Axel were Guardians. To many, that meant

they were terrorists – or 'internet insurgents' – but Sam knew the truth. She knew the Guardians were fighting for everyone's freedom. She believed in that cause, and was ready to fight for it.

But was she ready to die for it?

2

The ground shook beneath Jonah's blades, his ears were assailed by a blast of noise, and a wave of heat slammed his left side.

Jonah lost his balance. He tried to recover, but his body betrayed him. His arms and legs lashed out in an unco-ordinated flounder. His blades ran away with themselves, and sent him head over heels. Jonah landed on his back, struggling to breathe from the impact.

He looked up at the burning warehouse store, a thick plume of smoke billowing up to obscure the moon. The giant sign cracked and blistered until its words of encouragement were completely lost. A pulsating alarm pierced the night. Jonah didn't know if the explosion was an accident or the work of terrorists, but right now he didn't care.

A few other racers had been stopped in their tracks – the kid in the razor wire bled from where the debris had pushed his deadly decorations through his jacket – but the three leaders were surging ahead. Jonah clambered to his feet and pushed off again with all his strength. He couldn't give up now.

Against the orange glow of the burning building, Jonah spied two fleeing silhouettes. They ran out into the street, directly in front of him.

He crisscrossed his blades to avoid a collision, but instead thumped into a muscular racer, who shoved him back into one of the silhouettes. A girl.

Jonah reached around her body, almost hugging her to keep himself upright. He noticed her short red hair and her green eyes, which widened with alarm. She was beautiful, he thought – but she was also in his way.

The second silhouette – a man in black coveralls – appeared and pulled the girl away. They dashed across the street and disappeared into darkness.

Jonah turned his attention back to the race, but it was too late. He could see the first of the other racers now, skating past the row of recycling machines that marked the finishing line. It was over. Jonah had lost. Again.

He skated up to the organisers – a cabal of four rough-looking teenagers, not much older than him – to protest. 'Aren't you going to call a rerun?'

But they shook their heads in dismissal. The winner, a hulking kid, who, judging by his sleek six-wheel skates, didn't need the money, laughed at Jonah as he swiped his cash-card through the hand-held machine. It instantly transferred thousands of meta-dollars to his account.

'But the explosion,' he cried. 'That wasn't fair! I was… I could have won! If you knew how much I needed…'

His voice tailed off. No one was listening. Jonah's

14

cheeks burnt fiercely with the injustice of it all, but there was nothing he could do.

The racers were already dispersing, melting into the nocturnal shadows, and an older kid rolled up behind Jonah and suggested he do the same. 'Probably another terrorist attack,' said the kid, 'so you know there are going to be police bikes and fire-bots here any minute. You should get home before they see you.'

He was right, of course. The last thing Jonah needed right now, on top of everything else, was to be caught breaking curfew.

Sam sprinted away from the frantic boy on wheels. She looked back just once to see if she was being followed, but the boy had gone. *What if he could describe me to the police? she thought.*

The explosion had been bigger than she had expected. They had used too much plastique. Sam had said as much, but Axel had insisted it was better too much than too little. The important thing was that the servers were completely destroyed.

In the mouth of an adjacent alleyway, they checked themselves for injuries. In the light of the flickering fire, Sam checked herself over, then her father, for cuts and scrapes. They were both unscathed – which was something of a miracle. Axel didn't seem to care that they could have been hurt badly. More likely, he hadn't even thought about it.

Sam tugged at his sleeve, anxiously. 'The police will be on their way,' she reminded him, 'along with everybody else.'

Axel accepted the caution, and they raced for their bikes.

They had pedalled a good, safe ten blocks away before they heard the first sirens approaching.

'We could have been killed tonight,' said Sam, leading her father down a series of back streets that she had mapped out in advance. 'Was it worth the risk?'

'We hit the Millennials where it hurts,' said Axel. 'In the wallet. Those servers held the details of hundreds of thousands of their e-commerce operations.'

'Even so,' said Sam, 'it's just a drop in the ocean!'

'You wait, kiddo,' said Axel. 'You wait and see. We've just cost the Millennials a few million meta-dollars, and that's not even the important thing. The important thing is that the Metasphere will be buzzing with news of this tomorrow. We've made a statement tonight, struck a blow. For the Guardians. For freedom.'

'I guess so,' said Sam, although she wasn't convinced. She knew that every time the Guardians destroyed Millennial property they also eroded goodwill and polarised public opinion. She often wondered, silently, if there was a better way to achieve their goals.

'Don't worry, kiddo,' said Axel, sensing her anxiety, 'we leave England the day after tomorrow. Once we find those Four Corners, we'll swing this whole war our way.'

Jonah's mood sank even further as he rounded the last corner and saw the five hundred red buses huddled tightly together on what used to be called Clapham Common, but what Jonah now called home.

He had never imagined, growing up, that he would end up living somewhere like this. And now, it seemed that even this place – even a cramped bus-flat – might be more than he and his mum could afford.

The last few solar-powered lights were flickering, illuminating the bus-burb ahead of him. The wire mesh gate to the outside world hung open as it so often did, the padlock missing, no one bothering to replace it. His mum was always complaining about it. She said, one day, a burglar would march right through that gate, break into their bus and take everything they had. Jonah didn't agree. Every Londoner knew that bus-burb residents had nothing worth stealing.

Jonah's dad had told him once that, when he was a boy, this whole area had been grass and trees. He had come here to play football at the weekends. Jonah never quite knew if his father was kidding or not.

Of course, to hear Dad talk, everything had been different back then. Back before the world's population hit the big ten. Back when petrol had been plentiful, water flowed freely, and global warming was just a disputed theory and not a daily reality. Back when schools and medical care had been available to everyone, not just to the privileged few.

As Jonah threaded his way through the labyrinth of red metal, avoiding pools of stagnant rainwater and broken glass, he thought to himself that his father's childhood Britain sounded like it was out of a fairy tale. He still lost his way sometimes among the long-shuttered buses, but he could always find his bus by its number, 137, and by the name displayed in white lettering on its front: *Marble Arch*.

Dad was gone now. It was since he had died – since he had been killed three years ago – that everything had gone wrong for Jonah's family. His mum had been unable to keep up the rental payments on their little flat in Brockley so she took Jonah to live in the Battersea Power Shelter for months before she found them an upper-deck flat in the Boris Bus.

Jonah's bus was dark, both the upper and lower decks. He was relieved that his mum was asleep, and that his downstairs neighbours, Mr and Mrs Collins, who ran a meta-pub out of their flat, were too. He slipped off his blades, pried open the rear door to the bus and crept silently up the curved stairs. He was looking forward to getting a few hours of sleep before logging into school.

He quietly hid his skates under a dirty pile of laundry that his mum wouldn't dare rummage through and reached for his hammock.

And that's when he knew he'd been caught.

'Jonah Benedict Delacroix,' his mother's voice rang.

When she used his full name, Jonah knew he was in for it.

3

Over five thousand miles away from Jonah's cramped bus-flat, a rich man awoke in an equally cramped jail cell.

Matthew Granger could hear gunfire and explosions outside – the sounds, he thought with satisfaction, of a government falling. He checked his watch again. If he had timed this right, his supporters would be reaching him within the next ten minutes. He would be out of this prison in twenty, well away from California before an hour had passed.

Granger heard footsteps outside, running. The inspection hatch in his cell door was yanked open and a youthful pair of blue eyes peered in, brightening at the sight of him.

'You may want to stand back, sir,' said the youth. Granger did so, flattening himself against the white concrete wall. A small explosion blew the door off its hinges, and his rescuers – three of them, all young, all clad in combat fatigues – were revealed in the doorway. Granger's loyal followers, his Millennials. He righted himself on the poor excuse for a bed and addressed them as if from a throne.

'You have a plane waiting?' he said. It was an

assumption, not a question.

'Yes, sir.'

'And my legs?'

The young Millennials wheeled in a large aluminium case and opened it to reveal Granger's two cyber-kinetic walking legs. The prison had barred him from wearing them in case they were weaponised – which, of course, they were.

'And you remembered to put a 2012 vintage *cuvée de prestige* on ice?' Granger smiled – the charming, good-humoured smile that he had perfected to open doors for him ever since the accident. He had not yet turned forty, but he was aware he looked much younger with his tussled, dirty-blond hair and cherub-like complexion. 'Good champagne has been so hard to come by in this place.'

'It's an honour to meet you, Mr Granger.'

'I'm sure. And I can rely upon your continued support?' The three Millennials talked over each other in their haste to assure him that indeed he could. 'You see, my friends,' said Granger, 'today marks a bright day for the future of the Metasphere. It's languished in the hands of incompetents for too long. It is time to take back the world I created.'

'Some…some people have said,' the girl spoke up hesitantly, 'that, once you were freed, you would take over the Four…the Four Corners.'

Granger snapped his artificial legs onto his stumps

and smiled again. 'Yes,' he declared. 'And no one will stop me.'

Jonah squinted when the harsh, fluorescent light flickered on. His mum, Miriam, had turned it on from where she perched at the base of her bed at the front of the bus. She stared at Jonah with her sad eyes and, for a long minute, she said nothing more than his name.

Jonah hated her silence, which was more and more the norm – she would often sit across from him at their breakfast table as they shared a Pro-Meal pouch, and gaze into the middle distance. But not right now.

Tonight, Jonah's mum stared directly at Jonah with an expression he could guess was a mix of anger and disappointment.

'I thought I could win,' he explained, hoping it would make a difference.

'It's not safe out there, Jonah,' she finally said. 'I heard an explosion, and you weren't in your hammock.' She wiped the tears away on the sleeve of her dressing gown. 'I just can't lose you too.'

Jonah didn't know what to say. He felt himself seize up with his mother's sadness. 'Not to mention getting caught out after curfew!' she said in a raised whisper. 'Perhaps if I took away your Metasphere privileges...'

'It's not a privilege, it's a right!' Jonah shot back, harsher than he intended. His mum had threatened to keep him off-line before, but even though she was a metaphobe now, and never went online, Jonah's whole world was on the internet: his school, their digital gift shop, and his only other 'living' relative, his grandmother. She would never follow through on her threat, he guessed.

'I'm sorry,' Jonah said. 'I just really thought I would win, and then we'd have enough money…'

'I make money at the bank,' his mum said defensively.

'I know, I know, Mum, but you could make so much more if you actually went into the Metasphere. Real world jobs are for…' Jonah caught himself before he finished his thought. But Miriam knew what he was thinking even if he didn't say it aloud. She pushed back her long, black hair and exhaled slowly, shaking her head.

'Losers?' she asked. 'That's what you think of me, isn't it?'

'Of course not,' Jonah pleaded. 'It's just…it's just, I think you'd be much, well, happier if you went online.'

'A virtual world is not an escape from the real one.'

At last, Jonah agreed on something with his mum. To him, the virtual world wasn't an escape. It was a replacement. It was brighter and better in every way, and Jonah wished that he didn't have to live in the real world at all.

'You'll need to list the shop,' she said definitively. 'You know we need the money.'

'I can get us money,' Jonah pleaded. 'I can race again and—'

'No! We're not having this discussion. You have to sell the shop. There's just no other way.'

Jonah had known it was coming, and had hoped his win in the race would avoid or at least postpone this eventuality. But now, his mother had decided. It was time to sell the digital gift shop that she and Jonah's dad, Jason, had created when they first got married. It was the only thing left in the Metasphere that reminded Jonah of his father, and he was going to lose it.

4

Morning came too quickly. Jonah's mum had to wake him twice before he finally tilted himself out of his hammock, bleary-eyed.

Breakfast was the usual: strawberry Pro-Meal, a protein paste that came in a plastic pouch. Exhausted from the night before, Jonah slumped at the dining table, a thin sliver of wood that protruded from the wall in front of two plastic seats. He slurped the Pro-Meal directly from the packet. It was gritty and had probably never seen a strawberry, but real food had long been out of their budget.

Mum stood a hand-held monitor by Jonah's elbow and she tapped the co-ordinates of her favourite news channel. On the screen, an animated flamingo and an unfamiliar rhinoceros were delivering the headlines of the day. The butterfly, Jonah thought to himself, must have the day off.

'We can confirm that the American government has defaulted and collapsed,' explained the flamingo in a calm, female voice.

'And with other western governments on the brink of bankruptcy,' said the rhino in an agitated, gruff voice, 'the virtual world, once considered the ultimate safe harbour from the volatility of the real world, is poised to become a battleground between the Guardians and the Millennials.'

The Guardians and the Millennials!

Lately, everyone was talking about those two groups, about which of them was right. As if there could be any choice. Jonah didn't know how anyone could support the terrorist Guardians. Not after what they had done to his family.

'I thought they might say something about the explosion last night,' said Mum.

'It must've been those null-faced Guardians,' Jonah argued. 'Someone needs to stop them.'

Jonah's mum swiped off the monitor and put her coat on. 'I've got to get to work, and you've got to get to school. And don't forget to list the shop at auction afterwards. No excuses!'

'Can't we wait a few more months?'

'Wait for what? Until we starve?'

'But Dad would've wanted us to…'

'Dad's gone,' she said, cutting him off. 'And he's not coming back. We have to move on. You know that, Jonah.'

Mum kissed him on the forehead and disappeared down the spiral staircase. Jonah heard her tell Mrs Collins that he'd be putting the shop up for auction after school.

Jonah squeezed the Pro-Meal pouch, slurping the last remnants of strawberry-flavoured mush, and tossed it into the recycling container. Heavy footed, he descended the bus stairs and was greeted on the lower deck by Mrs Collins. She glanced at her watch and shook her head in friendly admonishment.

Jonah was late for school.

Again.

In the daytime, Mr and Mrs Collins ran their flat – the lower deck of Jonah's bus – as a meta-pub. They had left most of the old vinyl-covered seats in place, so their plugged-in patrons sat in rows, two by two.

Jonah yawned as he slipped into his usual seat near the front and felt for the Ethernet wire by its side. 'That explosion keep you up too?' asked Mr Collins. 'I bet it was them Guardians. Freedom fighters, my bottom! Terrorists, more like!'

He continued to mutter to himself about the state of the world as he handed Jonah a sterile Direct Internet adaptor packet. Jonah tore open the foil wrapper with his teeth. He snapped the nozzle-like adaptor onto the end of the Ethernet wire. Then he reached around to his lower back, pulled up his T-shirt and felt for the small plastic ring that guarded the opening to his spine.

To Jonah, this was nothing unusual. Like most people his age, he had had the Direct Interface or DI socket fitted as a baby. It was a part of him.

Jonah Delacroix had never known a world without the Metasphere.

England, like most countries, had all but run out of oil. Carbon rationing made it difficult, almost impossible, to go anywhere. And who wanted to see more of the real world, anyway? The real world was hot, crowded and violent. But inside, in the Metasphere, everything was different.

In the Metasphere, Jonah could fly. He could go where he liked – outside of school hours, that was.

'I'll be a bit late today. I've got to auction the shop after school,' he said, partly complaining and partly explaining.

'I know, dear. Your mum told me. Shame.' Mrs Collins tapped in CHANG ACADEMY into the datapad tethered to Jonah's monitor and held up the screen, showing Jonah's Point of Origin co-ordinates for his approval. 'We'd buy that place from you if we had the meta-dollars, but we don't. So that's that.'

Jonah carefully guided the nozzle into the plastic ring. He had done this a thousand times before, but the cold adaptor still gave him a shiver every time he twisted it in.

Click. The first ridge snapped into place. Jonah pushed it further inside until it made a connection with his spinal fluid.

Click. The adaptor would now transmit data through his central nervous system, directly interfacing with his brain.

'You're all set,' said Mrs Collins. 'Now make sure you

learn something in there.'

She tapped the screen of Jonah's datapad to confirm his entry into the Metasphere. With one tap of a finger, a familiar wave of nausea swept away the real world and plunged him into a dark vertigo.

Each of Jonah's five senses slipped away as his mind was pulled deeper into the computer network. It would take his brain a moment to adjust to its new reality, a virtual reality. He closed his blind eyes, and was dimly aware of his real-world body slumping in his seat. Jonah wouldn't need it where he was going.

5

Jonah's senses came back to him, starting with his vision. A bright, three-dimensional digital landscape unfolded around him – around his digital self.

He was standing in ivy-covered grounds before the stately facade of one of the best, and most expensive, public school franchises in the online world: the Chang Academy for Gifted Youths.

Jonah was just in time. The main doors were already closing. He took to the sky, leaving behind him a hovering, giant gold ring, his exit halo, his own personal portal between worlds. He felt the cool, sweet air of the Metasphere in his face and a familiar thrill in his stomach. In here, he felt at home.

Jonah guided his flight precisely, in control over every muscle in his virtual body. He swooped through the school doors, through the scanner that logged his arrival.

'*Jonah Benedict Delacroix,*' the automated scanner announced in a tinny voice as the doors clicked shut behind him. A forbidding padlock icon appeared over them, to lock the students in and keep the freeloaders out.

Jonah had attended a real-world school once, but it had been closed down and the next nearest had been a four-mile walk away. He had hated it there, anyway. He had been on the losing end of one too many schoolyard fights. His dad had hunted down a Chang scholarship for him. He could never have afforded to have come to a place like this, otherwise.

He came to a graceful landing in the entrance hall – flying in the corridors was against school rules. A red dialogue balloon popped up by Jonah's side, to notify him that his presence had been marked in the school register along with a demerit for his late arrival. He dismissed it with a flick of his fingers and hurried to his classroom, making sure that his feet touched the floor with every step.

He passed a silver centaur, which looked at him with disapproval. 'Late again, Mr Delacroix?' it said in a fluting, female voice.

'Yes, miss,' said Jonah. 'Sorry, miss.'

The rest of Jonah's class were already at their desks. He apologised to his teacher, a golden Chinese phoenix called Mr Peng, as he hurried to his usual seat at the back.

'Glad you could make it, humatar,' clucked Harry, whose desk was next to Jonah's. He had the shape of a fidgety rooster.

Jonah was, in fact, surrounded by all manner of creatures: cats and dogs, a panther, a yellow cow, even a seven-foot-tall robot. In the Metasphere, everyone

31

was represented by a unique avatar, some more bizarre than others.

Jonah's avatar, however, was human-form – a 'humatar' – a digital doppelgänger of his real-world body. It had the same freckled cheeks, the same tuft of dark hair that he could never quite get to lie down. It was a little taller than Jonah's real body – which was short for his age – and yet still shorter than the majority of the beasts around him. He was still waiting, impatiently, for a major growth spurt.

Jonah's was the only humatar in the school, much to his embarrassment. He hated the fact that he looked so ordinary. Not that there was anything he could have done about it. No one could control what their avatar looked like. Each one was born in a deep recess of its owner's subconscious mind.

He flexed his wrist, and an icon that only Jonah could see – a small iron safe – appeared before him. This was Jonah's inventory space, a private storage locker for his files, photos and apps. Jonah reached in and plucked out his virtual datapad. It downloaded the notes from the lesson so far.

The class had been discussing the only topic on everyone's minds: the fall of the United States government.

'My dad says it's a good thing the governments are collapsing,' said a panther from the far side of the classroom. His name was Mike Sawyer, and he was the only other student in the class from England. 'He says the sooner we get rid of ours too, the better.'

'They just want to poke their noses into our lives,' agreed a giant ladybird called Angela, 'and take our meta-dollars in taxes.'

'The whole Metasphere runs slower since the governments took over,' argued Mike.

Mr Peng raised a wing for silence. 'A lot of people do feel that way,' he acknowledged. 'They believe the real and the virtual worlds should remain entirely separate. All the same, events in one world can and do affect the other.'

Jonah scowled. Didn't he come here to escape the real world?

'So, if the Metasphere is no longer to be run by the real-world governments,' said Mr Peng, 'then who should control it?'

'It should go back to Matthew Granger and the Millennials,' asserted Mike. A few voices murmured their agreement to this, while others jeered in opposition.

'Why should any one person control it?' Kylie Ellis spoke up. Her avatar was a floating purple square, perfectly flat, which pulsed in time with her words. No one quite knew what that was about. 'The Metasphere belongs to its users,' she argued, sounding like a Guardian. 'It belongs to all of us!'

The class erupted into a heated debate, which Jonah tried to tune out:

'You can't just let everyone do what they like. There'd be chaos!'

'We can look after ourselves. We don't need anyone to do it for us.'

'But what about things like avatar fraud? What would you do about—?'

Everyone was shouting over each other, to get their opinions across. It was one of the things Jonah hated about politics: nobody ever listened, everybody just spoke.

'The Guardians say they'll set up communities to self-regulate—'

'—who'd regulate them?'

'—give anyone that kind of power, and the next thing you know they'll be keeping secrets from us, deciding what we can and can't know.'

'Matthew Granger wouldn't do that,' said Mike. 'He wouldn't censor content like the governments do. He—'

'—was sent to prison for tax evasion, wasn't he? He's no better than—'

Jonah couldn't bear to listen to any more of it.

The classroom fell silent as he leapt to his feet, his fists clenched, his shoulders trembling. 'If it wasn't for Matthew Granger,' he said in a quiet, angry voice, 'there wouldn't even be a Metasphere.'

'You're just saying that because your dad used to work for him,' said Davey Biggs, a hippopotamus, who sat behind Jonah.

'Am not,' protested Jonah. 'I'm saying it because it happens to be true. Mr Granger created the Metasphere, and he was doing a perfectly good job of running it till it was stolen from him.'

'Do you know what I heard?' boasted Mike. 'I heard that Matthew Granger busted out of his jail last night. He's coming back!'

Kylie's square icon gave a shudder that Jonah took to be a headshake. 'He can't just plug back in and expect to take over. The Guardians won't allow it.'

'Who cares what the Guardians think?' spat Jonah. 'They're terrorists!'

'They're fighting for us all,' insisted Kylie.

'They're just thugs and killers!' Jonah countered.

'The Metasphere shouldn't be controlled by a dictator,' shouted Kylie, 'and it won't be. I believe the Guardians will make it free, whatever it takes.'

'Including murder? Including bombing innocent people?' Jonah glared at his classmates, each in turn, challenging them to disagree with him. Most stared down at their desks in discomfort, and Kylie Ellis seemed to turn a slightly redder shade of purple.

'Yeah, my dad was Matthew Granger's pilot,' said Jonah. Tears were welling up inside him, remembering that day, three years ago, the airport bombings, the day his father didn't come home. 'And you all know what happened to him.' In one day, thirty-seven airports were destroyed, but London's Heathrow, where Jonah's father had been taxiing Matthew Granger's private jet, was the biggest target. 'He was murdered by the Guardians!'

Mr Peng stepped in to calm things down. 'Jonah, I'm sure no one meant to upset you,' he stammered. 'Let's move on to today's lesson. Please.'

Jonah couldn't concentrate on his teacher's lecture. He felt as if the classroom walls were closing in around him, threatening to crush him.

'Harry,' he whispered, 'do you still have that deconstruction virus?'

'Yeah,' said Harry the rooster, 'but I'm not using it again. I'll be kicked out for sure.'

'Then give it to me? Please?'

Harry had earned his Chang scholarship through his programming genius. He only seemed to use this talent, however, for the playing of elaborate practical jokes. Everyone still talked about the time he had deleted the staffroom door.

Harry opened his own inventory space, invisible to everyone else, and pulled out an app in the shape of a biscuit and dropped it into Jonah's hand. Jonah popped the cookie into his mouth, transferring the data it contained from Harry's computer terminal – wherever in the real world that was – to his own. Then he rose from his seat, and floated out of the classroom. Mr Peng called after him, concerned, but Jonah ignored him.

He flew down the school hallways, ignoring the rule,

until he was back at the padlocked entrance doors. He placed his hands against them and willed Harry's virus code to spread into them. The millions of pixels that held the doors together separated, and the tiny squares imploded at once with a *pop*. With the doors completely depixelated, Jonah pushed himself through the opening and emerged into the school grounds. He threw out his arms as far as they would extend, and lifted off.

The Chang Academy fell away beneath his feet. He could feel his anger, his frustration, falling away from him too, the way it always did when he flew like this.

Flying was Jonah's favourite thing in the Metasphere. He imagined that his dad must have loved it too, when he had flown his aeroplanes in the real world.

Up here, Jonah was free from the shame of his human-form avatar. Free from the responsibility he felt, being the only member of his family left online. And free from a real world where his father never came home any more.

For a few precious moments, Jonah soared above it all.

6

The Chang Academy was sited on its own private island, a little way out to sea.

Jonah made for the mainland. He passed over a ring of islands with sandy beaches, swaying coconut trees, and Tikitiki cocktail bars. He looked down to see oblivious avatars sunning themselves on their virtual holidays. As he reached the mainland, he swooped over a haunted forest, where a massive, multiplayer role-play game was in full swing. He spotted platoons of avatars chasing after transparent ghosts with rifles and electric nets. The game, Ghost Smackdown 3, was popular with some of Jonah's classmates, but when Jonah played a MMORPG, he preferred hunting 'Brain Sucking Zombies'.

As he gained height, the virtual world sprawled out beneath Jonah like a patchwork quilt. Anyone could buy a plot of virtual land in the Metasphere, and build whatever they wanted on it. These days, big developers were snapping up huge adjacent plots to create giant themed zones – but still, the bulk of the landscape was a hodgepodge of clashing designs and functions.

Jonah banked left above the bright, primary colours of Blockhead Headlock, a popular game zone that Jonah had long grown out of. The usual barrage of advertising pop-ups came screeching and hectoring after him, but he outpaced them easily.

The sky around him thronged with avatars of all shapes and sizes: animals, humatars and geometrical shapes. Most numerous were the birds and the winged insects, and Jonah thought he spotted a grinning helicopter. You didn't need to have wings or rotors to fly in the Metasphere, but those that did appeared to enjoy flying the most.

Jonah touched down in Venus Park: a manicured, Japanese-style cherry blossom paradise, where avatars hovered along the curving pathways or flew between the trees, two by two.

The park was a place for lovers. Separated by great distances in the real world, they could stroll together here, under blossom leaves and over the ornate bridges of the goldfish ponds. Jonah spotted a multi-coloured giraffe walking with a floating rhombus, and a woolly mammoth holding a bouquet of virtual flowers in its trunk, trying to impress a giggling bumblebee that hovered just out of reach.

He didn't understand why people chose to call that other world – that dull, grey place – the 'real' one. It didn't feel half as real or as vibrant as this world did to him. Venus Park reminded Jonah of better times. On one of the streets that faced the park was the Delacroix family gift shop. He had spent many happy weekends and school holidays working there with his mum and dad, selling digital trinkets to the park's long-distance couples.

As Jonah looked around, he saw the bumblebee kiss the mammoth and then they parted, diving through their respective exit halos and returning to their real-world lives.

Jonah often wondered who was behind those avatars. He tried to imagine their real-world bodies, like his body, slumped in meta-trances somewhere as their minds flew free. To him, it was unfair that other avatars disguised their users. Jonah's dad, whose own avatar had been a sleek red dragon, had always said he should be proud that his virtual and real selves were so close to one another. It meant he had nothing to hide.

He saw a group of protestors, marching back and forth in front of the park gates with an angry, mangy hyena at their head.

'Keep the Millennials off our freedoms!' barked the hyena. The protesting avatars cheered and applauded his words. It made Jonah so angry that some people could be so ignorant.

With a sigh, he headed for his family's shop. He didn't want to sell it. But his mother was right; he didn't want to starve to death either.

The windows of the shop were boarded up, pasted over

with digital leaflets from auctioneers and estate agents offering to sell the land. Jonah ripped down one flyer, promising 'fast sale, low fees', and the locked door opened for him with one scan of his avatar.

The shelves inside were almost empty, with just a handful of heart-shaped cakes, balloons and teddy bears left upon them. The gift shop had been closed for almost two years now. Mum had blamed governmental red tape, but Jonah knew this was only part of the story. The business had been failing, its brand of virtual gifts and apps considered old-fashioned now. Most days, there had been no more than one or two customers. It had become too much for Jonah's mum. She had found it too painful to be here, alone.

She had torn out her DI socket and joined the metaphobes and the luddites stuck in the real world. Jonah couldn't bear the fact that she had done that to herself, cut herself off from the Metasphere, the only reality that mattered, just when he had needed her most. He had tried to respect her decision, but he hadn't ever understood it.

Jonah spent the rest of the morning cleaning out the shop. He wanted it to be sale-ready for auction to fetch the highest bids. He collected the unsold teddy bears and trinkets, stuffed them into a box and coded them for recycling credits.

He tapped the leaflet, from which sprang a pop-up message asking him to confirm his listing. He tapped

YES and flicked the dialogue box away with a flick of his hand. And waited.

The leaflet flickered and scanned the property, generating a 3D blueprint of the shop that hovered above the leaflet. Another pop-up appeared, quoting Jonah an estimated sale price of two hundred and seven meta-dollars, *Barely worth it*, he thought. Before he had a chance to agree to the listing, another box appeared, flashing in red: WARNING – UNKNOWN APPLICATION DISCOVERED. The small print read:

An Unknown Application has been discovered in the property. This may be a virus. Please delete this application before proceeding to auction.

Jonah looked around the empty shop and couldn't see any apps, but he didn't want to look too hard. The unknown app gave him an excuse not to sell.

Then he noticed something strange about the 3D model. It showed a level below which Jonah was standing. The shop had a secret cellar.

Jonah pulled the empty display cabinets to the walls and stared hard at every centimetre of the virtual wooden floor, before shoving over each display cabinet to see what lay beneath. And there it was, below a cabinet in the centre of the shop – a trapdoor in the floor, with a metal ring for a handle.

Jonah had grown up in this shop. He thought he had

explored it thoroughly, poked his nose into every corner, every crevice. So how could there be something here he hadn't seen before?

Jonah's heart beat faster as he took the handle in his hand, pulled it, lifted the door open. He was greeted by a strong musty smell and, looking down, he could make out two brick walls, meeting at a corner. The cellar was as long and as wide as the shop itself.

Did Mum and Dad know about this?

It was dark down there, and Jonah wished he had a torch. There could have been anything hiding in that darkness. Some valuable treasure, he hoped – something left behind by the previous owners that could solve all the Delacroixes' problems. He shook his head; that was just stupid wishful thinking. All the same...

There was no ladder; Jonah dropped himself into the secret cellar. He stood there for a long moment, blinking, waiting for his eyes to adjust to the darkness. He noticed something. Something that caused his stomach to do a somersault.

He wasn't alone. There was somebody – or something – in the cellar with him.

A figure, crouching in the corner. One he had never thought he would see again.

It was a huge, red dragon. Its wings were folded behind its back. Its fierce yellow eyes were glaring right at Jonah. He took two steps back, away from the creature, then he stopped himself. And approached it instead.

He knew this avatar, knew it almost as well as he knew his own, but... But that was impossible. Wasn't it?

'*Dad?*'

7

The dragon gave no reply. Jonah took another step towards it, looked closer. His chest had tightened until he could hardly speak, hardly breathe, but he had to know.

'Dad... Is that you?'

'Jonah...' the dragon said in his father's low voice. Jonah had almost forgotten how soothing it was. Had his father been hiding down here all this time?

'Dad, why have you...' Jonah started to ask, relieved, happy and angry all at the same time at the discovery that his father had been in hiding. But when the dragon continued to speak over him, Jonah's heart sank with the realisation that this was just a copy of his dad's avatar reciting a recorded message.

'...If you have found this avatar, then I am gone. And I'm so sorry for that. I don't have time to explain now, but there are parts of my life that I didn't share with you. For your protection, Jonah. But if you're seeing this recording now, then I may not be able to protect you any more. I am sorry that I won't be there to see you grow up. You have so much potential, even if you don't see it in yourself just yet. But other people will spot it and you will be a guardian of hope in these confused worlds.'

Jonah's dad had never spoken to him like that when

45

he was alive, and Jonah caught himself reaching out and touching the avatar, as if by holding him it would make him come back.

'But, Jonah, there is something you must do for me, and for a higher cause. I need you to filter my avatar onto yours. Find my friend Axel; he'll know what to do next. I wish I could tell you more, but the less you know, the safer you and Miriam will be. Please do this for me, Jonah. I love you, my boy.'

The program stopped and the dragon held out both of its talons for Jonah to reciprocate. He knew that grabbling them would authorise the filtering process, illegally taking his father's avatar as his own.

It was the most dangerous decision of Jonah's life.

Matthew Granger had checked into the grandest, most expensive suite of a top Paris hotel. Money was no object to him. His now-defunct government may have thought they had seized his fortune, but they hadn't found a tenth of his online accounts.

The *directeur d'hôtel* had recognised him, of course, but for a price, he would keep the identity of his infamous guest to himself.

Granger's Millennials had kitted out the adjoining suite with the most advanced computers on the market. *His* computers. He had been out of circulation for years, but still his competitors hadn't caught up with him.

He had brought his best programmers here too,

those who had remained loyal to him during his imprisonment, none of them older than twenty-five. They were tapping away at their datapads, looking in on the Metasphere from the outside, sifting through terabytes of information.

It felt good to be out of prison, but Granger didn't feel free, not yet. He knew he wouldn't feel free until he was back where he belonged, back in control.

At the age of six, Matthew Granger had lost his whole world. A Marin County car crash had claimed the lives of both his parents. He had lain in the twisted wreckage of their people carrier for over four hours, expecting to die himself.

The doctors had amputated his legs at the quads. They had told him he was lucky to be alive. Granger hadn't felt lucky.

The uncle who had taken him in had been awkward with children, but brilliant with computers. Under his care, Granger had learned how to build a *new* world. A world to which he could escape. A world in which he could walk, and more.

A world in which he could fly.

His invention of Web 4.0 had made him rich: a billionaire by age twenty-six. He had had enough money, at last, to commission NASA to construct one of his earliest designs: his cyber-kinetic walking system. Matthew Granger had spent twenty years of his life confined to a wheeled prison. No longer.

How frustrating for him, then, to have swapped one type of prison for another.

Officially, the charge had been tax evasion. Granger knew the truth, however. The major governments of the world had been in trouble for some time. With more and more business being done online, they were struggling to collect enough tax income to sustain themselves. Granger, on the other hand, had been doing very nicely, thank you, from his small cut of every transaction conducted inside the Metasphere that he had built.

The governments had wanted that money. Granger had refused to give it to them, any of it. In a panic, they had invoked an obscure United Nations resolution, twisting its wording to suit their ends. They had effectively nationalised the Metasphere, taken over its running between them, while Granger had been arrested on their trumped-up charges and locked up safely out of their way.

He was caught by surprise, sold out by a traitor on the inside he had yet to discover. The feds had pounced on him and perp-walked him in front of all the cameras they could pack in front of the courtroom. He was caught by surprise, but not unprepared. Matthew Granger always had a contingency plan.

'It's confirmed, sir,' reported one of Granger's programmers, a petite young woman whose name he had never bothered to learn. 'It *is* him, the name from the watch list.'

Granger leaned over her shoulder, checked the data on her screen. 'So,' he breathed, 'he is alive, after all.'

'He's been doing his best to stay hidden,' said the programmer. 'His avatar hasn't been scanned anywhere for three years, two months and—'

'How did you find him?'

'His avatar code sequence was flagged in an error report. I don't understand, sir. Why would he resurface now, after all this time?'

'He must have heard I was free,' said Granger, who had always had faith in his own importance. 'It must have panicked him, made him careless. This could be a problem. He worked as my pilot for almost a decade. He flew me to every one of the Four Corners. He's the only man alive – apart from me – who can find them.'

'You think he might be a threat, sir?'

'I've always had my suspicions. The last time I saw him, he was running into a burning building. They never found his body. Why hide from me? Why, unless he has betrayed me? Why, unless he was a sleeper Guardian agent all along?'

'What should we do, sir?' asked the programmer.

'Trace the source of that error report,' instructed Granger. 'Find Jason Delacroix – in the real world, I mean – and kill him!'

8

Jonah felt a sickening surge in his head.

Images were flashing behind his eyelids, too fast for him to make out what any of them might be. He had a giddy sensation of falling, and for an instant he feared he might fall out of the Metasphere altogether.

He tried to let go, but his hands clenched uncontrollably around the talons. The dragon depixelated from head to tail and a rush of red cascaded towards him. Each new pixel sliced into Jonah like a shard of glass.

The pain subsided and Jonah came to his senses in the secret cellar of the gift shop, on his knees, trembling and flushed, fighting down a tidal wave of nausea. In the body of the red dragon. His father's body.

He could feel the dragon's wings behind him, like an extra pair of arms. He flexed his shoulders, unfolded the wings, spread them out until their tips touched the cellar walls. He put his hands – his claws, he supposed he should call them now – to his face, felt around the shape of his snout and gingerly touched his sharp teeth.

He still felt sick, a little dizzy, and somehow the world seemed smaller to him – although of course Jonah knew it was he who had grown bigger.

Jonah couldn't see his own avatar, his humatar, in front of him.

With a sense of trepidation, Jonah shuffled around to look behind him. He felt *too* big now, unable to turn his great, trunk-like neck, hardly able to move at all in this too-small space. His avatar wasn't there. It had gone, disappeared.

Jonah began to panic.

How could he have been so stupid? Everyone knew the penalty for filtering, for taking another avatar as your own. Exile. Jonah's DNA would be placed on a block list, forever denied access to the Metasphere. He would be forced to live out his life in the real world, never see his friends again because he didn't know where to find them or even what they looked like.

It would be like dying. No, it would be worse than that. *At least if I were dying*, he thought, *I could be Uploaded*.

Jonah had to get out of there – out of the Metasphere – before anyone found out what he had done. He flew up out of the cellar, through the gift shop door, and back towards his Point of Origin. As he flew, his new wings gave him power and lift that he'd never experienced in humatar form. He soared towards his school, terrified that someone he knew – or worse, who had known his father – would see him.

His golden exit halo hovered in the Chang Academy grounds, where he had left it. It was only one of many, but it glowed at Jonah's approach as if beckoning him towards it.

It still recognises me, he thought with relief. The halo was his only way out of the Metasphere, the only way to reconnect his conscious mind with his unconscious body. Without it, Jonah's avatar would be trapped in the Metasphcre forever, while his physical body slowly wasted away in the real world.

He dived through the ring of light.

Jonah was back on the bus, in the meta-pub. He was trapped once more in his awkward, real-world body – and, for once, he was thankful for this.

He was a little alarmed to find Mr Collins crouched beside him, frowning over a datapad. 'Was everything all right for you in there, son?' he asked.

Jonah didn't dare answer him. He just nodded dumbly.

'I think we must have a software glitch,' Mr Collins explained. 'For a while there, the system was showing two avatars registered to this terminal, which of course ain't possible. I've reported the error, but I'm gonna have to run some scans. Can't afford a virus on the loose.'

Mrs Collins click-clacked up to them in her high heels, concerned. She asked Jonah why he wasn't in school, and he told her he wasn't feeling well. It wasn't even a lie he realised as he said it. He had expected that, back here, his nausea might have subsided. No such luck.

Mrs Collins fussed over him. 'Maybe you should ring your mother,' she prodded.

'There's no need,' he said quickly, 'honestly. I just need to go upstairs and lie down for a bit. I'll be fine.'

'Sir, we've found him!' cried the programmer.

'Where?' asked Granger.

'London, sir.' On the programmer's screen, an aerial image was zooming in on an area once known as Clapham Common, to a wire-fenced compound filled with red London buses. To one bus in particular.

'Do we have agents near there?' asked Granger.

The programmer nodded, her fingers a blur over her datapad. 'Yes, sir. Sending them in now, sir. Do we have a description of Mr Delacroix to give them?'

'He could have changed his appearance by now,' said Granger. 'We can't afford to take any chances. I want everyone aboard that bus dead!'

As soon as Jonah closed his eyes, the flash-frame images came back: people and places he didn't recognise, memories that weren't his own. He wasn't sure if he was asleep or awake – but he could hear a terrible growling sound, and slowly he came to realise that this at least was real. The growl was coming from somewhere nearby.

He climbed out of his hammock and looked out of the window. He couldn't see anything at first, but the sound was growing louder and closer.

Then, two petrol-powered motorbikes – the first he had seen in years – shot into view, weaving between the surrounding buses. They skidded to a halt beneath Jonah's window, outside *his* bus, and their riders dismounted. They were wearing combat fatigues, and helmets with mirrored visors that concealed their faces.

They were carrying guns.

Jonah stared, open-mouthed, as the two men shouldered their way into the bus through its open back doors. He heard a scream from somewhere below him, from the lower deck. It sounded like Mrs Collins.

Jonah made for the stairwell, but he was only two steps down when another louder sound froze him in his tracks: machine-gun fire.

It seemed to go on forever, that sound, building from a chatter to a thunderous roar before, abruptly, it ceased. A dreadful silence fell.

Jonah couldn't believe it, couldn't quite process what his senses were telling him. He knew he wasn't dreaming. This was like playing an immersive game in the Metasphere, only it was really happening – and right here, of all places, in the bus-burb. In the real world.

Which meant, as Jonah now realised with a heart-freezing dread, that he wasn't protected. Unlike his avatar, his real body could be hurt, even killed.

As carefully, as quietly, as he could, he backed up the stairs. He grabbed his rollerblades and pulled them on. He ripped away the rubber seal of the emergency exit window at the back of the bus, and he pushed out the glass. It smashed on the ground outside, and immediately Jonah heard footsteps below.

Someone was climbing the stairs after him.

He hoisted himself up and out of the window, rolling himself on top of the bus. He scrambled to his feet and skated as hard as he could across the roof.

A blast of bullets exploded through the metal roof behind him. There was no doubt about it now. The motorbike men were trying to kill him. They must already have killed Mr and Mrs Collins, and everyone else aboard their shared bus.

Most of their victims would have been plugged in. They wouldn't even have seen it coming. And, less than an hour ago, Jonah would have been one of them.

He reached the front end of the bus, and launched himself across the gap to the neighbouring one. He landed hard, but kept going. He continued to jump from rooftop to rooftop, as fast as he could. He heard a roar from behind him, then another: a pair of motorbike engines, starting up. They were coming after him.

Jonah lost his footing on a slippery steel roof. He careened off the edge of the bus, and slammed into the vents of an adjacent bus. He hit the ground with a bone-jarring thud. Fortunately, he had managed to land on his feet.

But he could hear the roars of the two motorbikes, closing in on him.

He skated through the labyrinth of parked buses, no clear destination in mind, just desperate to shake off his pursuers. A few faces appeared at windows, drawn by the noise, but at this time of the day most people were plugged in, at work somewhere in the Metasphere, oblivious to the commotion of the real world. Nor did the motorbike men appear to be interested in these onlookers. It was Jonah they wanted. No matter how hard he pushed himself, how many twists and turns he made, he couldn't seem to shake them off.

He rounded the back corner of a Number 23 bus, and froze in fright to find the motorbikes in front of him, bearing down upon him.

Jonah shot off to the right, turned left, right, left again in rapid succession. The motorbikes were faster than he was, but they couldn't match his agility. He had begun to get the feel for his real-world legs again, to gain confidence. All that time he had spent practising on his blades... It might not have won him the night-time races, but it might yet save his life in a more immediate way.

Still, he couldn't elude the motorbike men forever.

They had split up – he could hear the roars of their engines on each side of him now. They were trying to close him down – and, as long as Jonah remained hemmed in by the bus-burb walls, they would certainly succeed.

He came around another bus, saw the compound gate hanging open in front of him, and he made a split-second decision.

He made a break for it.

9

Jonah knew he had made a big mistake.

The streets around the bus-burb looked different in the daytime, alien. The sun exposed all the grime and the litter, the graffiti and the broken windows.

It was crowded out here too, with rickshaws, bikes and other bladers, all stuck at ground level, jostling each other for the limited space available.

He hadn't been outside in the daylight for two years. Jonah had forgotten how daunting these streets could be, outside of curfew hours.

On the plus side, the crowd would hide him from his pursuers, the motorbike men. However, it also slowed him to a maddening crawl.

And what if there were more assassins waiting out here?

Jonah suspected everyone who came towards him, everyone who bumped his elbows as they skated by. He was accosted by beggars, who saw that his clothes were finer than their own rags – and, though he told them he had no money, he feared they wouldn't believe him. Jonah had heard dreadful stories about people slaughtered for handfuls of loose change, enough for their attackers to get online for an hour or two.

He heard a motorbike engine. It sounded close.

His pursuers must have split up to search for him. Jonah imagined them pushing towards him, flattening anyone who couldn't get out of their way. He couldn't let them see him. He knew he would have no hope of escaping them again.

He saw a green plastic skip by the side of the road. A recycling machine. As high as Jonah's chest. He didn't stop to think about it.

He hauled himself up over the lip of the green container, dropped into a mound of paper, tin cans, broken bottles and something cold and slimy that he didn't want to think about. He buried himself as best he could. Then he lay still and listened to the harsh rasp of his own breathing and his heart hammering in his chest.

And to one other sound: the growling of a motorbike engine, approaching.

The motorbike came closer, ever closer. It seemed to be right beside Jonah's head now, and to have stopped there. He held his breath, thinking about all the people – the scores of people – who had seen him getting into the skip, the strangers who could betray him. It seemed like minutes – long, terrifying minutes – before the motorbike moved on at last, and finally the sound of it had faded.

Jonah lay where he was for a good while longer, anyway. He couldn't make his muscles move, couldn't face what was waiting for him outside his hiding place.

He couldn't go back home. What if there was someone waiting for him there? Anyway, Jonah's bus was a massacre scene now. He couldn't *ever* go back. And nor could his mum. He had to tell her what had happened.

He only wished he understood it himself. Somehow, he felt responsible. Was it only a coincidence that his bus had been attacked after Jonah had filtered his dad's avatar? Was it his fault that the Collinses had died?

He heard an ominous thunk, followed by the whirl of a motor, and the rubbish around him shifted. Jonah realised, almost too late, that the recycling machine had activated itself. He scrambled out of it, before he could be drawn down into its blades and mulched.

He had no choice now. He couldn't keep hiding.

Keeping his head down, looking up only when he had to, Jonah headed north-east. He weaved through the crowds, gaining in confidence as he started to remember what this world was like. He passed the Tate Modern power plant, where London's waste was burned to generate electricity. He skated over the Millennium Bridge, and blagged his way past the St Paul's checkpoint.

Jonah was in the City now, London's financial district: a square mile of calmness and relative prosperity which stood isolated from the crumbling streets around it. He saw the City Tower looming over him, and he recalled the last time he had been inside that building: when his mother had dragged him around these streets three years ago, begging for a job.

Jonah rolled into the lobby, and waited to be cleared by the white, round explosives detector in the ceiling. When the red light on it turned green, he wheeled his way up to the reception desk, short of breath. 'I'm here to see my mum,' he panted.

A security guard looked up from the Metasphere monitor on which he had been watching virtual football. He seemed annoyed by the interruption.

'Miriam Delacroix,' said Jonah. 'She works on the sixty-first floor.'

The guard's expression cleared. 'Oh yeah, the nappy-changer, you mean,' he chuckled. 'You come to get your nappy changed, kid?'

Jonah tried to ignore the dig, but he could feel his cheeks burning bright red. He couldn't help but be ashamed of what his mum did for a living. There were so few jobs available, however, to metaphobes and off-liners.

He pressed his thumb to the scanner, signing into the building's guest book, stubbornly avoiding the chuckling guard's eyes. Then he rolled towards the lifts.

It was a long ride up to the sixty-first floor.

Jonah looked at himself in the mirror in the lift. He cut a sorry, dishevelled figure. The thought of all

61

that had happened to him made him feel panicked, claustrophobic. How could he explain to his mum that they had lost their home?

The lift doors whooshed open, to reveal a huge, white, open office space – and a hundred unconscious young bodies dangling in rope hammocks from the ceiling.

It was Miriam Delacroix's job to look after these bodies: these pyjama-clad traders, swaying in their cocoons while their minds were busy elsewhere. She attended to all their physical needs, so they didn't have to leave the Metasphere and its virtual markets for hours, even days, at a time. Time was money, after all.

'Mum? Where are you?' Jonah called.

She was the only other person on the floor not plugged in. She dropped a feeding tube when she saw her son, and ran to meet him. 'Jonah! What are you doing here?'

'I... I... Something's happened,' he stammered. 'Something bad.' Then, the words tumbled out of him: 'I found Dad's avatar and I filtered it and these men came into the bus and they shot everyone but I got to the roof and I skated—'

'Slow down, Jonah!' Mum put her hands on his shoulders and pushed down, to calm him, to keep him from hyperventilating. 'Catch your breath.'

She kissed him on the forehead and looked solemnly into his eyes. He knew she was sad any time Jonah mentioned his dad, and regretted talking about him earlier. But he could tell there was something else too.

'I've been waiting for this day,' she sighed. 'But you're still so young.'

'I don't understand,' said Jonah. 'You've been waiting for...for what?'

'Your father told me everything, Jonah.'

'You knew about the avatar? You knew he'd copied it?'

'He did much more than that. He copied far more than the avatar.'

'Can you tell me how to take it off? Can you tell me how to be myself again?'

Mum shook her head. 'Your father knew his life was in danger. He left the avatar for you to find, in case the worst happened. I wish you hadn't found it, Jonah, not yet.'

'I think it... I think his avatar did something to my head, Mum.'

Mum nodded. 'That'll be your father's memories, Jonah. He copied them. All of them. I don't know how – I don't know how he did it, without going to the Island, but he did. And they're your memories now.'

Jonah blinked. He recalled the stream of visions that had hit him when he had first filtered the dragon avatar, the strange dreams that had not been his own. Could they have been his father's dreams? How was that possible?

'Oh, Jonah,' his mum sighed, 'there's so much we've

kept from you. So much I should have told you before, but I thought… I didn't want you to have to grow up too soon, and now. Now, there's so little time.'

She chivvied him into one of the rope hammocks and thrust a sterile adaptor into his hands. She lowered her voice, as if the dangling bodies around them might hear. 'I can't protect you, Jonah,' she said, 'but there is someone who can.'

'Axel?'

His mum looked surprised when Jonah spoke the name. 'That's right. There is a man called Axel Kavanaugh. He was Jason's – your father's – best friend since flight school. You need to find him in the Metasphere, so that he can find you in the real world.'

'How?' asked Jonah. 'Where…?'

'The Icarus,' said Mum. 'Axel keeps a watch over it. You remember that place?'

Jonah did. The Icarus was a pilot's bar, not far from the gift shop. It had been his father's favourite hangout.

'Mum, who were those men?' he asked. 'The men who tried to kill me?'

'They were Millennial agents, Jonah.'

'But that doesn't make sense! Dad was a Millennial. He worked for Mr Granger for years. Why would they—?'

'Your father knew things, Jonah,' said Mum. She unfurled an Ethernet wire, helped Jonah plug himself into a terminal. 'Secrets that nobody else in the entire world knows, apart from Matthew Granger himself – and now, you know those things too.'

'But I don't,' protested Jonah. 'I swear, I don't know a thing!'

She stroked his head affectionately and smiled sadly. 'It's all in here, Jonah. You just haven't worked out how to access the knowledge yet.'

'I don't want it,' said Jonah. 'If I could just take off Dad's avatar—'

'It's too late,' Mum whispered. 'There's one more thing you need to know. Your father wasn't a Millennial. He only pretended to be in order to get close to Matthew Granger. He was a double agent, Jonah. Your father was a *Guardian*.'

Jonah opened his mouth to speak. He had a thousand questions, tripping over each other in his mind. But his connection with the Metasphere terminal had been made, and he felt his stomach tumbling as he descended into darkness.

10

It was the smell that hit Jonah first: a rank odour of spices and leather.

A vast market, like a Moroccan *souk* he had once seen in a movie, materialised around him. It was thronged with avatars, shouting and haggling.

The City Tower terminal had automatically sent him to the virtual trading floor. Many of the avatars buying and selling here must have belonged to the young bodies that Jonah's mother cared for in the real world.

He was still dressed in his father's red dragon avatar.

Unfurling his immense wingspan, Jonah took to the sky. He examined the souk from above, and noted the location of his glowing exit halo. It was easy to get lost in an unfamiliar part of the Metasphere.

He felt his whole body surge as he flapped his wings. Jonah felt strong, powerful, and a part of him couldn't help but relish this new sensation.

But he was also afraid and confused – and even angry. He was angry with himself for having been so quick to filter the dragon avatar. And he was angry with his parents for having hidden so much from him.

He was still trying to take it all in, everything his mum had said. His dad – a Guardian? How could that have been? The Guardians had killed his dad. That was what he had always believed. And what had Jason Delacroix known that was worth killing him for?

As he glided through the virtual air, Jonah let out a scream of frustration. His breath turned into a stream of fire, and the flames washed back over his red, scaly body.

Jonah flew over Venus Park, over his family's gift shop, and banked left. He was soaring over one of the oldest areas of the virtual world. They called it 'The Mirrors'. The buildings here had been coded to a lower resolution than was now customary, and felt flat, almost 2D, and lacked the realistic texture of the modern Metasphere. Beneath him, Jonah saw MetaOx Street, a copy of the real Oxford Street in London. In its earliest days, much of the Metasphere had been designed to replicate such real-world locations. Jonah couldn't imagine why.

A line of digital red buses inched their way along the busy shopping promenade, and he despaired at the sight of them. They all bore the number 137. His bus. His home. Gone forever.

The Icarus bar was a large, conical building. A neon sign outside depicted a man with winged feet, outlined by a bright orange circle. The entrance was up on the third floor; its patrons had no option but to fly in. Jonah's dad had often remarked that this was only fitting for a pilot's haunt.

Jonah touched down on the landing perch and collapsed his wings. He had waited outside the Icarus for his father many times before. But now, for the first time, he flew through its doors.

Inside, the bar resembled a giant birdcage. It was six storeys high – the entrance on a middle level – and it was packed with avatars, mostly birds or other winged creatures, chatting, drinking, reminiscing about days gone by. They rested on broad perches which jutted out from the sides of the cage at all levels, or on swings that hung from the high, caged domed ceiling.

'*Jason Benedict Delacroix*,' the tinny voice announced. Jonah had been scanned and his avatar identified, his father's avatar.

Suddenly, the chatter that had filled the Icarus ceased. The birds all turned to look at the new arrival as if they had just seen a ghost. As far as they were concerned, Jonah realised suddenly, they had.

He almost turned and flew out of there. The last thing he had wanted was to be the centre of attention. But if he fled now, he would never find Axel Kavanaugh, his dad's old friend. And Axel was the only hope he had, the only one who might be able to dig him out of this mess he was in.

Jonah floated, self-consciously, down to one of the three bars and landed on a perch. He could feel a hundred pairs of eyes burning into his back.

He was relieved when a tiny, red-winged blackbird

fluttered over and stood on the bar. 'Jason, is that really you?' asked the bird.

'Axel?' asked Jonah.

'You've been gone for over three years. We all thought you'd died that day.'

Jonah didn't know what to say. He supposed he ought to confess that he wasn't who everyone thought he was, he had only borrowed his father's body – but the blackbird seemed so excited to see him that he didn't let Jonah get a word in.

'So, where have you been hiding all this time? I want to know everything. We should meet up, face to face. Where are you now?'

'I'm in the City Tower building in London,' said Jonah, 'but—'

Before he could complete the sentence, the bird was whipped away by a giant eagle's wing. A few stray feathers remained in the air where he had been poised. 'Hey!' cried Jonah. He unfolded his own wings, about to fly to the aid of the stunned blackbird, but he was seized from behind by a pair of enormous paws.

'Hold up there, Ghost of Christmas Past,' growled a voice in Jonah's ear.

'Who are you?' cried Jonah. 'What are you doing?'

'It's me, you brain-dead dragon,' hissed the voice. 'It's Axel – and I'm savin' your scales!'

'Nice shot, Dad. I've got him now!' A winged unicorn swooped past Jonah and flew at the blackbird with her horn lowered. The bird, however, had recovered enough to dive out of the way. The unicorn slammed headfirst into the cage wall, hard enough to make the entire interior rattle. The blackbird glanced back at Jonah and laughed, then disappeared through an exit halo.

'You OK, kiddo?' Jonah's captor had let go of him, to go to the unicorn's side. Jonah could see him properly now: he had the body of a lion, but the wings and the head of an eagle. A gryphon.

'I missed him, Dad. He got away.' The unicorn was clearly dazed, but determined to stand on her own four hooves.

The gryphon rounded on Jonah. 'What the hell were you thinking, Jason? I thought you were smarter than that. Too smart to be taken in by some Millennial spy.'

'What... What do you mean?' Jonah stammered.

'What did you tell him?'

Jonah's throat dried. The gryphon was right. He had naively assumed that the blackbird was a friend – but, behind the avatar, he could have been anyone.

'You gave him your RWL, didn't you?' the gryphon growled – and all Jonah could do was nod dumbly as it sank in with him that he had just made a terrible mistake.

He had revealed his Real World Location.

*

'Not too bright, sir, this pilot friend of yours.' The Millennial agent turned to his boss with a grin, as he tugged the Ethernet cord out of his spine.

'What happened?' asked Granger. He was staring at a monitor connected to the agent's terminal. Although its user had logged off, it was still showing the inside of the Icarus – and the red dragon avatar of a man he had never expected to see again.

'Stupid dragon flew right into the joint and told me his RWL.'

Granger pondered on that for a moment. 'I wonder...?' he mused. 'It doesn't sound like him to be so careless. We should check it out, anyway. Where is he?'

'City Tower, London.'

'Send two remotes. Take out the whole building if you have to.'

The Millennial dashed away to a datapad to carry out his orders.

Granger's gaze was still fixed to the monitor. He was weighing up his options.

Jason Delacroix had escaped his assassins once already. He might do so again. He had become extremely adept at hiding, in the real world. But his avatar... His avatar was right there now, on Granger's screen.

It seemed a shame to waste this golden opportunity.

Granger snatched a datapad from a startled programmer, and began to tap in a sequence of commands. It took a moment for the other programmers to see what he was doing. Then, one by one, they turned to stare at him, open-mouthed. One girl even began to voice a protest, but she caught herself in time.

Granger didn't need to explain himself to any of them. If there was one thing he despised, it was being told what he could or couldn't do.

'You'd best get out of here, Jason,' said the gryphon. 'Get back through your halo, before—'

'No. No, wait!' said Jonah. 'How do I know who you really are? You could be a spy too, for all I know.' He was determined not to make the same mistake twice.

Before the gryphon could answer him, however, the roof collapsed.

The Icarus's customers scattered from their perches, flapping to avoid chunks of falling masonry and twisted metal. Jonah thought he could hear a high-pitched whirling sound over the clamour of frightened voices – and, a second later, the tip of an enormous drill head punched its way through the ceiling.

'A Recycler!' cried the unicorn. 'But what's it doing here?'

'Get to your halo, Sam,' the gryphon snapped. 'You too, buddy!' He pushed Jonah with his sharp beak. As they flew for the exit, two more drill heads came screaming through the bars of the great birdcage, one to each side of them.

Jonah thought he wouldn't make it. There was a crush at the doors, as everyone tried to squeeze through them at once.

Then, suddenly, he was outside in the daylight. He looked back, and he saw them: Recyclers, as the unicorn had said. They looked almost like giant metal birds themselves. They loomed over the Icarus on their long legs, pecking at it with their whirling drill 'beaks' – and, where they pecked, the building depixelated, collapsing in on itself until there was nothing left but a colourless void.

Jonah had seen Recyclers before, of course, but never like this. The Metasphere was constantly reconfiguring itself, building on the best of what had come before. The Recyclers were its means of picking through old programming code, deleting subroutines that had become obsolete and reprocessing the rest. Whenever a virtual building or a plot of land was earmarked for repurposing, that was when the Recyclers would move in. But they were supposed to only recycle empty buildings and abandoned plots of digital land.

There had been live avatars trapped inside the Icarus. Many of them, Jonah hoped, would have had their exit halos close by, would have been able to get out of there in time. The others...

If an avatar died inside the Metasphere – as rare an event as this was – then the mind of its user died with it, leaving the body a vegetable. But Jonah didn't have time to dwell on his guilt.

With the Icarus gone, the Recyclers turned their attention to the street where Jonah now hovered: MetaOx Street. They drilled their way through the virtual buses, scattering red pixels to the wind – and a number of pedestrians were caught in their remorseless paths and wiped out. Forever.

They were coming towards Jonah.

The gryphon and the unicorn dropped out of the sky, one to each side of him.

'It's the three of us they're after,' said the gryphon.

'Three of us, three of them,' said the unicorn. 'One for each of us.'

'They're killing everyone,' said Jonah, 'and it's all because of me.'

He was frozen in shock as people screamed and ran around him. He felt the gryphon's paw on his shoulder again.

'Follow me,' the gryphon shouted. 'Fly!'

11

Jonah didn't need telling twice.

He still didn't know if he could trust these new acquaintances. Right now, though, they were all he had. He flew with them, along the busy streets, through panicking crowds. He glanced back, to see the Recyclers right behind him. They had folded up their legs beneath them and were speeding after their three targets like rockets.

'We have to draw them away from the people!' Jonah shouted. The Recyclers were digesting everything – and everyone – in their paths.

Jonah pointed his dragon's snout upwards, beating his wings as hard as he could. The gryphon and the unicorn followed his lead, and the three of them soared into the sky. 'They're gaining on us!' cried the unicorn.

She was right. Jonah could feel a pull on his tail: a vortex effect from the whirling drills, threatening to suck him in.

He saw a startled budgie frozen in his path, and he ducked beneath it. He hoped he had given it a wide enough berth for the Recyclers to miss it as they followed him.

The gryphon fell in at Jonah's side. 'Time to face

facts, buddy,' he growled. 'The kid and me are done for.'

'No!'

'Our exit halos are back behind the Icarus,' said the gryphon. 'We'll never make it around these things, not a prayer!'

'But I'm the one they really want. I could lead them away from you.'

The gryphon shook his head. 'One for each of us, remember? I don't know what you were thinking, Jason, coming here. Best we can do now, though, is to get you back to the real world. Where's your exit halo? Tell me it's somewhere close!'

Jonah surveyed the destruction below him. A giant scar of nothingness cut through the heart of The Mirrors. Most of MetaOx Street was destroyed, and momentarily he thought his exit halo had been Recycled with it.

Then he remembered. He had materialised in the souk. That was where he had to get back to. Jonah's stomach turned to ice. It was too far away. He wouldn't make it!

He dived towards Venus Park instead. He swooped over the heads of the courting couples and the marching protestors, and straight into the Delacroix gift shop, its door dissolving at his approach. The gryphon and the unicorn were right behind him, and the secret trapdoor was still exposed, still open.

They dropped through the trapdoor, and Jonah pulled it shut behind them.

The gryphon blinked as he looked around the gloomy cellar. 'Where is it, then?' he asked. 'Your exit halo?'

'Not here,' said Jonah. 'I've had a better idea.'

'You're kidding me, right?' the gryphon cried.

'We can't hide from them,' said the unicorn. 'They'll eat right through these walls, then—'

'I know,' said Jonah. 'That's what I'm counting on.'

The cellar was already beginning to shake, as the first drill head bit into it from above. Jonah took a deep breath, placed his claws against the wall, and summoned up the virus code that his classmate Harry had given him. He felt the data coursing through his virtual body – his father's virtual body, rather – and into the source code of the cellar walls, which began to blur and distort.

In that same instant, the Recyclers arrived. They broke through the ceiling, bearing down upon their prey. Jonah and the others backed into a corner, but could go no further. Jonah wrapped his giant wings around his two new friends, in a hopeless attempt to protect them. A sharp drill tip pierced the scales on his back, and he screamed in pain and almost belched fire again, but stopped himself for fear of burning someone.

Suddenly, the drills stopped spinning. The Recyclers sputtered and shook, and at last depixelated and disappeared. Jonah's desperate plan had worked.

'Where'd you get a virus like that?' asked the gryphon, not waiting for an answer. 'You infected the whole shop with it, right? So, when the Recyclers gobbled up the walls, they were infected too.'

Jonah wasn't listening to him. He poked his dragon's head up above where the floor of the gift shop had been. There was nothing there now – literally, nothing.

'It's all gone,' he whispered.

'I'm so sorry,' said the unicorn. 'This was your place?'

Jonah didn't answer her. He felt numb. A few avatars had drifted over from the park, to stare curiously at the new, gift-shop-shaped hole in their world.

'How…how did this happen?' asked Jonah. 'Who sent the Recyclers after us?'

'It must have been that blackbird,' said the unicorn.

'He was staking out the Icarus,' said the gryphon, 'in case you appeared there.'

'Dad and I got there as quickly as we could,' said the unicorn, 'as soon as we got the alert that your avatar had been scanned by the Icarus's gate, but…'

'Listen, buddy,' said the gryphon, 'I'm sorry about this place too – I know you wanted to leave it to your son some day – but you're not out of the woods yet.'

'Dad's right,' said the unicorn. 'The Millennials know your RWL. They'll find your body in the real world. You have to log off and hide.'

'But how will I find you again?' asked Jonah.

'We're leaving England tomorrow at sunrise,' said the gryphon, 'and you need to come with us. Meet us at Delta House. And remember your oath as a Guardian –

because it's time to fulfil it. Now, get to it!'

'What's Delta House?' Jonah asked.

The gryphon roared his eagle head back with laughter and slapped Jonah on the wing with his lion's paw. 'I'm glad you haven't lost your sense of humour! Now go!'

Jonah didn't know what Delta House was, but he would have to figure that out later. Right now, he knew that the unicorn – Sam, as her father had called her – was right. He had to get back to the real world.

Jonah's exit halo was just where he had left it, in the crowded souk.

He was relieved to have reached it without more Recyclers coming after him.

He dived through the halo, and returned to his physical body in the City Tower. His eyes took a moment to refocus on the real world, as if he had woken suddenly from a deep dream. Everything he had been through – the Icarus, the chase, the destruction of the shop – felt like it *had* been a dream. Or a nightmare.

Jonah rubbed his eyes and looked around frantically. He couldn't see his mum.

He unplugged himself, toppled out of his hammock and ran through the sea of suspended traders' bodies, calling for her. He followed a crunching, splintering sound, and found her hacking her way through an office door with a fireman's axe.

'Jonah,' huffed Miriam Delacroix, 'get over here now!' She swung the axe into the door again, successfully amputating the handle. She kicked the door open, and burst into a furnished but unoccupied suite, an office purely for show.

'Mum, what are you doing?' cried Jonah. 'You're scaring me!'

He watched from the doorway as she threw open a metal cabinet in one corner of the room. She yanked out an aluminium and canvas contraption emblazoned with a Pegasus logo, hurried back to her son and began to strap it to his back.

'You *should* be scared,' she said. 'Put this on, Jonah. You have to go.'

'But, Mum, I need to tell you—'

'I already know, Jonah. I was watching you on a monitor. I saw the Recyclers. I saw everything. The Millennials know you're here, in this building.'

'Then let's go. I'll call the lift, and we'll—'

Mum placed her hands on Jonah's shoulders and held him still with the power of her urgent, sad gaze. 'There's no time, darling,' she said. 'Look!'

She pointed to the window. Jonah looked out and saw two unmarked, black lorries racing up the street below them. He had no idea what they were, or who might be inside them, but his mother was clearly terrified of them. She tightened straps around Jonah's waist, legs, chest and arms. A drawstring dangled over his stomach, and he reached for the red toggle at the end of it, to pull this tight too.

'Not yet,' said Mum, batting his hand away. 'Not until you're out. Cover your eyes, darling.'

She hefted the axe again, and swung it into the window. As it shattered, glass fragments blew back into Jonah's raised hands, scratching his palms. He was looking at the metal cabinet his mum had opened, and for the first time he saw the words stamped into its door: EXECUTIVE ESCAPE GLIDER.

A fierce wind blew into the sixty-first-floor office, forcing him to squint against it.

Mum bundled Jonah over to the smashed window. She took his hand and closed it around the red toggle on his harness. 'As soon as you're clear of the building,' she instructed him, 'pull the ripcord. Do you hear me, Jonah? Pull the ripcord!'

He was looking down at the street. Those black lorries were still coming. Too fast.

The first lorry smashed into the base of the City Tower, and exploded. A mushroom cloud of fire billowed up towards him. The building shook, and Jonah fell into his mother's arms, unbalanced by the weight on his back. She pushed him firmly away from her, back to the window. 'No, Mum, don't!' he screamed.

'It's the only way,' she insisted as she held him for the last time, too briefly. 'I love you, Jonah. Your father lives inside you now. Learn from him, but listen to your own heart, and you'll always do the right thing.'

Then she gave him one final shove, out through the window, and Jonah was falling. Falling towards the fire. He remembered his mum's instructions and pulled as hard as he could on the red toggle. The pack on his back sprung open. Two black wings unfurled above him, a series of aluminium poles snapping into place to form a frame.

For the first time, Jonah flew in the real world.

He felt the second explosion before he saw it, his hang-glider rising on a sudden wave of hot air. He turned to see what was happening behind him, but the wings turned with him like a kite and almost curved him back into the burning building. He quickly focused his gaze ahead, at the vast urban sprawl of south London, and the glider responded and banked him away from the collapsing tower to safety.

He didn't dare look back again. He couldn't bear to look, anyway. His mum was trapped in the inferno, lost to him. He should have refused the glider, put it on her instead, but he hadn't had time to think. It wasn't fair that she had sacrificed herself for him. It wasn't fair that he should lose his mum too.

As he soared across the river, Jonah spotted his bus-burb, a huddle of red rectangles. He leaned to his left and steered the hang-glider away from it. There was nothing for him there. In the past few hours, he had lost his homes in both the real and the virtual worlds. He had become an orphan – and all because of one stupid mistake.

He couldn't take it all in yet. He needed someone to talk to, someone to tell him what to do, but he was entirely alone. He had no one. At least, no one still alive.

I'll go to the Island of the Uploaded, he thought.

He would talk to the dead.

12

Jonah hit the ground hard.

He had glided nearly five miles south-east of the City of London and positioned himself to land on a straight stretch of road near the Crystal Palace shelter. In the air, he had felt as if he was going slowly, but the busy road had rushed up to meet him with alarming speed.

Jonah kept his knees bent, and let the eight rubber wheels still attached to his feet take the brunt of the impact for him.

His sudden drop out of the sky took a number of bicyclists and rickshaw drivers by surprise. Jonah heard their cries but kept his head down, didn't let them see his face. Any one of them, he thought, could have been a Millennial spy searching for him.

Somehow, he managed to remain upright and, miraculously, not collide with anyone. If only he could have said the same last night, he thought. If only!

As soon as he had slowed down, he unclipped his harness and ditched the glider pack. It was the last thing his mother had ever given him, and he couldn't bear to look at it. Jonah skated away as fast as he could. He needed to put more distance yet between himself and the City. He skated until his legs ached.

His mind was racing. He had a million questions, things he should have asked his mum when he had had the chance.

He found an open meta-pub and skated in. It was an old-style pub, with dark wood timbers and a low ceiling. An obese landlord glowered at Jonah's blades from behind the bar. 'Gotta take those things off, kid,' he grumbled.

Jonah obeyed, holding onto a polished brass railing as he untied his boots and surveyed the room. There were about a dozen other patrons, meta-tranced at their terminals, spread across the small, dimly-lit space.

Jonah looked hungrily at the Pro-Meal pouches hung behind the bar and asked about getting online. 'It's eighty meta-dollars an hour, kid,' said the landlord. 'And the protein is thirty.' Jonah didn't have enough money for both – but he needed the access now, and his real world body needed rest. Food would have to wait.

'Just the access,' he said. He took a seat at the last open terminal. 'And I need an adaptor.' The landlord snatched a foil packet from a clip-strip, tossed it across the room to him and watched as Jonah set his Point of Origin co-ordinates.

'Goin' to see the deadies, eh?' the landlord sniggered. 'Just don't go trying to Upload yerself. I run a respectable establishment, not a suicide bar.'

Jonah ignored the fat man's blathering. He inserted

the adaptor into his spine, and slumped out of the real world.

Jonah's red dragon avatar splashed down in warm water. His exit halo bobbed beside him like a buoy. He hadn't swum in this body before, and it took him a moment to realise that the dragon's stumpy arms alone wouldn't keep its bulk afloat. He had to use his wings.

He was caught by a wave and washed ashore. He landed face first and got a mouthful of sand. Another wave crashed down around him as he struggled to his feet. He was still gasping for air when he heard a familiar – and reassuring – chuckle.

'I hope you don't land your planes like that, son.'

It was Jonah's grandmother. The trunk of her grey elephant avatar flapped about as she shook with mirth.

Jonah trudged up the beach, a white sandy paradise that stretched as far as he could see. He sank into the wet sand with each of his heavy steps. The elephant came stomping up to meet him. She wrapped her dry, grey trunk around his shoulders, pulling his head into the crick of her neck. She couldn't fully envelop the dragon avatar in her hug, the way she had with Jonah's old humatar. Still, he had always found comfort in Nan's embrace, and he was grateful for it now. He didn't want to let her go.

'It's good to see you, son,' she said. 'You hardly ever

seem to visit any more.'

She thought he was his father. Of course she did. Jonah thought about telling her the truth, but he thought it would be too much for her to handle.

The Island of the Uploaded was where the dead lived on, at least in a sense. Millions of avatars spent their days here, basking in the virtual sunshine, between visits from friends and family. Most of them had been elderly, in the real world, or the victims of terminal illnesses. Jonah's grandmother had been both.

She had been the lucky one.

Jonah's parents weren't here. Neither of them had seen their deaths coming. They hadn't had time to prepare, to Upload their avatars and their memories to the Island.

'How is baby Jonah?' asked Nan. She had Uploaded before Jonah's first birthday; she only remembered him as an infant.

'Well,' said Jonah, not wanting to lie to her, 'he's... changed. Quite a lot.'

'They do at that age. I was always amazed at how fast you changed when you were growing up, Jason. One minute, you were a little boy, the next you were a little man, and now you have a family of your own. Is Miriam with you today?'

'No, she...she couldn't make it.'

'Shame. Well, give her my love, won't you?'

'Of course,' said Jonah, swallowing back tears.

'There's something wrong, isn't there?' said Nan. 'I could always tell with you.'

Jonah chose his words carefully. 'I've been asked to do something,' he said, 'and I don't know how. I don't know what this thing means, or where it will take me.'

'It sounds like an adventure,' said Nan. 'You've always loved an adventure, no matter how dangerous. I couldn't keep you indoors, however I tried – like this RAF nonsense. Is it that again, Jason? You aren't still thinking of joining up?'

Her mind had wandered to another time, a time before Jonah was even born. This happened to her a lot, and it was something Jonah had become used to. The Uploaded retained their memories from life, but accessed them at random. Sometimes, when Jonah had come here as himself, his grandmother had remembered him from his previous visits. Sometimes, he had had to explain to her who he was.

He envied her that, sometimes: the ability to live in a long-gone moment as if it were the present. He had often wished he could do the same: jump into his own past and lose himself in the memories of better days.

'Why don't you settle down,' suggested Nan, 'maybe start a family of your own?'

'I will,' said Jonah, playing his part, wanting to comfort her. 'I will. Soon. I promise. I'll even give you a grandson.'

'A grandson?' Her mind had wandered again.

'You're too young to be talking like that. You have your whole life ahead of you. Why can't you just enjoy being a boy?'

Her elephant eyes looked sharply at Jonah, and his heart leapt. For a moment, he was sure his grandmother had seen through his dragon mask and was talking directly to him – the real him. But, of course, that was impossible.

How could she understand everything that had happened to him? How could he explain to her that her son and her daughter-in-law were dead?

She didn't even understand the truth about herself.

No one talked about it much – about the fact that the process of Uploading killed the user in the real world. Everyone on this sunny shore had committed suicide to get here. But none of them remembered it. The Metasphere kept that crucial piece of information from them in case it drove them mad.

The Uploaded didn't know they were dead.

'Can I ask you a question?' asked Jonah, keen to get to the point of his visit.

'Of course you can, dear,' said Nan. 'Anything. You know that.'

'Do the words "Delta House" mean anything to you?'

Nan chuckled to herself as she swam in memories again. 'Pilot Officer Jason Delacroix,' she said. 'Every week. I write you a letter every week.'

'A letter?' Jonah asked. 'Like on *paper*?'

'Pilot Officer Jason Delacroix. Care of RAF Base Dover. Department of Defence. Delta House.'

Of course! His father's address at Flight School. Now, it made sense. That was where Dad had met Axel Kavanaugh. And it was where Axel, the gryphon, wanted Jonah to go now, to meet him.

'Thank you,' said Jonah, as he kissed his grandmother's wrinkled forehead.

'You give little Jonah a big kiss from his nan,' she said. 'I miss him.'

Jonah turned away from her. He flapped his wings, stirring up the hot sand on the beach, and pointed himself towards the breaking waves. A great wave crashed over his scales as he dived back through his exit halo. He knew what he had to do now.

Jonah had to get to Dover – by sunrise.

13

Jonah had skated through the night.

What choice had he had? Dover was over seventy miles from London – and, even if he could have afforded to take a train, they only ran there once a month since carbon rationing had been introduced.

The sun was rising as Jonah bladed through the deserted streets, and he feared he might be too late. But skating on instinct and adrenalin, he found the old RAF base on the eastern edge of town.

The base had been closed down some years ago. It was little more than an airstrip, really: a single runway, with a tilted control tower and a few decrepit bunkhouses. The tarmac was cracked and overgrown. No plane could have landed here now, even if any still flew to England.

An airship was hovering above the crumbling runway. Jonah stopped at the fence line and stared at it. It was massive, at least ten buses long. It was covered in reflective solar panels, and resembled a giant, shiny, black tortoise.

A bearded man dangled from the airship in a harness. He was thin, but clearly strong from the way he hoisted himself along the dirigible's underbelly. He wore black coveralls, with all manner of tools attached to his belt by carabiners. His wavy, grey hair was whipped by the wind that blew in from the nearby English Channel. He was tinkering with one of the propellers beneath the cockpit.

'Test it now, Sam!' he shouted, pushing himself out of the way. The propeller began to whirl, and the man looked pleased with himself. 'OK, kiddo, we're good to go!'

'Then let's get airborne, Axel.'

Jonah followed this new, gruff voice to a large man on the ground, who was belaying the suspended man. He had a black moustache and gnarly, dark hair, and he wore a long trench coat over a blue suit. Jonah didn't much like the look of him.

Axel hesitated. 'It's only just dawn,' he said. 'He could still make it.'

'We can't wait,' insisted the burly man on the ground. 'We're sitting ducks here.'

'You don't know Jason. He'll be here.'

It sounded like as good a cue as any. Jonah eased himself through the broken fence and skated across the uneven tarmac. As he neared the airship, he opened his mouth to introduce himself.

The burly man must have heard him coming. In a rapid motion that belied his size, he spun around, pulled a shotgun from inside his trench coat and pointed it at Jonah.

'On the ground!' he screamed. 'Hands on your head! Now!'

Startled, Jonah did as he was told. He dropped to his knees – something he had been close to doing anyway, from sheer exhaustion. Still suspended from the airship, Axel whipped out a smaller pistol and pointed it down at Jonah.

'Who are you?' he demanded. 'How did you find us?'

Jonah hadn't expected this. He understood, of course, that these men had been expecting to see his father, not a teenager on wheels. He had known they would be suspicious of him. But he hadn't expected guns – let alone two men who looked as if they would happily use them in an instant.

His heart was racing. He was panting for breath.

'You. You told me yourself,' he stammered. 'D-Delta. Delta House.'

A look of horror spread across Axel's face. 'That was you inside the Icarus?' he cried. 'Inside the dragon?'

The burly man scowled. 'What did I tell you, Axel?'

'I know. I know I should have verified his avatar, but there was no time. The Recyclers were after us, and—'

'Jason Delacroix died three years ago,' said the burly man, 'and you fell for a Millennial trick. You led them straight here to us!'

'No,' gasped Jonah, 'I…I'm not…'

'We should plug this little spy right now,' said the burly man.

'No! No, wait!' came another voice, a female voice.

Jonah looked up, thankfully. He saw a girl, not much older than he was, peering out of the airship's cockpit window. She had short, red hair, and he thought he had seen her somewhere before, and then it came to him. 'Can't you see he's scared?' said the girl. 'He's a kid, just a kid. Why would the Millennials send a kid after us?'

'Get back inside, Samantha!' ordered Axel. So, she was Sam, the unicorn!

'I'm just saying, Dad, does it make any sense to you?'

'She's right,' said Jonah, finding his voice. 'I'm Jonah. Jonah Delacroix. I'm Jason's son. It was me yesterday, in the Icarus and the gift shop. I saved us with the virus. I know I should have told you who I was, but I've skated all night to get here. My dad said to find you.'

'I don't know,' said Axel. 'What do you think, Bradbury?'

The burly man was losing patience. 'I still say we should plug him!'

'He might be telling the truth!' Sam protested.

'And he might be spinning us a line,' said the man called Bradbury. 'He might not be a Millennial, but he's not one of us – and his very presence here compromises our mission. I have a clear shot, Axel. I just need you to say the word.'

Jonah couldn't believe it. After all he had been

through, the deadly attacks he had survived, he was going to be killed by the very people he had come to for help. He closed his eyes and waited for the shot to come.

Axel sighed, exasperated. 'No, Bradbury. Guns down. Guns down. Sam is right. He might be telling the truth. Look at him! My God, he even looks like Jason.'

Jonah had never thought he looked like his father, and he couldn't tell if Axel was just saying this to defuse the tension. Either way, it worked. Bradbury lowered his gun, begrudgingly, as Axel rappelled to the ground and approached the relieved Jonah with an outstretched hand.

Jonah climbed, with some difficulty, to his feet and steadied himself on his blades. His every muscle was aching. He skated to meet Axel, carefully avoiding Bradbury's hostile glare, and they introduced themselves properly.

'You shouldn't have come here, kid,' said Axel. 'I don't know what you've been told, but we can't babysit you. The work we do, it's too dangerous. If you want my advice, you'll roll right back to London – and get rid of that dragon avatar, PDQ.'

'I don't know how!' cried Jonah.

'Then stay off-line till you do. It's not you the Millennials want, it's your daddy, but as long as you're dressed in his scales...' Axel's eyes clouded over, and he turned away. It occurred to Jonah that he had been expecting to meet more than an ally this morning. He had been expecting a reunion with one of his oldest friends.

'Come on, Bradbury,' said Axel, with a sad sigh. 'Let's go!'

And, at that very moment, Jonah heard the roar of engines behind him, and Sam cried out, 'Dad, behind you! Remotes!'

Jonah spun around and saw them too: two unmarked, black lorries. They flattened the rusted fence around the airstrip, and came barrelling up the runway. Jonah could see right through their windscreens, into the empty drivers' cabs. He was frozen, knowing exactly what horror was in store but helpless to prevent it.

He heard Bradbury's voice, raised urgently: 'Get us airborne, Axel!'

Jonah turned back to the airship, in time to see Axel swarming up a ladder, disappearing through a hatchway. Bradbury was untying a pair of taut ropes from the iron anchors that held the hovering behemoth in place. As the second rope came free, the airship began to drift away. Bradbury dived for the ladder himself, caught it, and hoisted himself upwards.

'Wait!' cried Jonah. 'Take me with you! Please!'

The airship was rising. The ladder was already out of Jonah's reach. He skated furiously to catch the dangling tethers. He missed.

'Grab my dad's harness!' called Sam.

With all the strength he could muster, Jonah

crisscrossed his legs and chased after Axel's discarded harness. It was being dragged along in the airship's wake, dancing before his eyes as if taunting him deliberately. The end of the runway was fast approaching, and Jonah realised with a start that beyond it was a cliff. If he didn't brake now, he would shoot right over the edge! But, behind him, the black lorries were drawing closer, ever closer with their deadly payloads.

Jonah grasped for the harness, but the closer he got to the runway's end the stronger was the wind, blowing his lifeline out of reach. He summoned the last vestige of his fading strength, lowered his head and thrust himself determinedly into the wind. He reached out and caught the harness at last.

Jonah entangled one arm in its canvas straps, so he couldn't be shaken loose. He kept his left blade on the tarmac, as he poked his right foot through the leg hole. He didn't need to skate now, just to let the airship pull him along.

As Jonah lifted his left leg into the harness, his right skate hit a pothole. He tumbled backwards and was dragged along on his back, unable to regain his footing. The tarmac shredded his shirt and cut into his flesh. Jonah cried out in pain but the wind stole his scream.

Then the ground fell away from beneath him, and he plummeted.

It felt like forever before the tethers of the harness snapped taut and arrested his fall. Secured by one leg and one arm, buffeted by the wind, Jonah clung to the canvas straps for dear life. His muscles seized in pain. Behind him, the two remote lorries lurched over the cliff edge and arced towards the choppy waters of the Channel below.

The first of the lorries was directly underneath Jonah when it blew. He braced himself for what he knew would happen next.

The wave of heat propelled him upwards, and smashed him into one of the solar panels on the airship's underbelly. He reached out, grabbed onto the vessel's frame and steadied himself. He looked up to see Axel, Bradbury and Sam staring at him from the cockpit. Below him, the second lorry hit the water and detonated harmlessly.

Looking back at the shore, Jonah saw the fabled White Cliffs of Dover, charred black from the explosions, shrinking into the distance. The very edge of his country.

For the first time in his life, he was no longer in England.

There was no going back now.

14

Jonah felt like he had closed his eyes for only a minute.

He was woken by Sam, shaking him. 'Ouch, careful,' he said. His whole body felt brittle. He was wearing a new, grey sweatshirt and lying on a bunk in a windowless cabin. 'Where am I?' he muttered.

'Somewhere over France,' Sam replied. 'You collapsed as soon as we'd pulled you inside the airship. Which was probably for the best, seeing the state of your back.'

Jonah felt beneath his shirt. His back was bandaged, and a terrible thought occurred to him. Sam must have seen it in his eyes, because she quickly reassured him, 'Don't worry, there's no damage to your DI. You could plug in right now if you wanted to.'

She offered Jonah a full-English-flavoured Pro-Meal pouch, which he accepted gratefully. He hadn't eaten since breakfast yesterday.

'Look – Jonah, is it?' said Sam. 'My dad and Bradbury, they've got questions that won't wait, and I thought you'd rather I was the one to ask them.'

Jonah nodded as he ate. He certainly didn't relish the idea of being grilled by the forbidding Bradbury.

'How did you find us?'

In a quiet voice, Jonah told Sam everything that

had happened to him, from his discovery of his father's avatar to his visit to the Icarus. He told her about his return to the City Tower in the real world, and the two black lorries like the ones at the airstrip that had brought it tumbling down. He choked as he told her about his mother's sacrifice, and Sam squeezed his hand and waited for him to compose himself and continue. She didn't say anything, but Jonah felt she understood.

'Wait,' said Sam, as Jonah neared the end of his story. 'When you logged in to see your grandmother on the Island – you were in a meta-pub?'

Jonah nodded.

'That explains it,' said Sam. 'Bradbury was right. He thought you must have led the Millennials to us, and you did.'

'No,' cried Jonah. 'No, I didn't. I wouldn't!'

'It's OK, kid.' She called him 'kid'. Like Axel had. Like she was *so* much older than he was. 'I know you didn't mean to do it. It's just that the public terminals aren't so secure these days. Your conversation with your grandmother was probably hacked.'

'Oh,' said Jonah. He felt stupid and embarrassed. He had never worried about privacy in the Metasphere. As far as Jonah knew, privacy on the internet was just another relic of his father's fairy-tale youth. 'I'm sorry. I didn't know. Do you think…your dad will believe me, right? That I'm not a spy?'

'Our dads go way back,' said Sam, 'back to the airlines

and the RAF before that. It was my dad who recruited yours into the Guardians. He'll believe you.'

'And Bradbury?'

Sam grinned. 'Don't worry about him. Bradbury's suspicious of everyone.'

'That's right. He is,' came a voice from the doorway. 'It's his job to be.'

Axel stepped into the room. Jonah wondered how long he had been standing outside, listening. 'Bradbury's in charge of security for this cell,' said Axel, 'and he takes his role seriously. He also happens to be the finest engineer I've ever known.'

'Dad,' said Sam, 'I think he's telling the truth – Jonah, I mean. He isn't working for the Millennials, he just—'

Axel nodded. He looked angry. 'Millennial spy or not, Bradbury was right, the kid's a liability to us. We can't risk having him around.'

'But…but you were the one who told me to come!' said Jonah.

'When I thought you were your father,' grumbled Axel. 'It's my own fault, I guess. I wanted so much to believe that Jason might be alive…' He sighed. 'Maybe we drop him in Tehran. He can find work there until—'

'But I don't want to… I mean, I can help you! I can… My dad, he knew something, didn't he? That's what my mum said, before she… She told me Dad knew things. Secrets. She said that, now, I know them too.'

Axel's eyes narrowed. 'What "secrets"?'

It was Sam who answered him. She repeated what Jonah had told her, about the images he had seen in his head – and, as she spoke, Axel Kavanaugh slowly lowered himself to sit on the bed beside Jonah, with a cautious new hope in his eyes.

'So, that's what he did,' breathed Axel, 'I should have guessed... Jason always had a back-up plan, and this must have been it. He couldn't tell anyone in the world what he knew, so he left a copy of his memories for the kid to find.'

'I'm not a kid,' Jonah protested.

'Jonah, listen,' said Sam, 'this is important. Have you heard of the Four Corners?'

'Of course,' said Jonah. He might have made some mistakes, but he wasn't an idiot.

'What do you know?' asked Axel.

'They're the four server farms that run the Metasphere,' said Jonah, as if he were answering one of Mr Peng's questions in school. 'But only Matthew Granger knows where they all are. He built them, and he kept their locations a secret.'

'That's not quite true, kid,' said Axel. 'Right now, those farms are in the hands of four different world governments, which is bad enough. And no one government is revealing their location.'

'Everything the Metasphere is,' said Sam, 'everything that happens in it, is defined by the Four Corners. Anyone who could find and control all four—'

'—would control the world,' concluded Axel. 'The virtual world. And you and I both know that that's the only world that matters these days.'

'Granger is out of jail,' said Sam. 'We think he's planning to retake those server farms with his Millennials.'

Jonah's first instinct was to retort *So what?* Until yesterday, after all, he had believed that Matthew Granger was the rightful steward of the Metasphere.

But then, the Millennials had killed Jonah's mother. They had tried to kill him. And he had discovered that his father was an agent for the Millennials' sworn enemies: the Guardians, whom Jonah had spent his entire life hating.

'No one man should have that power,' growled Axel, answering Jonah's unvoiced question. 'But we can't stop Granger unless we can find the Four Corners ourselves, and only one other man in the world ever knew where all four of them are.'

'A man who Granger had no choice but to tell,' continued Sam.

'His private pilot,' said Axel. 'Your father.'

Jonah looked at Axel. He looked at Sam.

'You said you have your father's memories,' said Sam. 'That means you can tell us where the Four Corners are.'

Jonah didn't know what to say to her. He didn't know what he should do. 'I can't...' he stammered. 'I've been told I have these memories, and I've seen a few flashes, but I don't...I don't know how to get at them.'

'Try!' demanded Axel.

'Please,' said Sam, more kindly.

Jonah tried. He closed his eyes and concentrated as hard as he could. He concentrated until his head hurt, but it was no use. It felt as if he *had* known where the Four Corners were, once, but he had forgotten.

'We're wasting our time,' Axel growled. He stood and made to leave the tiny cabin, but paused to round on Jonah in the doorway. 'I mean, what the hell was Jason thinking, entrusting all he knew to the kid? How is he supposed to cope with two sets of memories crammed into his little skull? No one can do that!'

Jonah's cheeks were burning again. 'I did my best,' he mumbled.

'We know you did, Jonah,' said Sam, letting out a sigh of disappointment.

'Either way, it makes no difference,' said Axel. 'The information we need, it's probably lost for ever.'

'Wait! I'm not so sure,' said Sam. 'Jonah, tell my dad how you found us – in the real world, I mean.'

'I already said,' said Jonah. 'I went to see my grandmother on the—'

'—Island of the Uploaded, yeah, and she told you about the RAF base in Dover. But how did you actually find it? The base?'

'I just followed the old road signs,' said Jonah, 'to Dover.'

104

'And then?'

'I don't understand.'

'I think I do,' said Axel. 'That base has been disused for years. I doubt there are any signposts left pointing the way to it.'

'I just... I don't know,' said Jonah. 'I just found it.'

'But how?' persisted Sam. 'You couldn't have been there before. You said you'd never left London in your life before yesterday. Did you ask someone for directions?'

'I don't know,' said Jonah helplessly. 'I don't...I don't remember.'

Axel turned to Sam. 'Are you thinking what I'm thinking, kiddo?'

'I'm thinking it's still there,' said Sam, 'everything that Jason Delacroix knew, and I'm thinking that Jonah *can* access those memories – he just doesn't know how. *Yet.*'

'I know how,' said Axel.

Sam's green eyes widened in concern. 'Oh, Dad, no.'

'There's no other way, Samantha.'

'What way?' asked Jonah, scared by the growing look of concern on Sam's face.

'There has to be, Dad. Jonah found his own way to the Air Force base. He must have accessed that memory of his father's without knowing it. We only have to work out how he did it, and then we can—'

'We don't have time.' Axel turned back to Jonah, who had been following this exchange with a queasy feeling in his stomach. 'Listen, kid,' he said, before correcting himself. 'I mean, *Jonah*, I wouldn't ask this of you normally, but we're down to the wire here. You're gonna help us, right? That's why you came looking for us. You're gonna help us stop Granger and the Millennials, like Jason would have wanted.'

'So it's really true, then,' stalled Jonah, 'what my mum said? That my dad was really… He was working as a double agent? He was really a…a Guardian?'

'You didn't know?' said Sam.

'Jonah was just a boy,' said Axel. 'Jason didn't want to drag him into all this, this war of ours, before he was ready. But, make no mistake, kid, everything Jason did, he did for you. He wanted you to grow up in a world that was free.'

Jonah's heart ached as if there was a hole in it. He was beginning to feel he hadn't known his father at all, as if he was a stranger to him.

'We should tell him, Dad,' said Sam. 'Tell Jonah what we're doing. He deserves – he needs – to know everything before he…' Her voice tailed off.

'What is it?' asked Jonah, nervously. 'What do I need to know? And…and what is it exactly you want me to do, anyway?'

But Axel never got the chance to answer his questions.

Jonah heard a muffled screaming of jet engines, and suddenly the airship was rocked violently. Axel steadied himself by hanging onto the door, but Jonah was pitched off his bunk and fell on top of Sam. He met her green eyes and realised at last where he had seen her before. She was the girl that had cost him the race.

An old speaker in one corner of the ceiling sputtered into life, and Bradbury's voice came through it: '*You'd best get up to the cockpit, Axel. We've got trouble!*'

15

A hawk-nosed jet fighter was hurtling right at the airship.

Jonah gaped at it in horror. He hadn't seen a real aeroplane in years – and now, he was on a collision course with one.

Bradbury was wrestling with the co-pilot's controls, and Axel leapt into the pilot's seat to assist him, but there was little either of them could do. Their fat, slow-moving vessel was easy prey for the sleek, grey hunter.

At the last possible second, however, the fighter sheared away from them, buffeting them in its jet stream. Jonah followed its progress through the cockpit's portside window, and was dismayed to see it banking to the right, coming around again.

'He's playing with us,' Axel growled.

'Not for long,' Bradbury said, tight-jawed. 'He's already fired a warning shot. He's giving us one last chance to transmit clearance codes.'

'I thought we had them,' said Sam, leaning between the two seats.

'Already tried,' said Bradbury. 'The codes we have are out of date.'

'They must have changed,' said Axel. 'If there's

anyone on board that plane, we're dead. Chances are, though, it's only a drone. Could we—?'

'Working on it, Axel, but it's gonna be a close one.'

Standing in the cockpit doorway, Jonah felt completely helpless. He didn't dare speak, or even move, for fear of getting in the way. He hadn't exactly been invited up here in the first place. He had just followed Sam.

Axel put a hand to his ear, listening to his headset. 'The Millennial plane is preparing to fire,' he announced, 'in five…four…three…'

Bradbury typed frantically at a datapad set into an instrument panel. The jet fighter was bearing down on them again, and the airship shuddered as if in anticipation. This time, however, the plane soared over them and kept on going.

'You did it!' cried Sam.

Axel punched the air in triumph.

Jonah couldn't restrain himself any longer. 'What? What did he do?'

'Instead of sending the clearance codes,' said Sam, 'Bradbury uploaded a virus to the fighter's systems. It severed the link between the fighter and its operator on the ground. It's flying on emergency autopilot now.'

'I bought us time,' said Bradbury, wrenching off his headset, clambering out of his seat, 'to bail out of this damn blimp.'

'No,' said Axel, 'not yet.'

'Are you crazy, Axel? The Millennials will regain

control of that plane and have it back on our tail before you know it!'

'I've been talking to the kid, Bradbury, to Jonah. He knows – at least, we figure he knows – the locations of the Four Corners.'

Bradbury shot Jonah a distrustful look. 'All the more reason,' he said, 'to jump for it before we're shot down.'

'No, no, no, you don't understand. Granger *knows* that he knows. That's why he sent those remotes to the RAF base, and why he's searching the skies for us now. It's not us the Millennials want dead, Bradbury, it's the kid!'

Bradbury looked straight at Jonah with contempt and anger. 'So you brought the war right to us?'

'They'll be combing the French countryside before we've buried our chutes,' said Axel. 'We won't stand a chance on foot unless...'

'Unless we get some local help,' said Sam.

'Delphine,' said Bradbury.

Axel nodded. 'Delphine knows the ground. She can get us past any Millennial search parties and over the border. But it won't be so easy to find her down there. If we want her help, we'll have to contact her first, and have her come to us.'

'I know where to find her,' offered Sam, 'in the Metasphere. I'll go.'

'I'll come with you,' said Jonah, quickly. He expected Axel or Bradbury to object to this, but neither of them did.

'Make sure you're quick about it,' Bradbury warned Sam. 'We've got maybe fifteen minutes before that fighter comes back – and, next time, I think it's safe to say its controller will be shooting first and asking questions later.'

Jonah and Sam plugged into a terminal in one of the empty cabins.

They arrived in the Metasphere in a sunny cornfield. The yellow cornstalks came up to Jonah's nose, and buried Sam completely. They flapped their wings and the dragon and the unicorn rose into the air.

'Are you sure this is the right place?' asked Jonah. The cornfield spread to the horizon in each direction. 'There's no one around for miles.'

'They're here,' said Sam. 'We just can't see them yet.'

She took a mental bearing from the position of the sun, and led Jonah north-east.

He hadn't noticed before how striking Sam's unicorn avatar was. It was dwarfed by Jonah's dragon, but would have been taller than his old humatar. Its hide was a pearly white, and its feathered wings shone where they caught the sunlight. The unicorn's mane was red. It had a splay of red tail hair too, the same shade as Sam's real hair. Jonah could almost have enjoyed this summer's day, flying through this cornfield with her, had it not been for the urgency of his real-world plight.

Then, in the blink of an eye, the cornfield disappeared.

Jonah was in the courtyard of a medieval castle – and there was a wall behind him, hemming him in.

Assorted avatars were gathered before him, many of them guardsmen armed with pikestaffs. They moved in to seize hold of him.

Jonah struggled, and surprised himself once more with the strength of his dragon avatar. He sent two of his would-be captors sprawling, but more came to their assistance. They pinned Jonah's wings to his side.

'It's OK, Jonah,' said Sam. 'They're friends.'

'Some friends,' scoffed Jonah, struggling to unfurl his wings.

'Identify yourselves!' a brawny guardsman demanded.

Sam gave her name and Jonah's, then reeled off a string of letters and numbers that Jonah took to be a password. 'We have to see Delphine,' said Sam.

'I'll have to verify your avatars,' said the guardsman, gruffly.

'Of course,' said Sam, 'but hurry, please. Our lives are in danger in the real world.'

The guardsman nodded. He gave a signal to the other avatars, and Jonah was prodded forward, towards the castle's forbidding grey towers.

From the conical roofs of those towers flew black and green flags, fluttering in the computer-generated breeze.

They were marched beneath a raised portcullis, across a marble-floored hallway, to a small, carpeted reception room. The door closed heavily behind them, and a yellow padlock icon appeared in the virtual stone.

Jonah hammered on the door with his wings. 'Hey!' he cried. 'Weren't you listening to what Sam said? This is urgent! You can't just lock us up in here!'

'They heard,' Sam assured him, 'and Delphine will be here. Soon.'

She didn't sound too confident herself – but there was nothing either of them could do about it. Nothing but wait.

Jonah floated up and down the room, anxiously. Sam used her unicorn's horn to skewer a red apple from a fruit bowl on the table. She flipped it into her mouth and crunched on it. Food in the Metasphere could be programmed to taste exquisite, but the eater had to remember that it wouldn't sustain his real-world body.

'Who is this Delphine, anyway?' asked Jonah. 'Another Guardian?'

'Not exactly,' said Sam, 'but her group, they...' Sam searched for the words. 'They share some enough of our goals to be allies in times of need.'

'And you're sure she will help us?'

'Once she realises what's at stake,' said Sam, 'I hope so.'

Jonah was still pondering on this when a dialogue balloon popped up in front of him. FIVE MINUTES, it said. A reminder from Bradbury, no doubt.

Sam butted the door with her horn. 'Hello?' she

called. 'Is there anyone out there? We're running out of time. We have to see Delphine. Hello?'

They heard a soft clunk from the door, and the padlock icon disappeared. Jonah and Sam stepped back as the door opened, and a knight in shining silver armour floated into the room. She was flanked by two guardsmen.

'Delphine?' guessed Jonah.

The knight gave a short bow of acknowledgement. Her visor was closed, hiding her face. Her helmet was crested by a single black and green feather.

'Little Samantha Kavanaugh,' said Delphine in a broad French accent. 'Still chasing after your papa?'

'More like the other way around these days,' said Sam coolly. 'So you verified our avatars and—'

'*C'est exact*. Your avatar checks out.' Delphine then turned to Jonah. 'Your dragon, on the other hand, is the avatar of a dead man.'

'Long story,' said Sam. 'You are looking at Jason Delacroix's avatar. But that isn't Jason Delacroix behind it, it's his son. Delphine, we need your help.'

Things happened quickly after that.

Sam explained to Delphine about the Millennial drone, and asked for refuge. She stressed that the knowledge in Jonah's brain was vital to the Guardians' cause. After that, Jonah noticed that Delphine could hardly keep her eyes off him and couldn't help but feel like a pawn in their dangerous games.

Sam handed Delphine an encrypted cookie, downloaded from the airship's systems. It contained their real-world co-ordinates. Delphine swallowed it right through her silver mask, and in return handed Sam a virtual croissant.

'Directions to a safe house,' she explained. 'I will meet you there.'

Then she had her guards escort Jonah and Sam back outside. They passed straight through the wall of the castle courtyard – and, when Jonah looked back, once more he could see nothing but the cornfield behind him.

They flew back to their exit halos and Jonah awoke in the airship cabin.

He had barely had time to adjust to the real world again when Bradbury thrust a heavy parachute pack at him. 'C'mon, kid,' he grunted, 'time we were outta here!'

As Jonah unplugged himself with one hand, he was relieved that Bradbury had said 'we' and not 'you'.

Jonah rose unsteadily to his feet. He hefted the parachute in front of him, tried to work out which of its many canvas straps went where. He panicked for a second. He didn't know what to do – and Axel, Bradbury and Sam were already racing out of the room.

Jonah stumbled after Sam, who was donning her own parachute like an expert on the run.

'Do what I do!' she shouted.

He followed what she was doing, and realised that the harness was similar to the one on the escape glider he had used yesterday. Once again, his thoughts wandered to those dreadful final moments when he had begged his mother not to push him from the building. But the wind whipped Jonah back to reality.

Axel had wrenched open the main hatchway. He and Bradbury dived through it without hesitation, and the wind reached in and almost snatched Jonah right out after them. Sam was still there next to him, and she checked over Jonah's pack, tightened a couple of his straps, grabbed his arm, and pulled him out of the airship.

Jonah was falling again.

Sam was right beside him, but angling her body away from Jonah's. She was trying to get away from him, so their parachutes wouldn't become tangled once they were deployed. And, over the screaming of the wind in his ears, Jonah could hear another sound: a horribly familiar sound. The sound of jet engines.

The next thing he heard was a staccato burst of gunfire. Jonah looked up, to see the airship listing alarmingly as the Millennial fighter swooped away from it in triumph. The airship had been punctured. There were flames licking about its starboard fin.

Sam pulled her ripcord. A large, white parachute billowed out of her pack and seemed to yank her upwards, away from Jonah. Of course, Sam was still falling – it was just that her rate of descent compared to Jonah's had slowed sharply.

Jonah tried to emulate Sam's lead, but couldn't find his cord. He searched frantically, beginning to panic. He was relieved when his sweaty hand closed around its prize at last. He closed his eyes and pulled.

Jonah now felt himself being hoisted upwards as the parachute unfurled above him. He felt as if he was floating now, safe. He could see the white discs of Bradbury and Axel's chutes, a surprisingly long way below him. They were descending towards a spread of green fields. Jonah couldn't see Sam.

The returning shriek of the jet fighter reminded Jonah that he wasn't out of danger. It was banking right for them. And high above, the stricken airship vented smoke and began to spiral downwards.

The airship was collapsing, shedding chunks of flaming debris and solar panels. Jonah held his breath. He knew that, should any of the wreckage tear through his parachute, it would be the end.

He was a little more prepared this time for the speed with which the ground approached. But unlike the day before, Jonah had no rubber wheels to absorb the impact. It was going to hurt.

He bent his knees, landed on his feet and rolled as quickly as he could. He felt as if a giant sledgehammer had struck his every bone simultaneously – but, as he came to rest face down in the prickly, sweet-smelling grass, Jonah judged that nothing was actually broken.

The parachute fluttered down over him, and it took him a breathless, blind minute to struggle free of its folds.

He was just in time to see the flaming remains of the airship disappearing behind a copse of trees, leaving a smoke trail behind it. The ground beneath Jonah trembled slightly as the wounded behemoth crashed into it, nose-first.

Then, for a short time, there was silence.

16

Matthew Granger was in a foul mood.

His dinner – his first decent meal in three years, a rare steak prepared by France's top chef – had just been interrupted. He had told his staff to alert him when Jason Delacroix was confirmed dead, but the fatigue-clad Millennial brought only speculation.

'We found the airship, sir,' he said.

'Survivors?' asked Granger, placing his fork gently on the table but making a point to keep a grip on his steak knife.

'We can't be sure,' replied the Millennial agent.

'Who was in charge of this operation?' asked Granger, rising to his feet and slipping the knife into a small hold built into his right cyber-kinetic leg.

A hush fell over Granger's operations room as he marched through the door. Two dozen Millennials hunched at their terminals and did their best to not catch their master's eye. They knew, either from experience or from rumours, that you did not want to be in Granger's line of vision when he had been given bad news.

'Who was flying the drone that engaged the Guardian

vessel?' he asked. A bespectacled youth with a mop of wiry hair raised a tentative hand.

Granger strode up to his terminal and scrolled quickly through a ream of densely-packed data on the screen.

'You had them in your sights,' he said quietly, dangerously.

'Y-yes, sir,' the programmer stammered, 'but I couldn't be sure—'

'You had them in your sights,' repeated Granger, 'and, according to this report, they transmitted an out-of-date clearance code. So, you fired a warning shot?'

'Yes, sir, I did, but—'

Granger spoke through gritted teeth. 'We are standing on the brink of a new world order. Everything we have worked for is ours for the taking. Only one man can keep us from claiming our prize – a traitor to our cause, a terrorist – and you had that man in your sights and *you fired a warning shot?*'

Granger's voice had risen as he spoke, until these last words came out as a scream. The young programmer was cowed into silence. He had turned quite pale.

'Begging your pardon, sir,' said the Millennial who had collected Granger, 'but the airship *was* destroyed and the target almost certainly killed.'

Granger rounded on him. 'Jason Delacroix has survived worse than this. He had all the time he needed to bail out of that airship and escape on the ground!'

'We've diverted all available drones to the area, sir, and we have sympathisers among the French *Gendarmerie* who can…' The Millennial tailed off, as Granger turned away from him with a snort of contempt.

'I have devoted my life to the fulfilment of a new world,' he raged, 'a better world for everyone. And when I put my trust in other people, they let me down. People like you—' He rounded on the trembling programmer. '—don't deserve to live in the world I built. And you won't!'

Granger grabbed hold of the programmer and pulled up the back of his shirt, revealing his standard DI socket. Granger reached for the steak knife and cut out the plastic ring embedded in his spine. His victim screamed as Granger pulled out his Direct Interface socket.

Granger dashed the blood-soaked DI socket to the floor. 'Don't let me see your avatar again!' he ordered, pointing with the knife to the door.

'Sir, please,' the boy snivelled. 'W-what will I do? Where will I…?'

'I don't know,' said Granger. 'I don't care. You're nobody now. Nothing. Live out your life in the dreary real world. You are not welcome in mine.'

Nobody spoke, nobody even breathed, as the programmer shuffled out. His head was bowed, his hands clutched to the hole in his back, and he was sobbing.

Granger addressed his remaining followers, more

calmly: 'I trust you have all learned something from this. We are not playing games here. This isn't a practise run. What happens in the next few days will decide the future of humanity. We will bring order to our existence, or perish in chaos. There is no room for doubt, because doubt leads to mistakes. If you cannot pledge your unswerving, unquestioning loyalty to me, you should leave this room now.'

As he had expected, nobody dared stir.

Granger waited for a moment for his words to sink in fully, then reminded his people that Jason Delacroix was their first priority. He wanted him found and killed, along with anyone he had been in contact with, anyone who could know his secrets.

Granger returned to his suite with a feeling of dread in his stomach. He sat back at his table, placed his napkin on his lap.

'I need a new knife!' he barked.

He hadn't planned for this. He had watched his enemies growing in number from his prison cell, but he didn't have a contingency plan for them finding a secret weapon.

He hadn't counted on the Guardians finding Jason Delacroix, alive.

He wouldn't let them beat him. He had waited too long, fought too hard, planned too well to let anyone stand in his way now.

There was a terminal in his room, of course. Granger

kicked off his shoes, lay on his bed, took a fresh adaptor from the drawer beside him and plugged himself in.

He closed his eyes and, when he opened them again, he was elsewhere: a white-walled conference room with a long, polished table, a video screen and a water cooler. He was looking through the eyes of his avatar: a fat, black, hairy spider, a metre and a half tall. Granger thought of this room as the centre of his web.

The room had no doors and no windows. The only way to reach it was to set the Point of Origin in the Metasphere to its exact co-ordinates – and these were known to only five people. As soon as he had adjusted to his new perspective, Granger ran a subroutine buried in his avatar code sequence, and messaged the other four.

As he waited for them to respond, he paced the conference room, luxuriating in the ability to stretch his eight legs. His cyber-kinetic walking system was at the bleeding edge of technology, but this felt like the real thing. This was freedom.

They arrived one by one, popping into existence around the table. A white Siberian tiger was first, followed by a slavering werewolf. The third avatar to appear was a spider, like Granger's, but smaller and red in hue. The fourth was a pyramid, with a single blue eye poised atop it.

These were Granger's most trusted lieutenants, the leaders of the four armies that would take back the

Metasphere for him. Squatting at the table head, he asked each of them in turn for a progress report.

'I have a force of sixty assembled in the west,' said the werewolf, 'with more on the way.'

'My force of eighty is en route to the Northern Corner,' said the tiger, 'though as you know it is a good march from our position here.'

'We have had no shortage of recruits to our cause in the east,' said the pyramid.

'That is good to hear,' said Granger, 'because I am moving up the schedule. I want our assault to begin in all four locations, twenty-four hours from now.'

'Sir,' protested the red spider, 'I'm not sure we can… As you know, our target down here is a thousand miles from any big city. Our equipment, our recruits, are—'

'Twenty-four hours,' said Granger. 'I don't care what it takes, or what it costs, you will be ready. Is that clear?'

'Yes, sir,' said the spider, meekly. The others confirmed their assent too, with the Siberian tiger boasting that her men would march through the night on her say-so.

'We need to move fast, people,' said Granger. 'Right now, the Four Corners are in the hands of the faltering governments, and therefore vulnerable. But the Guardians know the locations of all four and they won't wait long to make their move. I want those servers secured.

'Any intel on where they'll strike first?' asked the tiger.

'It could be anywhere, but the Southern holds the Uploaded, and if the Guardians are anything, they're sentimental. I will fly to the Southern Corner myself and take charge of the team there.'

The red spider opened his mouth to protest, but Granger silenced him with a glare.

He dismissed his lieutenants, who each dived through their exit halos and vanished. They had a great deal of work to do, in the real world.

Granger had work to do too, but he lingered for a moment. He brushed a hand over one wall of the conference room, and it became transparent. Through the wall, he could see the skyscrapers of a thriving meta-city, and flocks of avatars in the sky. He longed to fly with them, but that would have to wait.

Granger couldn't show himself in the Metasphere. His avatar was too well-known. The wall was transparent only from this side. Soon, though, when this world belonged to him again…

He smiled to himself. It had been irrational of him to worry about the Guardians. They were a disorganised rabble, clinging to outmoded dogma. They had no one with Granger's genius, leadership or vision. *So, let them come*, he thought. *Let them come for the Four Corners, and we'll just see who reaches them first!*

The race was on.

17

Another plane zoomed overhead.

The Guardians took cover beneath a scraggly hedgerow. Jonah lay in the dirt, with brambles scratching his cheeks. Still, he was glad to give his feet a short rest.

When the sound of jet engines had receded, they brushed down their clothes and walked on. Jonah felt as if they had been walking for hours. It couldn't have been all that long, though, because the sun was still high in the sky.

The others had landed not far from Jonah. He had clocked them from the air and found them quickly enough. They had covered Jonah's parachute with grass and soil, to keep it from being seen from above. Then they had set off across the French fields on foot.

Sam was leading the way, with a compass she had produced from a pocket of her black coveralls. She avoided well-trodden footpaths, and skirted fields rather than crossing them, keeping cover close at hand.

Jonah had never been in such a wide-open space before – not in the real world, anyway. It felt as if he, Sam, Axel and Bradbury were the only people in the world. They weren't, of course.

They had to hide in a ditch from a slow-grinding

tractor, driven by a grizzled old man in denims. He didn't look to Jonah like a Millennial agent. Still, Bradbury eased his shotgun out of his trench coat and held it ready. Jonah was relieved – for the old man's sake – when the tractor had passed them by.

They set off again, and soon came into view of a small, whitewashed farmhouse, with alternating green and black shutters.

'That's where we wait,' confirmed Sam. She pulled ahead of the others, and Jonah hurried to keep up with her, leaving Axel and Bradbury trailing behind them.

'You were going to tell me about your mission,' he said, glad of the chance to talk with Sam alone. 'Before the airship was attacked.'

Sam nodded. 'There's a man in Shanghai,' she said. 'He's invented a way to protect the Metasphere from outside control. A device. He calls it the Chang Bridge.'

'You were going to China?' said Jonah. 'In an airship?'

'This,' said Sam, 'this device, it's everything the Guardians have ever wanted, a way to keep the Metasphere free. The trouble is, we may have found it too late. Granger is out of jail – and, for the Chang Bridge to work, we still have to find the Four Corners. That was your father's job, but when he...when he died...'

'He took the information with him,' concluded Jonah.

'Until now.'

'Um,' said Jonah. 'Axel, your dad…he said there might be a way…?'

'He wants to do a full search,' said Sam, 'of your head.'

'You can do that? How?'

'With some software developed a few years back,' said Sam. 'We hook you up to a terminal, and the program goes through all the data in your brain, organising and indexing it. Once it's done, we can search for specific terms.'

'Terms like "The Four Corners",' Jonah guessed.

'If you really do know where they are – even if the information is buried deep in your subconscious – we can find it with a few keystrokes.'

'Wow!'

'Don't be too impressed,' said Sam. 'The process hurts like a vice grip to the grey matter, and it could…'

'Could what?'

'Damage you, Jonah. Permanently.'

Jonah recalled how eager Axel was to perform the search and wondered if he wasn't safer on his own after all.

'Thanks for sticking up for me,' Jonah said. 'Against your dad.'

'Don't mention it,' she said. Jonah smiled. 'Ever.'

*

The farmhouse had been abandoned long ago. A few pieces of broken furniture were piled into a corner of the main room, beside a fireplace, and a fine layer of dust covered the hard wood floors. Jonah noticed there were no footprints in it.

'You call this a safe house?' Bradbury mocked.

'This is more like a "wait house",' replied Axel. 'You don't go to Delphine. She comes to you.'

Bradbury shook his head and took up a position by the window, with his shotgun. 'If you want to be useful,' he said to Jonah, 'keep an eye out back for the *gendarmerie.*'

Sam noticed Jonah's confused look. 'Military police,' she explained.

'We're in France, kid,' grunted Bradbury. 'They still have some semblance of a real-world society here, at least on the ground.'

Axel concurred: 'And you can bet your sweet life they'll investigate an airship crash on their soil.'

Jonah cast his mind back to one of Mr Peng's lessons. He recalled that, thanks to a trading alliance with Iran and Russia, France was one of the few western countries that still had plentiful access to oil. Consequently, its government was more stable than most. And the Guardians...

The Guardians were an illegal organisation in most countries. Should Jonah be caught with three of them like this, he would probably end up in prison.

No wonder Bradbury was being so cautious, he thought. For the first time, Jonah realised the awful truth: that the whole world really was out to get them!

They sat in silence, the four weary fugitives, and Jonah watched as the daylight dimmed through the back windows. Much to his surprise, he started drifting towards sleep. He was woken by his own stomach, growling with hunger.

Then another growl – of a vehicle pulling up in the farmyard outside. Jonah heard a car door opening and a woman's voice called, 'If you want not the trouble, you should come with me.'

He recognised that voice. It was the voice of the knight avatar from the castle.

'Delphine!' he told the others. He was racing for the back door, heedless of Bradbury's whispered caution to him to wait.

Jonah stepped out of the farmhouse, and was blinded by a bright pair of headlights. He could just make out the shape of a dilapidated truck behind them, and a woman standing by the driver's door. She didn't look like Jonah had imagined she would. She was about nineteen years old, wore old-fashioned glasses, and had black hair that flowed gently down to her shoulders.

'It is you, isn't it?' he said, uncertainly. 'Delphine?'

'And you must be the *petit garçon* who dresses up in his father's clothing.'

Delphine fixed Jonah with a long and condescending stare. It felt like a stand-off. She looked even more mistrustful when his three friends emerged from the farmhouse behind him. Jonah noticed that Bradbury's hand was inside his trench coat, no doubt on his shotgun.

'*Merci de nous rencontre*,' said Sam, surprising Jonah with her French.

'You spoke of important information, inside this *garçon*'s head?'

'The most important,' said Axel, holding up four fingers.

'*Les quatre coins*,' she whispered. 'We must go quickly. The *gendarmerie*, they are searching the countryside for you.' She opened up the back of the khaki truck and ushered Sam and the two men inside, but not Jonah.

'You to me do not look very dangerous. You can ride *avec moi*.'

Jonah didn't know whether to take that as a compliment or an insult.

In contrast, there was no misunderstanding the warning look that Bradbury gave him: *Don't say too much!*

18

Delphine threw the truck at high speed around dark, winding country roads. The suspension was shot, bouncing Jonah around like a pinball despite his seatbelt.

'So,' she said at length, 'I am curious about this online disguise of yours. Tell me how it came to be that you could filter your father's avatar.'

Jonah didn't want to talk about it and didn't know if he could trust her anyhow. He remained tight-lipped.

As they approached the lights of a small town, the roads became smoother and straighter.

'So, you decided to join the Revolution?'

'I...I don't know,' mumbled Jonah. 'Maybe.'

'Your Guardians are fighting for a free, open Metasphere. This is good for our planet, I think. Here in France, as in many other countries, there are still those who champion the old selfish, destructive ways. But a virtual lifestyle is carbon-free.'

'You're an eco-warrior?' said Jonah.

Delphine pursed her lips in amusement. 'Samantha did not tell you?'

'Only that you're a Guardian ally.'

'Perhaps you have heard the name *GuerreVert*?'

Jonah had – and the sound of it filled him with horror. 'That hotel bombing in Vienna last year? Wasn't that…?'

'I did not take part in the operation myself, but I celebrate it as a glorious blow struck for our cause.'

'But…but a lot of people died in that explosion. Innocent bystanders.'

'Not *innocent*,' snapped Delphine. 'And not *a lot* compared to the hundreds of thousands lost yearly to the effects of global warming. There was a conference in that hotel, between the world's remaining oil producers. They are the ones who chose to wage war upon the Earth – and, in any war, there must be casualties.'

'I think you're wrong,' he said.

Delphine pointed to the glove box. Jonah opened it and pulled out a black canvas bag.

'Put it on,' she said. Jonah realised it was a hood. 'I'm not asking.'

Jonah rode the remainder of the journey in silence and in darkness.

Jonah felt Delphine swing the truck onto a gravel road and then briefly onto a smooth surface before switching off.

'Put that back where you found it,' she ordered.

Jonah took off the hood and found himself in a garage. Sam, Axel and Bradbury climbed out of the back, rubbing their bruised arms and legs.

Delphine locked up the garage, then led the way through a maze of dark back streets, to a cobbled alleyway behind a row of old, crumbling houses. She hauled herself up onto a rusted fire-escape ladder, climbed two storeys, then disappeared through an open sash window. Sam and Axel followed immediately, but Jonah hesitated.

He was still thinking about *GuerreVert*.

Jonah had been prepared to follow Axel, even though he was a Guardian, because he had been his dad's best friend. Sam, he had liked from the start. Jonah had been ready to accept that he might have been wrong all his life, that the Guardians weren't the bad guys, because after all how else could his dad have been one of them?

But *GuerreVert*… There was no doubting what they were.

A large part of Jonah wanted to run while he could, before he got even deeper into trouble. He might have tried it too, had it not been for the daunting presence of Bradbury, behind him, waiting to climb the ladder last.

Where could Jonah have run to in this strange country, anyway? Who else was there to help him?

The window opened onto a narrow landing, in a faded guesthouse. Delphine had disappeared, but a younger girl with a blue bow in her straw-coloured hair showed Jonah upstairs to a cramped attic room with a sink and a bed.

He sat on the side of the bed and buried his face in his hands. He felt confused and alone. What was he doing here, in the middle of France, with known terrorists?

A few minutes later, Sam knocked on his door to tell Jonah that a meal had been prepared for everyone downstairs. He didn't want to go. He couldn't face anyone at the moment, not even Sam and especially not Delphine. He only wanted to sleep, in the futile hope that things might look a little clearer to him in the morning. However, the gnawing hunger in Jonah's stomach won out over his weariness.

Dinner was stew: the usual artificial protein, but served with hunks of real, crusty bread. Jonah sat round a table with Sam, Axel, Bradbury, Delphine, the girl with the bow and two more strangers, a man and a woman.

The others talked about the states of the world governments, and about the rumour that Matthew Granger was in Paris – though there had been alleged sightings of him in three other cities too. Jonah gulped down his food, taking no part in the discussion. However, his ears pricked up at the sound of his surname.

'—always suspected he was one of yours,' Delphine was saying.

'One of the best,' said Axel.

'He must have been,' agreed Delphine, 'to have worked so deep undercover for so long. For how long was he Matthew Granger's pilot?' They were talking about Jonah's dad. 'He must have been a source of much useful information.'

'He might have been,' said Bradbury, bluntly, 'if he had survived long enough to bring it to us.'

'Yes, yes,' said Delphine, 'a regrettable turn of events – but all is not lost, I hear? Jason Delacroix was able to pass on what he knew to the *garçon?*'

Jonah almost choked on his stew. Bradbury shot him an accusing glare, and Jonah wanted to protest that he hadn't told Delphine anything, she was just guessing. By the time he could speak, however, it was too late.

Delphine had continued: 'The problem must be accessing that knowledge. If you wish, I will contact a specialist who can—'

'It's all in hand,' Axel grunted through a mouthful of bread. 'We're gonna run a search of the kid's brain. Tonight.'

Jonah looked across the table at Sam, in alarm. She seemed as surprised as he was by her father's pronouncement.

'A pity,' sighed Delphine, 'that your agent couldn't kill Granger when he had the chance. How careless of him to lose his own life instead. Had he been one of ours—'

'That's my dad you're talking about.'

Jonah hadn't meant to say the words out loud. He just hadn't been able to keep them inside. He had muttered them under his breath, but everyone had heard all the same, and everyone had turned to look at him. At first,

Jonah squirmed under the unwanted attention. But quickly a defiant spirit rose within him.

'I said, that's my dad you're talking about!' he repeated, more boldly. 'And, Guardian or not, he would never have... I know he couldn't have killed anyone, no matter who they were. And he wouldn't have worked with anyone who could. It was people like you who killed him!'

He pushed his bowl away from him, stood up, marched to the door with his fists clenched.

He heard Sam's voice behind him: 'Jonah...' He stopped in the doorway, turned back to them all, their astonished faces staring up at him.

He looked at Axel. 'And you. I don't know what my father saw in you, but I won't let you touch my brain.'

Then he turned, and walked calmly up the stairs to his attic room.

19

There was an unwelcome knock on Jonah's door.

'Go away!' he shouted.

He was lying on his bed, his arms wrapped around his pillows. His heartbeat was still racing after the scene in the dining room downstairs.

The door opened. Jonah looked up, hoping despite himself that it might be Sam who had come to see him. It was Axel.

'Pretty tough words,' said Axel. 'Can't say that maybe I don't deserve them.'

'Maybe?' replied Jonah.

'OK, probably. And that's the best you'll get.'

Jonah didn't say anything. He knew Axel wanted to get inside his head, and he wasn't going to let him.

Axel turned a chair around and sat on it, resting his elbows on its back. Jonah didn't move. 'Listen, I just came to check you were all right.'

'No,' said Jonah, 'you didn't. You came to talk me into letting you search my brain. To find more places to blow up. More people to kill. Well, you're wasting your time.'

'Now listen here, son,' said Axel.

'I'm not your son,' snapped Jonah. 'I'm not anybody's

son! Not any more.'

'I know you're upset by what Delphine said, but I think—'

'You almost had me believing… On the airship, you said my dad was one of you, that he died for the Guardians. But he didn't. My dad didn't die for the Guardians. The Guardians killed him!'

'No. No, Jonah, that's not what happened.'

'If the Guardians didn't do it, then someone like *GuerreVert* did, someone like Delphine, and you… You're happy to work with them, knowing what they are.'

'Jonah, no one ever claimed responsibility for the airport bombings,' said Axel. 'You must know that. The media blamed the Guardians, but—'

'Who else should they have blamed? The Millennials? Do you think they'd try to kill their own leader? The Millennials would have known Mr Granger was flying into London that day – that my dad was flying him into Heathrow.'

'The Millennials killed your mother, Jonah. That much, we do know.'

As if Jonah had needed reminding. He pushed his face deeper into his pillows and willed himself not to cry.

'It might not help you to hear this,' said Axel, 'but Delphine lost her parents too. She was six when Mauritius finally sank into the sea. There weren't enough rescue boats. She was sent away with the other kids. Her mother promised her she would follow. That's what drives Delphine, Jonah. She blames everyone who flies a plane or drills for oil or who manufactures plastic for the genocide of her people and the murder of her family.'

'Sounds right up her street, then,' said Jonah, 'to bomb an airport.'

'Maybe,' conceded Axel, 'but if *GuerreVert* had done something like that, I figure they'd be shouting it from the rooftops, don't you?'

Once again, Jonah found he had nothing to say to that.

'We need Delphine,' said Axel. 'Hell, I wish we didn't. You know this wasn't the plan. We were meant to take the airship to Iran, hop a plane to China from there. No can do, not any more. Our contact in Tehran won't wait for us. Too much Millennial heat. Only Delphine can help us.'

'How?'

'She can get us on a plane as far as Moscow.' Jonah raised his head, looked at Axel, who grinned. 'Yeah, I know. She says as long as it's in a righteous cause...'

Jonah sat up on the bed, drew his knees up to his chest. 'What happens in Moscow?'

'We have contacts there too,' said Axel.

'More killers?'

'I know how you feel, believe me,' said Axel, 'but Delphine is right about one thing. We are fighting a war here, for the future of our world – of both our worlds – and we cannot afford to lose it. If that means we make a few compromises, if it means some people get hurt… Well, I hope, in time, you will come to understand that, or at the very least, accept it.'

'I don't want to kill anybody,' said Jonah firmly. 'It's not right.'

'You sound like your dad.'

'You knew him well, didn't you?' said Jonah.

'We were best mates,' said Axel, 'back to RAF Flight School. We always watched each other's backs. We used to fly escort missions together, for the old oil tankers sailing from the Persian Gulf.'

'I remember,' said Jonah. 'Dad used to say the tankers were easy targets for the pirates and rival governments and the…the eco-terrorists.'

'Don't tell Delphine,' said Axel with a conspiratorial wink, 'but Jason and me, between us, we must have sunk at least a dozen *GuerreVert* ships in our time.'

'Why did Dad leave the Air Force?' asked Jonah.

'Isn't it obvious?' said Axel. 'The Metasphere was starting to take off, back then. Jason and me, we spent our off-hours surfing. We believed in what Matthew Granger was building. Everyone did. In the real world, the tankers were sailing less and less often, and fewer of them were making it to the UK. There were food shortages and riots. We were fighting a losing battle. But, in the virtual world, Jason met a girl.'

'My mum,' said Jonah. That story, he had heard.

'Jason wanted to get back to London,' said Axel, 'where Miriam was. He resigned his commission, went to work for a commercial airline out of Heathrow. He found me a job there, too. Those were good days, hanging out at the Icarus. That was the beauty of the Metasphere. You could have a layover in Singapore or Hong Kong, but still hook up with your mates for a virtual drink in the evening.'

'And was this when…? I mean, how did you…?'

'How did we wind up with the Guardians?'

Jonah nodded. 'Was it Dad who…?'

'They approached me first,' said Axel. 'Jason wasn't around much at the time. A little matter of Miriam being pregnant.'

'Oh,' said Jonah.

'The thing about your dad was, Jonah, he was always thinking about the future. Not like me. I don't think long past where my next pint is coming from. You ask Sam about that. But Jason, he could see the way the world was turning. No need for pilots any more, when nobody can afford to fly.'

'You were the last of your kind,' said Jonah.

'You remember him saying that too?'

'I'm not sure. I'm not sure if that was my memory or…or his.'

'He was right, too. Jason saw it coming. He cashed out his pension, turned it into meta-dollars, bought the gift shop, did pretty well with it for a while too.'

'You were saying,' prompted Jonah, 'about the Guardians.'

'Jason was always talking,' said Axel, 'especially after you were born. He could see how Granger was taking more and more. He used to say, by the time you grew up—'

'—that the virtual world would be in as big a mess as the real one,' said Jonah.

'That's right.'

'I can feel it,' said Jonah. 'How frustrated Dad felt, how he wanted...'

'I joined the Guardians on an impulse,' said Axel. 'It sounded like fun, and it was a way to keep on flying. That's me. But Jason... He made me believe in the cause. So, when they needed someone... When the job as Granger's pilot came up, and it looked like Jason was the only one of us with a snowball's chance of actually landing it, they asked me to recruit him.'

'He didn't want to do it at first,' said Jonah. 'He knew it would be dangerous. He...he didn't want me to have to grow up without him.'

Jonah felt like he was in two places at once. He could see Axel in the attic room, greying and tired looking, but he could also see him as a younger man, full of energy and enthusiasm.

'You're accessing his memories, aren't you, son?' said Axel.

That was it. Jonah was reliving moments of his father's life. Flashes of memories: talking to Axel, a discussion, then an argument with his mum, and a job interview with Matthew Granger. It was disorienting and confusing, and Jonah couldn't control it, but it was all in there. His father's memories, stored in his own brain.

'Maybe Sam was right. Maybe we don't need the search program after all. If you can—'

'No,' said Jonah. 'I can only remember bits and pieces. I…I want you to do it. The search.'

Axel raised an eyebrow. 'You're sure about this?'

'I'm sure,' said Jonah.

The truth was, he wasn't sure at all. He wasn't sure of anything. But Jonah had touched his father's memories, and he had felt the depth of his father's love for him. After everything he had been through, everything he had lost, it was a very special gift. And he had felt how determined Jason Delacroix had been to create a better world, a world for his son to live in, no matter the risk.

Jonah thought he knew, now, what his dad would have wanted him to do.

'Let's do the search,' he repeated. 'Before I change my mind.'

'OK, son,' said Axel. 'Let's get to it.'

Sam's room in the guesthouse was a floor down from Jonah's, and twice its size. It contained a dusty armchair and an inbuilt wardrobe. More importantly, it had a computer terminal. Jonah sat in the armchair, gripping its arms nervously.

He had plugged himself in, but hadn't set a Point of Origin. As a result, he couldn't complete his transition into the Metasphere. Nor did he feel fully grounded in the real world. The room had taken on a weird, dreamlike quality.

Bradbury had plugged his own datapad into the terminal, and was scowling over it. Axel was hovering by the door. He had asked Jonah four more times if he was sure he wanted to do this. Sam sat on the bed beside Jonah. Gently, she detached his right hand from the chair and held it. He appreciated her support.

'There's something wrong,' muttered Bradbury.

Axel started towards Jonah. 'Get him out of there, now!'

'No, that's not what I meant. The kid's safe enough. It's the program.'

'What's up?' asked Sam.

Bradbury ground his teeth in frustration. 'The program keeps freezing on me. I've generated an error report, but it makes no sense. It's as if...'

Axel leaned over Bradbury's shoulder. 'The computer's showing two avatars: Jason's and... Is that you, kid? You had a humatar?'

Jonah giggled involuntarily, feeling light-headed and disconnected from what was happening around him.

'That's what Mr Collins said, on the bus, back home. Two avatars.'

'I don't know how this is possible,' said Bradbury, 'but it looks to me as if your friend's avatar code sequence didn't overwrite the kid's. Somehow – I don't know how, but – I think he's holding them both in his brain at once.'

'That's impossible,' said Sam. 'No one can hold two avatars in their brain.'

'Bradbury, you ever hear of that happening before?' asked Axel.

Bradbury shook his head. 'Nor has the computer. It can't separate the kid's memories from his dad's. It won't execute the search.'

'There's no way?' asked Axel.

'No way,' said Bradbury. He yanked his pad out of the terminal by the lead. 'May as well face it, Axel. We're not gonna find the Four Corners this way – which means we've no hope of reaching them before Granger and the Millennials do.'

'Which means we might lose this war,' said Axel.

20

They left the guesthouse by the fire escape, the next morning. Delphine was waiting for them at the bottom with the truck. There was no one else around.

Jonah didn't say a word to Delphine. He rode in the back with the others, this time. He felt better after a night's rest, though also a little guilty. He knew it was irrational, but he felt he had let everyone down. He had let his dad down.

He asked Axel where they were going. 'I told you last night,' said Axel. 'Delphine has laid on a plane for us.'

'We're still going to Moscow?' said Jonah. 'I thought...'

'We aren't the only Guardians looking for the Four Corners,' said Sam. 'There are other agents out there.'

'And, when they find them—' said Axel.

'If they find them,' Sam corrected him.

'It'll happen one day,' said Bradbury. 'When it does, we must be ready. We'll need the Chang Bridge.'

Delphine's driving was as aggressive as ever, and Jonah had to wedge himself behind the wheel arch to keep from being thrown about. He was glad when the truck came to a halt and, a moment later, the back doors were wrenched open.

'We're here!' announced Delphine.

Jonah could still hear engines. He stepped out of the truck onto an asphalt surface, and his jaw dropped open in astonishment.

He had never seen so many aeroplanes in his life. They were huddled around him, eight or nine of them. Delphine had driven right into their midst.

One of the planes was suckling at a fuel truck. The unfamiliar stink of gasoline fumes burnt Jonah's throat. Another plane was being guided out of a hangar by a man in green coveralls holding a pair of paddles. There were several other people running about, shouting to each other in French. One of them, a man who looked too young to have a moustache, came up to Delphine and discreetly swiped his meta-card in Delphine's handheld. The machine dinged, the transaction complete, and only then did he acknowledge her four companions with a curt nod and lead them towards the parked aircrafts.

By the time Jonah realised Delphine wasn't coming with them, they had left her behind. He saw her getting back into her truck. He wasn't sorry.

He found it hard to imagine a *GuerreVert* supporter owning an aircraft at all. He was only a little surprised, then, to be taken past the gleaming white and silver jets, to a corner in which stood a beaten-up old turbo-prop. It was bulky and inelegant next to the gleaming jets, with its chipped red, white and blue paint.

'Hiram!' shouted the moustached youth. *'Ils sont ici!'*

The pilot leapt out of the cockpit to greet them. He was about fifty, grey-haired, with healthy bronze skin. He wore an open-necked shirt and shorts.

'Howdy folks,' said the pilot in an American drawl, 'and welcome aboard the *Fourth of July*. The name's Hiram. I hear you're Moscow-bound.'

Jonah placed a hand on the fuselage of the plane. A stream of memories flooded into his brain, memories that weren't his own. He saw himself at the controls of a hundred planes like this one, performing all manner of aerobatic manoeuvres.

The images threatened to overwhelm him, and he quickly snatched his hand away and shook his head to clear it.

Jonah had never flown in a real plane before.

It wasn't like flying in the Metasphere. It didn't feel like the airship had, either.

His stomach sank into his shoes as the plane left the ground. Once it was in the air, its small size made it easy prey to air turbulence. It was buffeted by every crosswind and bumped by every air pocket until Jonah feared he might be sick.

It didn't help that there were only four seats in the cockpit. He had ended up wedged between the back two, between Sam and Bradbury.

'I've filed a flight plan to Tunisia,' Hiram yelled over the screaming engines. 'So we'll be heading due south more or less, but changing course once we're safely out over the Med. Should keep those Millennial snoopers off our backs!'

Sam kept looking at Jonah, concerned. He returned her glances, forcing himself to smile, pretending there was nothing wrong with him. He feared he wasn't fooling her.

Just when he thought he could take no more, however, Jonah felt a great calmness rising from somewhere within him. His father's memories. Dad had loved this. Jonah closed his eyes and dreamed – or was it remembered – a thousand other flights like this one, a thousand open skies. It was an amazing sensation and this time he tried to hold on to it. The harder he tried, however, the faster it slipped away.

'Earth to Jonah!' joked Sam. 'Where were you?'

'Nowhere,' muttered Jonah, 'and everywhere.'

Bradbury was slumped in a meta-trance beside him. It was good to know that even an old wreck like this one had a satellite uplink. The cockpit was too noisy for Axel and Hiram to hear much, so Jonah had another chance to speak to Sam privately.

'So,' he said, 'this device, this Chang Bridge – what is it?'

'It's a back-up device,' said Sam, 'but a very special back-up device: the first with enough memory to back up the whole of the virtual world.'

'A copy of the Metasphere?' Jonah was awestruck

by the sheer magnitude of the possibility, but didn't understand why the Guardians would want it. 'But why? What good would that do?'

'Don't you see? If we can take a back-up of the Metasphere, we can build new server farms to power it, out of Granger's reach.'

'You're planning to build your own Four Corners!' Jonah realised.

'Not just four. Millions.'

'Then, who...who'd be in charge of them?'

'No one would,' said Sam. 'That's the whole point, Jonah. No one would know – no one person should ever know. If the Metasphere were powered by millions of servers, distributed all around the world, then no one person could ever control it.'

'So, the Metasphere would be...'

'As it should be. Free!' Sam declared. 'Democratic. Owned by the users, not the governments, and certainly not the Millennials. The only way anyone could tamper with its source code would be with everyone's agreement.'

Jonah nodded, thoughtfully. 'You need to act fast, then, before Mr Granger has the same idea and gets his own back-up device.'

'It could happen one day,' Sam agreed, 'although hopefully we've some time yet. As far as the Guardians know, Mr Chang is the only one with the technology to—'

'Mr Chang?' echoed Jonah. 'You mean *the* Mr Chang?'

'Of course. Who else did you think?'

'I suppose I should have realised, when you mentioned the Chang Bridge.'

'Mr Chang is Matthew Granger's fiercest rival,' said Sam. 'He's always said it was wrong that Granger had a monopoly on meta-life. Are you so surprised he should support the Guardians' cause?'

'No, I guess not,' said Jonah. 'I go... I used to go to one of his schools.'

'A Chang Academy?' Sam actually sounded impressed.

'Another place I can never go back to,' Jonah sighed.

'You don't know. Maybe, one day, when this is all over...'

'Maybe,' said Jonah. 'It's all just memories now, though, isn't it?'

Memories... He had had an idea.

He wasn't able to conjure up his father's memories consciously, but what about subconsciously? It had happened before, in Dover, and when he had talked to Axel. And on the Island of the Uploaded. Each time, Jonah realised, when he had encountered something that his dad would have found familiar, he tapped into his father's memories.

'Do you mind if I log on?' he asked Sam.

Sam shrugged. 'Be careful in there,' she said. 'Don't get scanned. And definitely don't talk to any blackbirds.'

Jonah took an adaptor pack from a pouch in Sam's seat, reached for the wire that was coiled up beneath it. 'There's someone I have to see,' he explained.

He was ready for the water, this time.

Jonah swooped low over the sea, landing gracefully on the shore of the Island of the Uploaded. He furled his dragon's wings behind him, and looked for his grandmother.

He couldn't see her, at first.

Normally, this wouldn't have worried him. Nan did wander inland sometimes, though never for long and she always returned to this spot. Jonah couldn't help but notice, however – as if for the first time – how crowded this stretch of beach was.

Most of the avatars around him were Uploaded themselves, of course, but others were visitors like him – and what, thought Jonah, if some of them were Millennial spies on the lookout for a red dragon? He checked behind him for his exit halo. This time, he wouldn't make the mistake of straying too far from it – and he certainly wouldn't reveal his Real World Location to anyone.

He felt relieved when he heard his grandmother's chuckle.

'It's good to see you, Jason,' said Nan as she drew Jonah into the embrace of her dry elephant's trunk. 'You hardly ever seem to visit any more.'

They lay in the shade of a palm tree, and talked.

Nan's memory seemed stuck in her younger days today. She reminisced about old school friends, and the sweet boy from Manchester she had known before she had met Jonah's grandfather. 'Of course, back then,' said Nan, 'we could only see each other on flat computer screens, through these gadgets we called webcams.'

Any other time, Jonah would have been happy to listen to her stories of the past; today, he had more important things on his mind.

'What was *my* school like, Mum?' he asked. He didn't like pretending to be his father, not with her, but it was the simplest way.

Nan looked at Jonah, confused, as if trying to remember who he was. Then her eyes cleared and she said, 'I know you aren't happy there, Jason. I wish we could afford to have you tutored online, but...'

'I know.' Jonah smiled. 'I was always the restless one. I hated sitting in dark, stuffy classrooms, looking out at the sky and longing to be up there, free.'

It was happening already. Just talking about his father, hearing about his life, was stirring up the memories buried in Jonah's brain, bringing them to the surface.

He urged Nan to say more. He prompted her with little details about Dad that he remembered from his own childhood, and with some he was 'remembering' now for the first time. They talked about the RAF, Jonah's mum and the gift shop.

Then he tried to remember the locations of the Four Corners.

He couldn't do it.

'There's something wrong, isn't there?' said Nan. 'I could always tell with you.'

'I think I need… The memories, they're too old. I need to talk about what happened next, after we bought the gift shop. After Jonah was born.'

'How is little Jonah? I miss him so much. Is he walking yet? They change so fast at that age. I was always amazed at how fast you changed, Jason.'

'Please try to remember. I know you…I know you weren't around then, but Dad used to… I mean, I came here every week to visit you. I must have told you things, about my life. Did I mention a man named Granger? Matthew Granger? I must have talked about him. Do you remember what I said about him?'

Nan chuckled. 'Oh, my dear, you know what it's like when you reach my age. The memory plays tricks on you. Why, I can hardly—'

'Please. It's important. I need you to remember!'

'Really?' Nan looked at Jonah. It was the same look she had given him the last time he had come here. The one that made him feel like she knew a lot more than she should. 'Because it seems to me, my dear, you are the one who has forgotten.'

'I…I suppose you're right,' said Jonah.

'Then let's see what we can do about that together,

shall we? There's a little trick I use, when I really, really must remember something I have forgotten. Close your eyes, dear. Close your eyes and take slow, deep breaths and listen to my voice…'

Jonah followed his grandmother's directions.

He sat on the beach with his chin slumped on his dragon's chest, the warm sun on his scales, and he let her quiet, soothing tones wash over him until he was no longer listening to her words but swimming through a sea of dreams.

There were faces, places, sweeping by in a blur. He resisted the urge to try to focus on any one of them, because he knew that if he did they would slip out of his grasp. Jonah waited patiently, until the barrage of images slowed down of their own accord and he could begin to make some sense of them all.

Then Nan as a young woman, walking Jason to school along a busy road filled with cars and buses. An image of his mother, also younger than he had seen her before: she was holding her round belly proudly. Then, a baby. Jonah caught his breath as he realised that he was looking down at himself, as a newborn.

In the hospital waiting room, a man offered him a cigar. It was Axel, before the grey hair and the beard. The sight of him opened up a door to another flood of memories: Flight School, training exercises with the RAF, the Icarus. Images of airports and runways came next. Jonah's first instinct was to try to go back, to see more of his family, but he made himself resist it. He followed the set of memories related to flying, or perhaps more accurately let himself be carried in their tide.

Sitting in the cockpit of a private plane, with Matthew Granger alongside him. Jonah felt a rush of anger at the sight of his cherubic face, and almost lost the memory because of it. Granger was saying something to him, however. He was giving him directions. Four sets of directions.

A white wasteland. A red desert. An island of skyscrapers. A tropical city.

He snapped out of his trance, sitting bolt upright, gasping for air. 'It...it worked, Nan,' he cried. 'It really worked. We did it!'

Jonah struggled to focus his real-world eyes.

He saw three blurry white faces hovering over him. 'Is something wrong?' he asked.

'Not any more.' Sam's voice. 'You were gone for hours. We were worried... Jonah, we're here. In Moscow. We're coming in to land.'

'Already?' Jonah sat up, confused. 'I thought... It only seemed like a few minutes to me. But listen, Sam, everyone. I did it! We did it, I mean. Nan and me.'

'Did what?' asked Bradbury, impatiently.

'I remembered,' said Jonah. 'I accessed my dad's memories.'

Axel craned around from his seat up front. 'You mean...?'

Jonah was still sifting through the images from his meditation. He recognised the red desert, parched and dry, from his father's memories. The Southern Corner. The one server farm that stored the Uploaded. Home to his Nan.

Jonah nodded. 'I've found...' He caught himself. It was something about the way Bradbury was frowning at him, something that made him cautious. *What do I really know about these people?* he asked himself. *Can I really trust them?*

'I've found...one of the Four Corners,' he said, at that moment deciding to keep the full truth back from the eager Guardians. 'I saw it from the air, as Dad would have remembered seeing it. A giant red rock with nothing around it. In Australia.'

21

Granger's destination was in sight, at last.

He had flown for over twenty hours, stopping only twice to refuel his chartered plane. It was still late morning in Paris, but here in the Northern Territories of Australia, the sun was already setting. Its fading rays glinted red off the vast arrays of solar reflectors that covered the rusty desert sands.

Granger was pleased to see a tight column of military jeeps crawling along the dusty Lasseter Highway below him. His southern strike team was on schedule, although the size of the force was rather less than he had hoped for. He instructed his pilot to wait to hear from him at Alice Springs, the nearest town, almost three hundred miles away. Then he opened the aft door and jumped out of the plane.

The broad, flat top of Ayers Rock was an irresistible target, the only geological feature of note for hundreds of miles around. It was largely covered in solar panels, but Granger angled his descent towards a gap between them. He executed a flawless landing, his cyber-kinetic legs absorbing the bulk of the impact, and he shed his parachute as if it were an overcoat he no longer needed.

Granger sat with his back to the metal entrance

hatch, and enjoyed the beautiful sunset. Some three hundred and fifty metres below him, he could see his people just passing the first of the two perimeter fences.

He picked himself up and casually trekked down the well-trodden, now-abandoned climbing path that sloped to the base of the rock. He could have parachuted straight to the bottom, of course – but he liked the symbolism of coming down from the rock to meet his followers.

Ayers Rock was many hundreds of millions of years old. It had endured while the rest of the mountain range had been eroded to sand. Granger was confident his own legacy to the world would last as long.

That was one of the reasons why he had built a part of that legacy here.

Granger remembered when Ayers Rock had been a tourist attraction – until the prohibitive cost of transport had caused the tourist trade to drop off. Today, it was well known that it now housed a much-needed solar power plant.

But only a handful of people in the world knew the rock's real secret.

Granger stood at the base of the huge rock and waited for the first of the approaching jeeps to grind to a halt at his titanium feet. A blond teenager in combat fatigues scrambled out of the passenger seat. His eyes were purple-rimmed with tiredness, and he blinked a little too often. He threw up a salute in Granger's direction – not strictly necessary, but Granger accepted the compliment.

'Southern strike team reporting as ordered, sir,' said Warren, the possessor of the red spider avatar. He looked as Granger had always imagined he would.

'Is this all you have?' sniffed Granger.

There were five jeeps in all, each with five or six men packed into them. They were flanked by four quad bikes, each bearing a rider and passenger.

Warren's face fell. 'As I tried to explain, sir, when you moved up the timetable—'

'Yes, yes,' said Granger impatiently, 'I remember. I had hoped, however—'

'I even brokered a deal with a religious militia in Perth to transport thirty volunteers across the Outback. If we could only wait twelve more hours, sir—'

'No,' said Granger. 'The attacks on the Four Corners must be synchronised, to give us the element of surprise.' He did a quick headcount. 'Even thirty-seven agents should be more than enough to take out a handful of government stooges.'

'I'm sure you're right, sir.'

Granger checked his watch. 'T minus thirty-four minutes,' he said. 'It'll take you almost thirty to climb this rock. You'd best get started.'

'Sir, I thought you said you would be leading the assault?'

'I said I would be taking charge here, Warren. I do

not propose to get myself killed in action. That would rather harm our long-term goals, don't you think?'

The other Millennials had disembarked from their vehicles and were awaiting instructions. They were a motley bunch. Some had the look of professional mercenaries, alert and well-equipped. Others were just kids, enthusiastic followers who had probably never fired a gun outside of a virtual training range.

Warren relayed Granger's orders to them: 'We're going in through the access hatch up top. Once we're inside, we try for the lifts, but we'll have to act fast before they're locked down. It's a ninety-five-storey climb down to the control room. If you need to familiarise yourself with the schematics of the inside, now's your last chance.' He raised his voice more than was required by the size of the grouping – an attempt to re-establish his authority after Granger's belittling of him.

Warren was not the most able of Granger's lieutenants. He was probably the most loyal, though, and this counted for a lot. The truth was, it was flattering to Granger's ego to have someone around who so obviously wanted to be him.

The Millennial army, such as it was, began to shuffle their way up the climbing path. Some of them shone torches, though the night sky was clear and bright. Granger picked out two of the more capable-seeming men as they passed him.

He led these two, a tall, muscular Kiwi and a compact,

wiry Australian, along the dirt road that wound around the base of the rock. He didn't bother to ask their names.

'Your job is to protect me at all costs,' explained Granger, 'including your own lives. And you aren't being paid extra to talk.'

He turned off the dirt road and made for a narrow gulley in the rock's side. He pushed his way through the scrub, until he found a series of natural handholds in the sandstone and hauled himself upwards.

A short climb later, Granger eased himself into a crevice in the rock face. The cave into which he and his new bodyguards emerged was invisible from the ground.

The walls of the cave were adorned with Aboriginal paintings, although Granger could barely discern these in the gloom. He was aware, of course, of the local superstitions that held this rock to be a sacred place. The rock's original Aboriginal owners believed it was hollow, an abode to the souls of the dead.

He found it amusing that, in part at least, he had made those old legends come true. The rock was indeed hollow – now – and the servers that ran the Island of the Uploaded, along with the rest of one quarter of the Metasphere, were housed within it.

Granger led the way into a deep recess of the cave, disturbing a nest of bats, which skittered and shrieked away from him. He pressed his hand against a section of the cave wall. It slid back with a rumbling, scraping sound, and a harsh white light spilled out and streamed over him.

'Tweedle-dee and Tweedle-dum. Inside. Shoot anyone that moves.'

Granger sent his two bodyguards through the opening, their weapons raised. When he was sure it was safe to do so, he followed them. He stepped out of the natural, dark cave into a smooth and well-lit service corridor. Lines of gas and water pipes, electrical wires and data cables hugged the walls above his head.

Granger pulled the cave door shut, leaving barely a seam in the wall to betray its position. He was standing in the heart of Ayers Rock now – its new, metal heart.

'The first rule of building a facility like this one,' he said with a cocksure grin. 'Always leave yourself a back way in.'

They proceeded cautiously after that. The big Kiwi went a few steps ahead of Granger, while the small Australian lagged behind to guard his rear. Granger himself had no weapon. Though he preferred to do most things himself, when it came to a fight he let others bloody their hands for him.

The Kiwi reached a T-junction with a long corridor, and signalled a halt. Dropping back, he walked two fingers on his palm, letting Granger know that there was a man around the corner to the left.

'Can you take him out quietly?' mouthed Granger.

The mercenary grunted an affirmative and, with a questioning look, drew his index finger across his neck. Granger nodded. He wanted the man dead. It was the only way to be sure.

He waited as the Kiwi crept up to the junction again and slipped around the corner out of Granger's sight. A moment later, he heard a quiet, strangulated whine, and seconds after that the Kiwi reappeared with an all-clear sign.

They moved on, walking quietly but quickly past rows of upright computer servers. 'The machines that make the Metaworld go round,' the Australian breathed.

He was wrong, but Granger didn't bother correcting him. These servers only managed the solar array up top. *His* servers were stacked vertically in the centre of Ayers Rock, reaching over a mile down into the ground.

They heard footsteps ahead of them, and a couple of voices.

They flattened themselves in the mouth of a side passageway as two armed men walked by. They were talking about a recent virtual rugby league match, Titans versus Broncos, too absorbed in their conversation to notice the intruders.

The Australian slipped out into the corridor behind them, and felled them with two near-silent shots to their backs. 'I would'a just shot out their legs if they'd been Broncos supporters,' he seethed, 'but man, I hate the Titans!'

Granger had come far enough.

He had almost reached the main control room. Every step he and his men took now would increase their risk of being discovered. He had them wait instead.

The minutes crawled by in silence, but for the low thrum of powerful servers from somewhere close by. Granger fancied that, if he leaned his head against the wall, he could feel that power throbbing through him.

The quiet was suddenly shattered by a klaxon alarm.

The mercenaries looked at Granger for permission to act. He shook his head: *Not yet*. They heard raised voices, and booted footsteps running through the corridors, but still Granger waited, counting under his breath.

He made his move, at last. He led the way to a lobby area in which a number of passageways met. He indicated two of these to his men, who stood guard by them. Three elevators formed a row along one wall, their displays indicating that two were in use, rising. The current security shift, no doubt, rushing to engage Warren's team up top. That left the off-duty shift, roused to action by the intruder alarm.

They came running from the bunkrooms and the common room. They were still struggling into their flak jackets, loading rifles as they rushed into the central lobby. Government lackeys. There were even fewer of them, looking even more hapless, than Granger had anticipated.

They thought the enemy was at the gate. They hadn't bargained on him already being inside with them.

The two mercenaries stepped into the mouths of the corridors, filled them with sprays of bullets. Their targets were lined up like skittles and fell almost as easily. As far as Granger could see, not one of them had got off a return shot.

He waited for the echoes of machine-gun chatter to die down. Then he marched purposefully to the control room. Its steel door was locked down, but Granger had the original code to the keypad. The government stooges could have changed the pass-code on the tap-pad a million times but Granger's code would still override any changes. He tapped in a sixteen-digit number and waited as the inner bolts in the door retracted.

'No gunfire inside this room,' Granger ordered. 'Not even in self-defence.'

The mercenaries went in first, the Australian screaming, 'On the floor!'

The room was staffed by five pasty-faced middle-aged technicians, all men, and all unarmed. They didn't try to put up a fight. 'Please,' one of them whined as he lay on his stomach with the big Kiwi holding a knife to his throat. 'We won't try to stop you. Why should we? We're just doing our jobs, and we haven't even been paid in months!'

'I can't let you leave,' said Granger. The young men

closed their eyes, expecting the worst. 'But if you work for me, I will let you live.'

It was another twenty minutes before Warren's ragtag army arrived in the control room.

Four Millennials appeared, in firing formation, in the doorway. They looked shocked to find Granger standing waiting for them, and the former government technicians back at their posts, working nervously.

'Whoa!' one of them cried, impressed. 'You're already here!'

Granger didn't wait for the rest of the Millennials to arrive, didn't wait to see how many had survived the battle with the government troops above. He knew all he needed to know.

He lowered himself into a comfortable leather seat at the primary control console. He let his eyes rove over the displays on the many screens around him, and he smiled as he took in the familiar initials stitched into the chair's right arm: *MG*.

Granger felt as if he had just come home. Better than that, he was one-quarter of the way to reclaiming his creation, his world.

The Southern Corner was his.

22

The streets of Moscow were broader than those of London, but just as crowded.

It seemed, however, that fewer people were on wheels. Most were trudging along the pavements with their shoulders stooped, sparing barely a glance for each other.

Of course, Russia still had oil and therefore public transport, although Jonah had blanched at the price of four single tickets from Sheremetyevo Airport to the Savyolovsky Rail Terminal on a clapped-out, sighing old train.

Bradbury had paid with a dog-eared plastic card, the same one with which he had bribed a weary airport official to overlook Jonah's lack of a passport. Jonah decided not to ask where the money was coming from, or indeed if the card was genuine.

They had waited an hour for a train, which had had standing room only and had proceeded gingerly along poorly maintained tracks. By the time they had reached the city, it was early evening and there was a distinct chill in the air. Jonah welcomed the fading of the day. He began to feel almost safe, anonymous, among the crowds.

Jonah had been to Meta-Moscow once. It had been better than this: an idealised version of what this city had once been. In real-world Moscow, as population levels had soared, the fairy-tale towers and domes of old had been crowded out of the skyline by massive concrete housing complexes. They passed snaking queues of people waiting for handouts at mission halls, watched over by armed guards.

They had walked for almost an hour and a half when Axel announced they had reached their destination. Sokolniki Park was neglected; overgrown, like other real-world parks, those that hadn't been built over. The fast-food stands around its entrance were untended, paint peeling from wooden shutters. A rusted Ferris wheel towered over the park. It reminded Jonah of the London Eye, a giant wheel that had once loomed over the Thames before it was felled during the food riots and sank into the river.

Jonah's dad had taken him on the London Eye on his sixth birthday. 'If you like this,' he had said as they had soared high over London, 'you'll love flying for real!'

'He's late,' said Axel, presently.

'He'll be here,' said Bradbury. 'He knows how important this is.'

'Are you sure we can trust him?' asked Sam.

'He'll be here,' Bradbury repeated. 'Dimitry believes in a free Metasphere as much as we do. Regulation is bad for his business.'

'Business?' said Jonah, warily. 'What business?'

No one answered him, and Jonah decided not to push the question.

He passed the time by trying to meditate again, as his grandmother had taught him. He closed his eyes, tried to empty his mind, but he couldn't do it. Jonah was too aware of the real world around him. He couldn't fully relax.

He realised that Bradbury was staring at him. 'Any lead on those other three Corners yet?' he asked. Jonah shook his head quickly.

'We know where one of the Four Corners is,' said Sam. 'That's something.'

'Enough to protect a quarter of the Metasphere,' said Axel.

'*If* we can procure the Chang Bridge,' grunted Bradbury, 'and if we can get it to that Corner before the Millennials.'

Any further discussion was forestalled by the sound of an approaching engine.

Bradbury was the first to his feet, his shotgun drawn again.

They were caught in the glare of headlights. A large, dusty black van came roaring up the pathway towards them. It skidded to a halt, kicking up chips of gravel as it spun around to face the way it had come. Its back doors flew open, and a stocky man in black beckoned to the quartet to join him inside.

They had barely climbed into the van when it roared off again.

The interior of the van was lined with computer equipment. Active monitors and flashing hard-drive lights glowed dimly. Four swivel chairs were bolted to the floor; as the last man in, Jonah found himself without a seat, and had to squat in the middle.

'I apologise I am late,' said the stocky man. He must have been about twenty. Jonah had thought him older at first glance, because of his unshaven appearance.

'What happened, Dimitry?' asked Axel.

'Andrey suspected we were followed. We had to be sure to lose pursuit before we came to meet you.'

'Andrey', presumably, was their driver. Jonah could only see him from the side: an older, muscular man with a thick black beard. He didn't even glance around at the mention of his name, focusing on the road. They had left the park now, turning south.

'Millennial spies?' asked Bradbury.

'I think not,' said Dimitry. 'We have our own enemies, *da*?'

He turned to Sam and introduced himself, kissing her hand. Axel and Bradbury, it seemed he already knew – while Jonah, he happily ignored. Bradbury asked if arrangements had been made. Dimitry said they had. A plane was waiting for the Guardians at a private airport, some twenty miles outside the city.

'What is all this equipment for?' asked Jonah. 'What do you do in here?'

'Dimitry runs a broadcasting network,' Axel replied for him. 'How is business, Dimitry?'

'Dangerous but profitable,' Dimitry replied. 'A Luke Wexler game comes out in a few months. Zombies Four. That will be very big for us.'

'Broadcasting?' asked Jonah.

'Yes,' said Dimitry. 'Many vehicles like this one, with satellite uplinks, always moving, uploading content to the Metasphere twenty-four hours of every day.'

'Pirated content, you mean,' guessed Jonah. 'You're pirates, aren't you?'

'We make information, culture, ideas, available to all,' said Dimitry, 'not just to *bourgeoisie*.'

'You can call it what you want,' said Jonah. 'But it's still stealing.'

Dimitry scowled. 'Our philosophies are not so different, I think. You are Guardians, *da*? You wish the Metasphere to be free to all?'

'We do,' said Bradbury. He shot Jonah a fierce glare, his meaning as crystal clear as always. Jonah chose to heed the warning and fell silent, but he couldn't help but wonder if there shouldn't be limits on some kinds of 'freedoms'.

For the second time in as many days, he found himself profoundly uncomfortable with the allies of his Guardian friends.

*

They drove through the centre of Moscow. Dimitry pointed out the green spires of the Kremlin, the fortified seat of Russian leaders going back centuries. The streets were quieter than when they had walked them earlier, and there was little illumination.

The van slowed down as it approached a T-junction. There were one-way windows in the back doors, and suddenly a harsh light spilled in through them. Another vehicle was coming up behind. It took Jonah a second to realise it wasn't stopping.

'Look out!' he yelled. But his warning came too late.

The van was rammed from behind. There hadn't been time to do anything except, in Jonah's case, to grab onto the pedestal of Sam's seat for support.

They were shunted forward, across the junction. Andrey slammed on the brakes and threw the steering wheel around. The tyres screamed, and Jonah smelled burning rubber. He thought they were going to hit the housing block opposite. He closed his eyes and prepared himself for the impact, but they skidded to a halt with centimetres to spare.

The van had spun almost nose to tail, and through the windscreen Jonah could see the car that had hit them: a sleek, black limousine, fitted with bull bars.

It was backing up, as if to escape the scene of the accident it had caused. But then it stopped, its engine revved, and it came charging at the van for a second time.

Meanwhile, the van had stalled. Andrey turned the key in the ignition, frantically. The engine hiccoughed and caught. Andrey stamped on the accelerator, and they were jolted forward, just out of the path of the hurtling limo. They roared off, back the way they had come. Through the back windows, Jonah saw the limousine performing an awkward three-point turn. It was hunting them.

'What the hell's going on?' cried Axel, rubbing his head. Jonah spotted blood was trickling down his temple. He must have knocked it on the computers, he reckoned.

'Chang Corporation,' Andrey snarled.

'That car was theirs,' Dimitry confirmed. 'It must have been them following us earlier. They will not give up until they drive us off the road.'

'But that doesn't make sense,' cried Jonah. 'I thought Mr Chang... He's supposed to be our ally!'

'*Your* ally, perhaps,' said Dimitry. 'No friend of my organisation.'

'Mr Chang owns most of the major movie studios,' explained Sam. 'It's his films that Dimitry has been pirating.'

Another car was coming towards them. Just as Jonah realised it was another black limo, it swerved onto the wrong side of the road and barrelled right at them.

Andrey's reactions were faster. He wrenched the wheel around again, veered the van across the pavement and drove into a side street.

He wasn't fast enough. The bull bars of the second limo clipped the back of the van, almost sending it into another spin. Andrey fought to keep the van on course, but Jonah could hear something dragging from the van's underside.

They tore around the city streets, the limousines close behind them. Jonah held his breath as they approached a crossroads and saw a truck bearing down on them from the right. Instead of stopping, Andrey put his foot down again and tried to beat the truck across. Jonah winced, sure they wouldn't make it. He heard the blaring of the truck's horn, the screech of its tyres, then, miraculously, they were through and the truck was stalled across the junction behind them, blocking their pursuers.

Andrey made four turns in quick succession, then backed the van into a narrow, cobbled alleyway and killed the engine and the lights.

Sam was the first to break the ensuing silence. 'What do we do now?' she asked.

'We abandon the van, of course,' said Axel.

'We cannot do that!' said Dimitry. 'The equipment in this van is worth many metas. Also, Chang Corp has agents everywhere and my face is known. We will be, as you English say, sitting on ducks.'

'So, what do you suggest?' said Bradbury, not

stopping to correct the Russian.

'We have a workshop across town. We can be having this van re-sprayed, new plates, within an hour. They will not be recognising us then.'

'Across town?' echoed Sam. Jonah had been thinking the same thing. How were they supposed to cross Moscow, in a damaged van, with at least two Chang Corporation vehicles on the lookout for them?

'Why don't we just talk to them?' Jonah spoke up. It seemed like the obvious solution.

Andrey glared at Jonah over his shoulder, and said something in Russian that Jonah assumed was an insult. 'No, I mean it,' said Jonah. 'Mr Chang knows we're on our way to collect the Chang Bridge from him. He knows how important it is. If we can just explain to his men who we are…'

'If they capture me,' said Dimitry, flatly, 'they will kill me.'

Jonah wasn't put off so easily. 'What about in the Metasphere, then? You have all the equipment here. What if someone went into the Metasphere and spoke to Mr Chang personally? They could ask him to call his men off.'

Axel shook his head. 'Nice idea, kid,' he said, 'but you don't just "speak to" someone like Mr Chang.'

'A man in Mr Chang's position,' said Bradbury, 'can't afford to be associated with outlaws like us, in either world. What little contact we have had with him at all

177

has been through a network of agents. By the time we could get a message to him—'

If they weren't going to try, Jonah was. He hadn't come this far to be gunned down on the streets of Moscow.

'I'll do it,' said Jonah. 'I know a friend of Mr Chang's. I think I can arrange a meeting with him.'

Everyone looked at him. Sam was the first to speak. 'Well, we've nothing to lose,' she pointed out.

'It's worth a shot,' confessed Bradbury. It was hardly a ringing endorsement, but Jonah wasn't looking for permission.

'You've got an adaptor?' asked Jonah.

Dimitry nodded. He produced a fresh DI adaptor pack and gave up his seat to Jonah. As Jonah plugged himself in, Dimitry showed him the datapad on which he was to enter his Point of Origin co-ordinates. Jonah knew the numbers well – better than any others. They were the co-ordinates for one particular franchise of the Chang Academy for Gifted Youths.

He was going back to school.

23

The school grounds looked different to Jonah.

It took him a moment to realise what was wrong. Of course, he hadn't been back here since he had filtered his father's avatar. He had not grown used to looking at the virtual world through the dragon's yellow eyes, to being bigger than he had been.

He felt as if he had outgrown this place.

A wave of doubt crashed over him. Jonah had affected to be so confident in the real world, in the broadcasting van, in front of Sam. Now, he was a kid again.

A dialogue balloon popped up beside him: No visitors without appointment. The school's security software didn't recognise him as a pupil here.

The main doors were closed, the padlock icon in place. Even if the doors were open, Jonah wasn't going to risk being scanned. But he still had Harry the rooster's virus.

He placed his talons against the brick wall, transferred the virus and pushed his way through into the school's entrance hall. He hesitated there, unsure what to do next. What if a teacher caught him here? How would he explain himself? What if they reported him? He was risking exile.

The school bell rang. Jonah panicked, and looked for somewhere to hide. There was nowhere. He was too big – and, already, the corridors were filling up with avatars released from their lessons. Some of them cast curious, even admiring, glances at the red dragon in their midst.

To most, Jonah realised, he was just a visitor touring the school, of no importance to them. Emboldened a little by this, he set out towards his old classroom.

The school clock read 11:00 local time, but 'local time' for the Chang Academy shifted throughout the day. Once Jonah, his classmates and the rest of their school went home, a second intake of pupils arrived from different time zones.

The Chang Academy had three school days altogether, to each real-world day. Fortunately for Jonah, the man he had come to see worked two of these.

Mr Peng was seated at his desk, marking class work on a datapad. He had a pair of *pince-nez* spectacles perched on his beak.

Jonah knocked tentatively on the open classroom door.

Mr Peng looked up at his visitor and frowned. 'Can I help you, sir?'

Jonah tucked in his giant wings and stepped through the door into the classroom he had escaped from just days ago. 'Mr Peng,' he said, 'it's me. It's Jonah Delacroix.' He knew that only the truth could help him now, whatever the risk of telling it.

Mr Peng rose slowly and waddled forward. The spectacles disappeared as he regarded Jonah through astonished eyes. 'My goodness me,' he breathed. 'I have seen this avatar before, have I not? Your father, I think.'

Jonah nodded, looking over his shoulder to be sure no one was eavesdropping. 'Please, sir, don't tell anyone.'

'On that, my boy, you have my word. But pray, tell me how—?'

'There's no time to explain, sir. I'm in Moscow with... friends, and I need to speak with Mr Chang, because his people are trying to kill us, and I remember how you said once you knew him and I thought maybe you could—'

'Slow down, my boy. One thing at a time. These "friends" of yours. Who...?'

Jonah couldn't say the words: *they're Guardians. I'm working with the Guardians.*

'Ah,' said Mr Peng, noting Jonah's silence. 'We are talking about associates of your father's?'

Jonah gaped in surprise. He wondered how much his teacher knew.

'In our classroom debates,' said Mr Peng, 'you always spoke up for stricter regulation of the Metasphere. You were strongly opposed to the views of Mr Chang and those of like mind to him. Am I to infer you have had a change of heart?'

It occurred to Jonah that Sam, Axel and the rest were probably watching him on a monitor, in the van. 'Mr Peng, please,' he said. 'We're in trouble, real trouble, and only Mr Chang can help us. Can you take me to see him?'

'I cannot do that, Jonah. I just don't move about as… freely as I would like to.'

So it was true, thought Jonah, what everyone said about Mr Peng. The rumours had been going around the school for as long as Jonah had been a pupil. They said that Jonah's teacher was a political prisoner in China. His real-world body was confined to a cell and his avatar to the co-ordinates of his workplace.

'Mr Chang and I were friends once, it is true,' said Mr Peng. 'He was kind enough to arrange my employment here. It has been some time, however, since we were last in touch, let alone able to meet. You understand, a man in his position—'

Jonah groaned. 'I know. He can't afford to be associated with an outlaw.'

'I prefer to use the word "dissident".'

'Isn't there anything you can do, sir?' pleaded Jonah. 'Can't you tell me how to find Mr Chang for myself, or… or, I don't know, get a message to him somehow? I know he'd agree it was important – crucial, even.'

Mr Peng considered this for a moment, then nodded. He closed the classroom door for privacy. He reached into his inventory space and produced a small, golden statuette, which he handed to Jonah. 'A good luck charm,' he said.

Jonah looked at the statuette. It was a cat. A golden cat. It had two faces, one looking each way. From one side, the cat was smiling, a paw raised as if in greeting. From the other, the cat was scowling and holding up a broom.

'The paw is to attract fortune,' Mr Peng explained, 'the broom to ward off evil.'

'I don't understand, sir. How...?'

Mr Peng smiled indulgently. He took the charm back and manipulated it deftly with his talons. The cat's two-faced head popped open, to reveal a small button beneath it.

Mr Peng handed the statuette back to Jonah. 'Press the button,' he instructed. 'It is pre-programmed to take you to the one you are seeking.'

'We've lost him!'

Sam and the others had been watching Jonah's progress. A moment ago, his red dragon avatar had been in a schoolroom, talking to a wise-looking old bird. Now, all Sam could see was the reflection of Bradbury's glowering face in a blank screen.

'Where'd he go?' asked Axel.

'The teacher had some kind of a figurine. The kid pressed a button in its neck, and everything went screwy.' Bradbury was shifting icons around on a datapad. The monitor flared to life again, but with a stream of error reports.

Sam leaned forward. 'It's saying – is this right? – it's saying there's no avatar registered to this terminal. But...'

'But the computer's still holding Point of Origin co-ordinates,' said Bradbury. 'It's maintaining the kid's exit halo. It's as if—'

'No,' breathed Sam. 'He couldn't have...' She looked at Jonah's lifeless body. She didn't dare put her fears into words. Everyone knew what happened when an avatar was destroyed – or, almost as bad, when it became detached from its user.

'It might just be a glitch,' she hoped.

Suddenly, there were headlights approaching. A black limousine drove across the end of the alleyway, and Sam heard it braking.

'Looks like we've been made,' groaned Axel.

Dimitry vaulted into the front passenger seat. 'Go, go, go!' he yelled.

Andrey restarted the engine and threw the van into reverse. Sam held onto Jonah as they bounced along the cobbles of the alleyway. The worst, she thought, might not yet have happened – and if it hadn't, then the last thing Jonah needed was to be thrown from his chair, accidentally disconnected.

The limousine backed up too, turned into the alleyway, and followed the van down it. Sam could see it gaining on them, its bull bars almost kissing the van's front bumper.

They emerged into another broad road. Andrey wrestled the van around, crunching its gears. They surged forward, but the limousine was right on their tail.

Bradbury elbowed his way down the van, past Sam. She opened her mouth to ask him what he was doing, but the answer became obvious. Bradbury whipped out his shotgun, smashed the butt through one of the back windows. He rested the gun barrel on the window's lip and fired.

Bradbury peppered the Chang limo with explosive pellets. Its windscreen and one of its headlights shattered, but it kept on coming. It must have been armour plated, thought Sam. Bradbury swore under his breath, ejected his spent magazine, smacked a new one into place. The shotgun flared again and again, and a line of holes appeared in the limo's bonnet. Suddenly, a geyser of steam erupted from its engine, blowing the hood open, and the limo swerved off the road and collided with a stone bollard.

'That'll teach them!' Axel whooped as they left their crippled pursuer behind.

The words were barely out of his mouth when the van ran over something in the road, shuddered and began to slow.

'Spike strip!' cried Dimitry.

'A trap,' said Sam, realising too late that the Chang crew had anticipated their route.

It lay across the road behind them: a narrow strip, black – Andrey wouldn't have seen it even in his headlights – studded with metal barbs. It must have been deployed by somebody on the pavement, although Sam hadn't noticed anyone.

'The tyres, they are shredded!' Andrey reported.

He kept on driving anyway, but the van was suddenly impossible to control. It almost missed the next corner, sliding across the road. 'This is hopeless,' cried Sam. 'Dad was right before. We'd be better off taking our chances on foot!'

In response, Andrey put his foot down, until the screeching of the van's wheel rims against the tarmac set Sam's teeth on edge.

And, suddenly, there was another Chang limousine in front of them, and another one turning out of a side road to their left, and Sam knew the chase was over.

Andrey wasn't ready to accept it. He tried to swerve between the two black cars. He didn't make it. The van struck the kerb and, for a heart-stopping instant, was hurtling through the air. It landed with a jolt, scraped a recycling machine and rolled to a despondent halt with its nose to a concrete wall. Sam and Jonah were spilled from their seats, and the wire to Jonah's back pulled dangerously taut.

The limousines pulled up behind the van, blocking

its escape. They emptied out four men each, in dark fatigues and balaclavas.

The men were all armed. They raised their guns, aiming them at the broadcasting van. Sam remembered what Dimitry had said: *If they capture me, they will kill me.*

It looked as if that moment had come.

24

Jonah opened his eyes. He felt disoriented. His senses were adjusting, as they always did when he switched between the real and the virtual worlds. However, this time he had made no such transition. At least, he didn't think he had.

He had to glance down, to check what he looked like. He was wearing the dragon avatar. He was still in the Metasphere, just a different part of it.

Jonah appeared to be in a temple. He could hear a melodious prayer chant, but from where he couldn't tell. There were Chinese characters carved into the woodwork, and a black-and-white yin/yang symbol woven into the rug on which he stood. He could see a lantern sitting on an altar, golden statues of a dragon and a tiger, neatly tended flower boxes and no exit.

Jonah floated to a window, peered out, found himself faced with an almost sheer drop. He was in a Chinese temple, all right; if he craned his neck to look upwards, he could see the stacked layers of a pagoda-style roof above him. But the temple was set into a treacherous mountainside, and he could see no way down.

'Hello?' called Jonah, softly, fearing he might be alone in here. 'Mr Chang?'

The cat statuette was still clutched in his claw, its head open. He concentrated upon it, as if it might come to life and tell him what to do.

A shadow shifted. Jonah started. He flipped the statuette into his inventory space and looked around. 'Hello? Is someone there?'

It floated out from behind a bamboo screen: a golden dragon, towering even over Jonah's dragon avatar. Its body was long, like a snake's, and two enormous horns protruded from its head. The golden dragon had a wispy, white beard and wise eyes. It regarded Jonah with a pursed smile.

'I do not believe we have met, little dragon,' it said.

'Are...are you...?' Jonah didn't complete the question. There seemed to be no point. *Who else could this be*, he thought, *but the mysterious Mr Chang?*

He took a deep breath and told himself not to babble. There was no time. He pictured his mum in front of him, her hands on Jonah's shoulders, keeping him calm.

'Please, sir,' said Jonah. 'I'll explain who I am, I'll explain everything, but first I need your help. It's urgent. My friends are—'

'Your friends are quite safe for the present, Mr Delacroix. I have called off the assault on their broadcasting van.'

'You know...?' Another question went unvoiced. *Of course he knows who I am*, thought Jonah. He was Mr Chang. He was reputed to be as smart as Matthew

Granger himself. It was one of the few things that was known about him.

Mr Chang, unlike Granger, had always avoided the spotlight. The directors of his multinational corporation did his talking for him.

'So, you see,' said the golden dragon, 'there is always time for tea, and the making of new acquaintances.'

He had produced a silver tray on which sat a teapot and two wide, shallow cups. It floated before him and, as Mr Chang gestured with his claws, the teapot tipped to pour steaming, green liquid into each of the cups. Another gesture, and a cup floated towards Jonah. Jonah hadn't tried to drink as a dragon before. His arms were too short to hold the cup to his lips, so he had to follow Mr Chang's example and let it float up to him. The tea tasted bitter and grassy; Jonah didn't like it much.

'The charm that brought you here – I left it in the care of an old friend, just in case. And today appears to be the "*in case*", does it not?'

'Mr Peng,' said Jonah, 'he's my teacher at school. I asked him if—'

The golden dragon's smile broadened.

'There is no need to explain,' said Mr Chang. 'I trust you appreciate how special you are, young Master Delacroix? Yours is the only brain I have heard of that can store two avatars at once. Well, of course, you know this. This is why you were granted your scholarship with me.'

Jonah *hadn't* known that. He had only been told his dad had 'pulled some strings' to get him into the Chang Academy. He hadn't known how high those strings had gone.

'Now, then,' said Mr Chang, looking sharply down his ridged snout at Jonah. 'Perhaps you would be so kind as to explain your presence in Moscow. I am sure you know that you are associating with a young thief whose activities have caused me no small inconvenience.'

It must have been the statuette, decided Jonah. As well as transporting him here, and alerting Mr Chang to his arrival, it must have gathered information from his avatar, including his identity and his Real World Location.

He related the relevant parts of his story to Mr Chang: finding the avatar, the attack on the bus, his mother's death, his grandmother helping him to find the Guardians, and their journey across Europe to Moscow. He was careful to emphasise that the Guardians' alliance with Dimitry was only one of necessity. At the mention of the Russian pirate's name, Mr Chang's eyes narrowed, and a wisp of angry black smoke curled up from his nostrils.

'You are certainly a resourceful young man,' said Mr Chang, when Jonah had finished his tale. Jonah thanked him, genuinely flattered. 'One thing, however, I do not understand,' said Mr Chang. 'You say your Uploaded grandmother helped you access your father's memories, and that through this process you uncovered the location of one of the Four Corners?'

'That's right,' said Jonah, warily.

'I would have expected the Four Corners to be linked in your father's mind. Surely the memory of one should have led you to the memories of the others?'

'I…I don't know what you're saying.'

The golden dragon chuckled. 'You are still young,' he said, 'still unsure of the path you wish to tread through life, and yet already wise in many ways. I look forward to our promised meeting in the real world.'

'You mean,' said Jonah, 'you mean you'll tell your men to let us go?'

'More than that,' said Mr Chang. 'I will have them escort you to the Myachkovo Airport – that is where your aeroplane is waiting to bring you here to Shanghai? I will also arrange your onward journey from my country, once I know your destination…?'

'I'm not sure,' said Jonah. 'I'm not sure where we go next.'

'Come, come,' said Mr Chang. 'Your associates will have the Chang Bridge, and knowledge of the location of one of the Four Corners. Where else would they go?'

'I mean…'

'You mean you are not certain you can trust me either, to share this knowledge with me.' Mr Chang sounded more amused than angry.

Jonah tried to deny the charge, but he found himself tongue-tied.

'Let me see,' said Mr Chang, thoughtfully. 'If I were in your shoes, if I had determined the locations of the Four Corners... Which one would I choose to reveal to the Guardians? Which Corner would I most desire to see in safe hands?'

Jonah shifted nervously from foot to foot. He felt as if Mr Chang's shrewd eyes were looking right into his mind, reading his memories as he had read his dad's.

'The Southern Corner, I think,' said Mr Chang. 'Have I guessed correctly? Your slightly perplexed expression tells me that I have.'

'How did you know?' asked Jonah.

'From the way you spoke of your grandmother. This, too, I understand. She is the only link you have remaining to the family you have lost. You wish to protect her.'

'They...they say it's the Southern Corner that powers the Island of the Uploaded.'

'I believe this to be true,' said Mr Chang. 'I also believe the Southern Corner to be hidden somewhere on the Australian continent.'

'It is,' said Jonah quietly. He saw no point in withholding the truth any longer, but he didn't need to tell him where. 'And we need your help.'

Mr Chang inclined his dragon's head, inquisitively.

'We need to get there before Granger does,' said Jonah.

*

Matthew Granger sat in the control room of the Southern Corner.

Around him, the facility was abuzz with activity. His Millennials were searching the service corridors for any government lackeys who might have been left behind. There were systems to familiarise themselves with, and bodies to shift.

There were also security arrangements to make. To begin with, Granger wanted guards stationed around the perimeter fence. It wasn't that he thought any government had the resources or the willpower to try to take back what they had lost. But the Guardians were another matter.

Granger had two kids running system diagnostics. Every few seconds, one of them felt the need to report another discovered fault to him. The servers had been long neglected, apparently, and were in a poor state of repair. The software that ran them was outdated and buggy. Granger wasn't surprised.

There was a lot of work to do.

For the moment, however, none of that mattered. Matthew Granger sat still, as everyone rushed about him. He looked at the datapad nestled in his lap, drummed his fingers on the arm of his chair. He was waiting for a message.

It appeared at last, with a soft computer chime. Just three words of text, from the head of Granger's northern strike team. The last of the teams to report in.

It is ours, read the message. Granger smiled.

He sat for a few minutes longer, savouring his moment in private. Then, he mentally engaged his cyber-kinetic legs, pushed himself to his feet, cleared his throat for attention. The room fell silent, expectant. He allowed that expectation to build, before satisfying it with a grin and a nod of his head.

Granger's Millennials were cheering, applauding, before he could begin to speak. He felt the occasion should be marked with a few words, anyway. *Not here, though*, he thought. No, his maiden speech of this brand-new era should be heard by the largest possible audience. It should be recorded for posterity.

Granger tore open a fresh DI adaptor pack and plugged himself into a terminal. He left his real-world followers to their celebrations as, at last, he returned to the world he had created. The world that was now his again.

25

About five minutes had passed. It felt more like five hours.

Sam lay in the back of the broadcasting van. Jonah was sprawled beside her, still in his meta-trance. Axel and Bradbury, too, had flattened themselves to the floor.

They had expected the Chang Corp gunmen to open fire. Axel was the first to raise his head when they didn't. He peered through the shattered back window, saw something he didn't like and dropped again.

'They're still out there,' he hissed. 'They've got us outnumbered, outgunned and cornered. I don't know why the hell they don't just—'

He was interrupted by a voice, mechanically augmented. *'You in the van,'* said the voice. *'Come out now with your hands in the air and you will not be harmed.'*

'They are lying,' said Dimitry, his head down in the passenger seat. 'They will shoot us as soon as we step outside.'

'We don't know that,' said Sam.

'If they wanted to kill us,' said Bradbury, 'they'd have done it by now. I would've.'

'Then it is only because they do not realise who I am,'

said Dimitry. He was stiff with fright. 'Once they see me, they will surely—'

'What choice do we have?' said Sam, exasperated. 'They're offering us a chance, and I...I'm going to take it. I'll go out there first. I'll talk to them.'

As she picked herself up, she realised she was trembling inside. She half expected her father to stop her from putting herself at risk.

Instead, it was Bradbury who barred her way. 'No,' he said gruffly. 'I should be the one to go. It is my responsibility to protect—'

Dimitry had wound down his window. He leaned out of it and shouted: 'You will not take us alive. We have explosives, many quantities of explosives. They are powerful enough to destroy this van and you also. So, it is you who who will lay down your guns an' back away, please.'

Sam stared at him in horror. She didn't know if Dimitry was bluffing or not. Either way, this wasn't good.

Everyone waited with breath held, until the augmented voice came again: '*I repeat, you will not be harmed. We have orders to that effect from Mr Chang himself.*'

A pause, and then the voice continued: '*It appears you have a mutual friend – a Mr Jonah Delacroix. Where is he?*'

*

Jonah had hoped the cat figurine would teleport him back to his school, back to his exit halo.

'This device only works one way,' Mr Chang explained. 'But you can find your own way back to your halo through here.' He guided Jonah to a wall-hanging tapestry. It depicted a dragon not unlike Mr Chang's own avatar, surrounded by heaps of gold and jewels.

Behind the tapestry, there was a secret door.

'Thank you,' Jonah said, before stepping through the door.

Jonah emerged into a deserted alleyway, and turned to find a brick wall behind him. It was solid to his touch; there was no way back to the mountain temple through there. Rather than walk the streets, Jonah took to the sky to survey his surroundings.

He was in a Chinese-themed zone. He soared between skyscrapers and through archways decorated with singing paper lanterns. He was greeted joyously by many other dragons of varied shapes and colours.

Desperate to get back to Sam in the real world, he climbed higher and flew faster than ever before. He whipped through the digital clouds until he spotted the Chang Academy island in the distance.

He hardly noticed that an exit halo had opened in front of him.

He swerved around it, kept flying. A moment later, though, another halo opened to Jonah's right. He could see two, three more halos, suspended in the air around him.

In the mouth of the nearest halo, an avatar was forming: an enormous, black spider. It had elongated fangs and eight round, glistening black eyes: four in the sides of its head and four more in a square pattern glaring directly at Jonah.

Jonah's heart leapt into his mouth. He recognised the spider. It was probably the most recognisable avatar in the virtual world.

Matthew Granger had found him, and had come for him personally.

Jonah flew around the halo. He had to get away from here before the spider avatar became fully formed, before Granger's senses transferred fully from the real world to this one. He pulled up short as he saw another black spider, climbing out of one of the other exit halos – and another and another.

There were spiders below Jonah, too. The land below was crawling with them.

There was no escape. Matthew Granger was everywhere.

The sensation was overwhelming.

Granger could see the whole of the Metasphere from hundreds of thousands of points of view at once. He could hear it too: billions of voices raised in surprise and adulation – and, yes, some in anger towards him, but there were always those who resisted progress.

He closed his eyes, focused his mind. He could control the images, control them like a slide show. He could choose which of his many avatars' eyes to look through.

Granger went on a tour of his virtual world. He satisfied himself that, from the call centres to the game zones, he had everyone's attention. Concerts had been suspended; all trading on the stock markets had ceased.

Everyone was waiting to hear what he had to say.

The spiders all spoke at once, in one voice. Granger's voice.

'For those of you who don't know me,' they said, *'or have forgotten me after all this time, let me introduce myself. I am Matthew Granger.'*

Jonah, like everyone else, was just floating, listening. He didn't have much choice.

'Twenty years ago, I created Web 4.0, the beta version of what we now call the Metasphere. My intent was to create a better life for all, a better world than the one we had. It was to have been an ordered world, an efficient world, a world in which – to put it bluntly – things worked.'

At first, Jonah had just been relieved that the spiders hadn't come for him. Now, however, he felt queasy with anticipation. For Granger to be doing this, showing himself like this, there had to be a good reason. Something big.

'Three years ago,' said the spiders, 'that world was taken from me. Our governments – the very bodies that had ruined their world – believed they could do a better job than I of managing this one. We have seen how wrong they were.'

Many avatars cheered at this – and the thing was, as hard as he tried, Jonah couldn't think of a reason to disagree with them.

'Well, those dark times are over. You have no doubt heard that, three days ago, in the wake of the collapse of the United States government, I escaped from the prison to which I had been unjustly confined. I have been busy since then.

'We have traversed the real world, my followers and I. We have returned to the sites of the four server farms that I built to run the Metasphere two decades ago. We have retaken those sites from the governments who—'

The rest of Granger's words were drowned out by a tremendous roar.

Jonah had never heard so many voices raised at once. It sounded as if the whole world was screaming, some in celebration, some in fury, each faction determined to outdo the other.

'My friends,' Matthew Granger boomed over the hubbub, through the mouths of his many spider avatars, 'the Four Corners are mine again. I am back in control. Today is the beginning of a bright new era.'

Jonah had to get back to the others.

He continued to the Chang Academy. His route was lined by more spider avatars. They floated in the air, bobbed on the water. Jonah couldn't escape their combined voice.

Bradbury was the first out of the broadcasting van, his hands in the air. When the Chang Corp men didn't gun him down at once, Axel followed his example.

Two Chang Corp men came forward and frisked them. They took Bradbury's shotgun and Axel's pistol, then motioned them towards the waiting limousines.

The other six gunmen hadn't moved. They were crouched behind their vehicles, their weapons trained on the prisoners.

Sam emerged next. The first two men searched her and finding no weapons, holstered their own.

'He's inside,' she said. 'Inside the van, and inside the Metasphere. And we're not going anywhere until he comes out of his meta-trance.'

Dimitry and Andrey climbed out of the passenger and driver doors. Dimitry held his head low, avoiding eye contact with the gunmen. None of the Chang Corp men reacted to his appearance, so either they didn't recognise him or – more likely – they knew who he was and just didn't care.

Sam heard a groan from inside the van. Before anyone could stop her, she had run back to it, pulled the van doors open.

Jonah was coming round, and had evidently discovered the fresh bruises on his body. Sam picked him up, unplugged his Ethernet cord and helped him outside. 'What happened?' asked Jonah, a little groggily. 'No, actually, never mind that. There's something I have to tell you. Granger...Matthew Granger has taken back the Metasphere.'

Jonah walked between the van and the limousines and told his story. Dimitry and Andrey listened too, as did the Chang Corp men, who came out from behind their cars and lowered their guns. Axel and Bradbury came with them; no one tried to stop them.

They started asking Jonah questions. One thin-faced man, wearing an earpiece, came forward to say that he had checked and it was true.

They stood together in silence for a time, these former enemies.

'So, what now?' asked Sam.

'Our instructions,' said the thin-faced Chang Corp man, 'are to escort you to the Myachkovo Airport.'

'Why?' asked Jonah. 'What's the point now? It's too late!'

Dimitry glared at him. Sam knew what the Russian pirate was thinking. Those 'instructions' were all that was keeping him alive. The rest of them too, most likely.

'No,' said Axel. 'It's not too late, it's just a different mission. So Granger has the first mover advantage. He's got the Four Corners now. And, before him, the governments had them. We always knew this fight was coming. If we had got there first, we'd be defending. But now…'

'Now,' said Sam quietly, finishing her father's thoughts, 'we'll be attacking. We'll have to fight the Millennials head-on.'

26

Dimitry's plane was larger than Hiram's had been, and a great deal more comfortable. It had a spacious passenger compartment, with eight padded chairs arranged around glass-topped tables. There was a fridge stocked with drinks and snacks.

It looked like Jonah had always imagined Granger's plane would look. The one his dad had flown. He guessed there was a lot of money in Dimitry's line of work.

Dimitry was flying the jet himself. Jonah had hoped to leave him behind at the airport, along with Andrey. No such luck. He couldn't help but notice the way Dimitry looked at Sam. He had already invited her to join him in the cockpit. 'Maybe later,' she had said, faking a yawn.

They had been airborne for twenty minutes when Axel decided to log on. He located a Metasphere terminal under his seat, and unwound its Ethernet cord.

'I wanna have a quick recce, see what's going on in there,' he said. 'Anyway, I need a drink, and I can't have a real one. Need to keep a clear head.'

'Where are you going?' asked Sam.

Axel pulled a face. 'I guess it can't be the Icarus.'

'You should steer clear of that area,' said Sam. 'We know there are Millennial spies around there, and they've seen us with Jason Delacroix's avatar.'

'I know a place for tonight, off the beaten track, no questions asked,' said Axel. 'You coming with me, kiddo?'

Sam said she would, for an hour. It was only as she was logging on that Jonah realised this would leave him alone with Bradbury. He nearly asked Sam if he could go with her, but he was tired and decided to rest instead. He didn't have to talk to Bradbury, he told himself.

Bradbury had stripped down his recently returned shotgun and was cleaning and oiling it, making sure the Chang Corp men hadn't damaged it. Jonah lay back in his chair and was asleep before he knew it.

Jonah was half woken just once, he wasn't sure when.

He could hear voices. Axel's was a little too loud, his words slurred. He had probably got his avatar extremely drunk and was still feeling a knock-on effect. Of course, back in his real-world body, he was soon sober again.

Axel was describing street parties and fireworks. Half the Metasphere, he said, was celebrating Granger's return. Bradbury was annoyed by this. He said something about sheep, about how some people were too stupid to know what was good for them. Sam pointed out that she and Axel had witnessed furious protests too. They had even seen avatars fighting.

Jonah drifted back to sleep. He was woken by Sam, to find sunlight streaming through the aeroplane's windows. 'Dad says we'll be touching down in forty minutes,' said Sam. 'I thought you'd want to get cleaned up and eat something.'

Axel had disappeared from the passenger compartment. He must have been at the controls, because Dimitry was sleeping in his seat. Sam woke him, too. Bradbury had found a kettle and was brewing up a pot of Stimucaff, a coffee substitute.

Dimitry said something to Sam in Russian that made her laugh. Sam surprised Jonah by answering in the same language.

'What did he say?' Jonah asked Sam.

'Oh, nothing important,' she replied before quickly adding, 'he's just being macho.'

Jonah had preferred it when Sam was acting cool towards their pilot. What could he say about it, though? *It's not like she's my girlfriend or anything!*

Bradbury handed Dimitry a Stimucaff. 'No problems with the Chinese authorities?'

Dimitry shook his head. 'They radioed as soon as we flew into their airspace, but I was able to bluff them. I said I was carrying an American businessman.'

'And you're sure they believed you?' asked Sam.

'If they hadn't,' said Bradbury, 'they'd have blown us to pieces by now.'

'Or maybe Mr Chang told them to let us land,' said

Jonah, not wanting to let Dimitry get all the credit for their safe descent. It was he, after all, that had found Mr Chang in the Metasphere.

They landed at another private airfield, outside Shanghai.

They said their goodbyes inside the plane. Dimitry was keen to get back to Moscow and his work there. He had a broadcasting van to replace, he said, and he shook his head at the thought of how much this would cost him. He wished the Guardians good fortune, and he kissed Sam on the cheek.

He turned to Jonah and said, 'My resourceful young comrade. Had it not been for you, I would not be here now. I am in your debt forever.'

Jonah was taken aback. It was the first time Dimitry had addressed him directly, and he hadn't expected such kind words. He almost felt guilty for having disliked the Russian so much.

'What did you say to Sam, in Russian?'

'I asked her not to go on. Instead to return with me to Moscow.'

Jonah stopped feeling guilty. He really didn't like this Russian at all.

'And what did she say?'

'Why don't you ask her?' he replied.

Jonah disembarked behind the others.

They had barely set foot on the tarmac when two

black limousines came racing to meet them. Jonah froze, remembering the black remotes that had chased after him at the Dover airstrip. Then four men jumped out of the first limo, dressed in fatigues and armed like the Chang Corp men in Moscow.

Jonah's heart sank as they marched up to the plane. It looked like Mr Chang had betrayed him after all. He was about to raise his hands in surrender, but the four men brushed past him. 'Hey, what's going on?' cried Axel. He started after the armed men, but Bradbury held him back.

Dimitry had been quicker on the uptake. He had been standing in the hatchway behind Jonah and the others. However, when Jonah looked now, he was gone. The Chang Corp men disappeared into the plane after him.

An elderly Chinese man stepped out of the second limousine. He wore a grey suit and a chauffeur's cap, which he tipped in Jonah's direction. 'Master Delacroix and company, I presume? If you would be so kind as to step this way, please, my employer is eager to meet you.'

Jonah looked at Sam, looked at Axel, looked back at the plane. He started forward.

He was stopped in his tracks by the sound of a gunshot.

He turned back.

'Master Delacroix, please,' said the chauffeur. 'Mr

Chang would prefer you not to involve yourself in his private business.'

Jonah stammered, 'But…'

Bradbury took his arm, propelled him towards the limo. 'The gentleman is correct,' he said gruffly. 'Dimitry isn't one of us. We had a deal with him. That deal is done. What happens to him now is none of our concern.'

'We have a deal with Mr Chang, too,' added Axel.

Jonah was shocked by their uncaring attitude. He turned to Sam for support. She looked as dismayed as he was by this turn of events, but she didn't speak up. Catching Jonah's eye, Sam shook her head.

He got the message: *what could we do, anyway?*

The chauffeur held open the back door of his limo. Bradbury pushed Jonah inside. The others joined him. They sat on an L-shaped seat, real leather, around a minibar and entertainment console. Jonah squirmed around to look through the side window.

The Chang Corp men were emerging from Dimitry's plane. To his relief, Dimitry was with them. He was very much a prisoner, his hands on his head, four guns trained on him, but he was alive – for now, anyway.

The limo pulled away, leaving the Russian pirate to his fate. Jonah couldn't help but wonder what might have happened – what the others might have done – had the Chang Corp men come for him instead.

After all, he wasn't really 'one of them' either, was he?

The streets of Shanghai were even quieter than Jonah had expected.

He knew from school that China had the highest population of any country – but that the Chinese people, looking to escape their overcrowded real-world cities, had been among the first to truly embrace the Metasphere.

Jonah had heard of people here hooking themselves up to drips to spend days at a time online. They even slept online, recording their dreams to watch later. Like the traders at London's City Tower, they often employed servants – digital holdouts and metaphobes like Jonah's mum – to look after their meta-tranced bodies.

Shanghai was an odd mixture of Art Deco-style townhouses and more modern glass and steel skyscrapers. As they approached the Pudong district – Jonah was following an interactive map on the console in the limo – the skyscrapers grew taller and grander, until they crowded out the smaller buildings altogether.

In the course of their journey, they passed only two other cars, and both of these were also Chang Corp limousines.

They pulled up at the blue and grey Shanghai Tower. Jonah looked at it in awe as they made for the entranceway. The tower was the tallest building in the world, once topped only by the now-crumbled towers of Dubai. It spiralled up into the clouds.

'Do you see anything familiar?' asked the chauffeur with an indulgent smile. 'The building was designed in the image of a coiled dragon.'

He ushered Jonah and the three Guardians into the building's lobby. They were met by a security guard and escorted to an elevator.

They travelled up over a hundred floors in silence, and Jonah winced as he felt his ears popping. Sam noticed his discomfort and grinned at him. She showed him what to do, holding her nose and blowing out, making her face red and her cheeks puffed. Jonah laughed aloud. Bradbury glared at him, but for once Jonah didn't care what the surly engineer thought. It felt good to laugh, if only for an instant.

The lift opened and they stepped out into a sunlit atrium. Behind them, the core of the tower continued to rise, but now they were standing in a ring-shaped space between its outer and inner glass walls. There were trees here, but also tables and chairs arranged around the edge of the ring.

The security guard stayed inside the elevator. The doors slid shut and Jonah heard the cab descending. For a moment, he thought they had been left alone. Then a boy came to greet them. He was Jonah's age, Chinese, with an impish grin, and he carried himself with a confidence that Jonah envied. He wore a tailored black business suit and a tie with a golden dragon embroidered in the red silk.

He bowed to the four visitors. 'Good afternoon, Miss Kavanaugh, gentlemen. I thought this might make a more agreeable meeting place than the airport.'

'I've never been in a building this tall,' said Sam. 'The views are breathtaking.'

'We didn't come here to admire the scenery,' said Bradbury, bluntly. 'We were promised Mr Chang would meet us personally.'

'Of course,' said the boy. 'Mr Bradbury, I presume? Then your friend here must be Mr Kavanaugh, while you...' He turned to Jonah and his smile grew broader, warmer. 'You must be young Master Delacroix – or may I call you Jonah? It is an honour to make your acquaintance in the real world.'

'I, um... Nice to meet you too,' said Jonah, 'but I don't understand...'

'Of course. I have neglected to introduce myself. Forgive my lapse in manners. Sometimes I forget my real-world form is so unlike my true self.' The boy didn't look apologetic. He looked as if he was enjoying Jonah's confusion.

'You mean you're...?'

Sam was the first to say it. 'You're Mr Chang, aren't you?'

The boy bowed his head again. 'And I am at your service,' he said.

213

27

High up in the sky, they sat beneath a potted tree, around a meeting table.

Axel was still having trouble taking it all in. 'So, you're Mr Chang,' he repeated. 'CEO of the Chang Corporation. The third richest man in the world.'

'The second, I believe,' said the Chinese boy. 'If you check today's stock price.'

'You're just a kid!' said Axel.

'What my dad means to say,' said Sam, diplomatically, 'is that Chang Corp has been in business for over twenty years. You couldn't have been born when—'

'My father built up the company,' said the boy. 'He was Mr Chang too, of course. I inherited Chang Corp on my fourteenth birthday.'

'And you've doubled its size in two and a half years,' said Sam.

'I had excellent tutors, my father included. At school, I learned everything I needed to know about science and technology. At home, I was instructed in business.'

Jonah couldn't quite believe it. He still had no idea what he wanted to do with his life and the events of the past few days had confused him all the more. And yet,

Mr Chang had it all sorted out.

'So, you're the inventor of the Chang Bridge,' said Bradbury.

'Straight to the point,' said Mr Chang. 'My father would have approved. Of course, since Jonah and I spoke in the Metasphere, a few things have changed.'

'Not as far as we're concerned,' said Axel. 'Our plans remain the same.'

'I am most pleased to hear it. Having Matthew Granger back in control of the virtual world is, shall we say, bad for my business.'

'It's bad news for everyone,' said Bradbury. 'That's why we're here, Mr Chang. We have to act now. We need your invention.'

Mr Chang reached into his suit jacket. He produced a small, thin, silver box. It was no larger than a personal hard drive. It had a row of LEDs on its front edge, three ports on the rear. Etched into its top surface was a hologram of a coiled, golden dragon, similar to Mr Chang's own avatar.

'That's it?' said Jonah.

'Indeed,' said Mr Chang. 'You were expecting something...?'

'Bigger,' said Sam. 'Definitely much bigger.'

'Gotta hand it to you, kid,' said Axel, quickly correcting himself, 'I mean, Mr Chang. If that box does half of what you claim it does, then I don't care how old you are or where you went to school. You're a genius!'

Bradbury had picked up the device. He turned it over in his hands, inspecting it. 'What do we do with it?' he asked.

'The Chang Bridge must be physically interfaced with the servers of any of the Four Corners,' said Mr Chang. 'Once this has been achieved, the rest is automatic. The device will take a little under a minute to do its work.'

'Less than a minute?' said Bradbury. He looked at Mr Chang, suspiciously. 'To back up one-quarter of the Metasphere's data?'

'My goodness, no. That would be quite impossible.'

Axel and Bradbury exchanged a glance. They both leapt to their feet. Jonah spotted Bradbury's hand twitching in the direction of his concealed shotgun, and he felt his stomach tightening. He looked around for more Chang Corp men. He couldn't see any, but he knew they couldn't be too far away. He didn't want to end up in the middle of another armed standoff.

'What are you trying to pull here, kid?' growled Axel.

'I fail to see your meaning.' Mr Chang remained seated and calm.

'We came here for a reason. We were told you had a device that could back up the Metasphere, a device that could—'

'Mr Kavanaugh, please,' said Mr Chang. 'The size of the Metasphere is measured in Geopbytes, even

Saganbytes. The device that could store such a quantity of data would be the size of an island. It would be the size of the Four Corners combined.'

'I knew it all along,' snarled Bradbury. 'I said it was too good to be true. We're wasting our time, Axel.'

'No, wait,' said Sam. 'Mr Chang, obviously there has been a mix-up here, but I'm sure we can still—'

'Evidently so,' said Mr Chang, 'and to my lasting regret. I can assure you, Miss Kavanaugh, it was never my intention to deceive.'

'Of course not, no.'

'Of course, the nature of our alliance has demanded that, until this moment, our communications have been made through intermediaries.'

'So, you're saying it's not your fault,' said Bradbury. 'One of your people or ours got the wrong end of the stick?' He looked far from convinced.

'We've been on a wild goose chase,' said Axel, 'while Granger has been—'

'What *does* it do?'

Axel broke off in mid-sentence. Jonah had spoken quietly, but now everyone's eyes were on him. He cleared his throat.

'The Chang Bridge,' Jonah said. 'You knew exactly why we wanted it – we talked about it in your temple, in the Metasphere – and you said, well as good as said, that it would help us. So, if the Chang Bridge isn't a back-up device, then what is it?'

Mr Chang smiled at him. 'You are a shrewd young man indeed, Jonah Delacroix.'

'Well?' said Bradbury.

'My Chang Bridge,' said Mr Chang, 'does exactly as its name suggests. It will create a bridge between the Metasphere and a new virtual world.'

'A new...?' Axel sat down again, nonplussed.

'A better world,' said Mr Chang. 'Matthew Granger is a genius, do not misunderstand me – but, in maintaining a monopoly over meta-technologies, in stifling any and all competition, he has stunted his own creation. As for the real-world governments, the less said about their stewardship of the Metasphere the better.'

'And this new world,' said Sam, 'it already...exists?'

'My Changsphere has ten times the Metasphere's processing power, and employs it more efficiently. The user experience is thus heightened by—'

'Your "Changsphere"!' exclaimed Bradbury.

'Think of it as a yang to the Metasphere's yin,' Mr Chang explained, as if his visitors would know what he meant by that.

'No, no, no, no, *no!*' Axel palmed his face in frustration. 'No, this wasn't the deal, Chang-boy. We were supposed to be making the Metasphere free for everyone, not just swapping a world with one dictator for another.'

Mr Chang's eyes darkened. 'I have no lust for power, Mr Kavanaugh. I hoped you would understand this by

218

now. The source code of the Changsphere would be available upon request, the development of third-party applications positively encouraged. Most importantly of all, users would have a choice – between the old world and the new. Mr Granger's monopoly would be broken.'

'But one man – you – would still be in control,' protested Axel.

'Through my corporation, yes. I believe the world – any world – needs leadership, a man with vision, else it can only stagnate. We have seen how—'

'So, even if we trusted you,' said Bradbury, 'what about the future? What happens if a megalomaniac inherits your *Yang*sphere?'

'Even in such a circumstance,' said Mr Chang, 'by then there would likely be another new virtual world to compete with mine. The circle would begin again.'

It all sounded quite reasonable to Jonah. It sounded good, in fact. A whole new virtual world to explore… An even better one… He could see, however, that Axel and Bradbury weren't convinced. They had wanted to save the Metasphere, not replace it with a new model.

Mr Chang stood up. 'Of course, you need to consider my proposal. Take all the time you need. Keep in mind, however, that my device will give you what you seek – freedom from a world controlled by Matthew Granger.'

'Where is it?' asked Sam. 'If the Changsphere already exists, then where is it?'

'Where else, my dear?' said Mr Chang. '"The size of

an island", I said. And I am sure you are aware, through the online news services, of a purchase I made some eighteen months ago. My first acquisition for Chang Corp, as it happens.'

'Hong Kong!' recalled Axel. 'You bought Hong Kong!'

'And,' breathed Sam, 'you turned it… The whole city? You turned it into a giant server farm?'

Mr Chang just smiled, bowed to his guests and left. He stepped through a doorway, disappearing into the core of the Shanghai Tower. And for a minute or more after he had gone, no one said a word.

'OK,' said Sam at length. 'Dad, I know you're not going to like this, but—'

'Too damn right I don't,' said Axel. 'We schlepped halfway across the world to meet some kid fresh out of nappies, who tells us the device we were promised doesn't even exist! And did anyone swallow that "misunderstanding" guff?'

Bradbury shook his head. 'Mr Chang knew what we wanted. He let the Guardians believe he had it.'

'Then why tell us the truth now?' asked Jonah.

'Because we had the device,' said Bradbury, 'and I was suspicious as soon as I saw it. Chang knew damn well I would take it apart and work out what it did.'

'But why? Why try to trick you in the first place?'

'He thinks we have no choice now,' said Axel.

'Granger has the Four Corners.'

'We're supposed to shrug our shoulders and go along with Chang's plan,' said Bradbury. 'We're supposed to create a portal to his virtual world, his *Yang-ville*, because it's the best we can do and because at least it's something.'

'Well…well, isn't it?' Sam hazarded. 'If it gives people a choice, it loosens Granger's grip…'

'I meant what I said,' said Axel. 'I've spent my life fighting for a principle. The virtual world should be free. No half-measures, no compromises. I refuse to just…just hand it over to Mr Chang or to anyone.'

'You realise we still need him,' said Sam.

'He said he'd get us to Australia,' said Jonah.

'Every contact we have in China reports to Mr Chang. Without him—'

Bradbury scowled. 'They have a point, Axel.'

'OK, OK, I get it.' Axel sighed. 'We've no choice for now but to suck it up – to smile at this Chang kid and say "Yes, sir", "No, sir", "Three bags full, sir". I'll even take his damn Chang Bridge if I have to. I'll tell the kid to his face that we've discussed it and decided to trust him.'

'But?' said Sam.

'We install that device over my dead body,' said Axel. 'As soon as we don't need Mr Chang any more, we destroy the Chang Bridge. Totally. Forever.'

28

'I am putting the fate of the world in your hands, Master Delacroix,' Mr Chang said. He deliberately handed the device over to Jonah, even though Axel stood with his hand outstretched and his palm up.

'I'll make good use of it,' Jonah promised. He felt guilty about deceiving his newfound friend – especially as Mr Chang was keeping Jonah's own secret that he knew where the other three Corners were.

'You will travel to Australia on one of my shipping vessels. It's docked now and will sail as soon as you board.'

'By sea?' Axel objected. 'That'll take days—'

'Four and a half,' replied Mr Chang.

'That gives Granger more time to entrench himself,' argued Axel. 'It's too long!'

'But far safer than travelling by air,' Mr Chang said.

Out of Mr Chang's earshot, Bradbury whispered to Axel, 'It ain't us he's concerned with, it's that little box.'

Mr Chang escorted the group back to the elevator and Jonah couldn't hold back any longer. 'What will you do to Dimitry?' he asked.

'He will serve as an example to others,' Mr Chang said.

'You don't have to...to kill him, you know.'

'You are right. I do have that choice.' Mr Chang smiled. 'It's good to have a choice, isn't it, Master Delacroix?'

The lift doors opened, and Jonah and his three Guardian allies stepped through them. As they rode back down to the ground floor, Jonah pondered on Mr Chang's words, but didn't know what to make of them.

The limousine was still waiting at the door.

Mr Chang must have sent instructions to its driver, because he knew where to go without being told. He drove Jonah and the others eastwards to the coast.

The evening was drawing in as they reached the docks of the Yangshan Deep-Water Port. The skeletons of cranes and derricks moved in silhouette against the greying sky.

Men in red boiler suits were shouting orders to the crane operators. The cranes screeched as they lifted giant metal containers the size of Jonah's bus over to a hulking black freighter, stacking them on the deck like building blocks.

Axel threaded his way confidently through the bustle, the others behind him. They climbed the ship's gangway and were met at its top by a slight, bearded man. He also wore a red boiler suit, with a golden dragon logo sewn into its breast pocket.

'I am Captain Teng,' he said. 'We sail for Sydney and I have my instructions to ensure safe passage. This is not a passenger ship, but we do have basic amenities, such as showers.'

Jonah realised he had been wearing the same clothes for four days straight, and had not showered. It must've shown.

Teng instructed a young crewmember, called Quek, to show them to their cabins, one level beneath the giant bridge castle that overlooked the containers being stacked onto the ship like building blocks.

'Can we get online?' asked Sam.

Quek nodded as they descended the steel staircase under the deck.

'We'll need to recruit an army, Dad,' she whispered to Axel.

'Then we had better get plugged in,' he replied.

Jonah was pleased to have a bed of his own again. The room was stark but clean, and to his surprise a change of clothes had been laid out for him. He was looking forward to a long, hot shower and then some rest. For the past few days he had been swept along by events, lurching from one fraught situation to another. He needed time to think.

The freighter was loaded up, the hatches battened down. Now, it chugged out into the harbour. The boat was an old-fashioned diesel model. To Jonah's surprise and discomfort, it had dirty black funnels, pumping exhaust clouds into the air.

He climbed up seven flights of steel stairs, ascending the bridge castle that overlooked the tightly packed containers, and watched the lights of Shanghai recede as the ship navigated out of the harbour. The freighter picked up speed as the waters of the East China Sea opened out before it. Its prow swung around to point south-east.

Sam, Axel and Bradbury spent much of the next four days online.

'We're activating different cells, pulling in agents where we can,' Sam explained. They meta-tranced for hours at a time, negotiating deals and brokering for equipment. At first, Jonah was barred from those sessions, but on their third day at sea, Axel finally invited Jonah to attend.

'We want you to feel one with the cause,' he said.

But Jonah wasn't sure if it was just that he was growing impatient of Jonah's line of questioning every time they logged off.

The rendezvous spot was a seedy, backstreet bar, with the usual riot of colourful avatars present. A couple of them – a large, white pig with sagging jowls and a dreadlocked humatar covered in moving tattoos – appeared to be extremely high up in the Guardian movement. Jonah wasn't told their names and he didn't ask.

Jonah was familiar with Axel's gryphon avatar and Sam's unicorn, of course. However, he had not seen Bradbury in the Metasphere before. He was surprised to find that the burly engineer took the shape of a Clydesdale horse, chestnut brown with a white nose and legs. Was that really how his inner mind saw himself?

More than once, Bradbury harrumphed and opined that 'the kid' shouldn't be here. Jonah resented this bitterly. So, he wasn't a Guardian. Hadn't he proved himself, all the same? Hadn't he saved them all from the Chang Corp men in Moscow? And the white pig, in particular, seemed delighted to meet him – although, of course, his real interest was in the knowledge that Jonah had, or rather had inherited, his father's knowledge.

The knowledge that, in part at least, he was still keeping to himself.

Jonah discovered that the Guardians were assembling at a place called Woomera – those who could reach it in the real world and were prepared to fight. From there, Axel would lead an assault on the Southern Corner at Ayers Rock.

There had been some debate about the wisdom of this course. The Guardians had pinned their hopes on the Chang Bridge device, and had been let down. Even if they could take the Southern Corner, they couldn't back up its data. They couldn't transfer its operations to one of their waiting server farms. They would have to hold the Ayers Rock facility, by force, indefinitely.

Axel had been one of the first to point out, however, that the longer they delayed, the more time the Millennials had to become entrenched within the rock themselves. Doubtless, they would be swelling their forces too, improving their security.

The sooner the Guardians made their move, said Axel, the better.

Back on the black freighter, Bradbury took Jonah to one side.

'This isn't your fight,' he said with his usual bluntness.

'But...' said Jonah.

'I mean it, kid,' said Bradbury. 'You've done fine so far, I'm not saying you haven't, but you're just a kid.'

'I stopped being a kid when my mum pushed me out of that building,' said Jonah, defensively, 'and Sam's barely older than I am—'

'Samantha has been training for this half her life,' said Bradbury. 'She's a talented mechanic, a promising pilot, and she's probably more mature than Axel is. She's also one hundred per cent committed to the cause. Can you honestly say the same?'

Jonah couldn't, and his silence betrayed him.

'I'm doing you a favour, kid, if only you could see it,' said Bradbury. 'It's gonna get rough out there, and you ain't prepared. If you want another reason, try this one for size: we can't afford to lose you. This mission, it's just the beginning. There are three more Corners out there, three more server farms in Granger's hands. You're the only person in the world who can direct us to them.'

Jonah hadn't come this far to be sidelined, but at the same time, he wondered if he should listen to Bradbury. It might keep him alive.

Apart from that one meeting, Jonah had been avoiding the Metasphere. Tensions in the virtual world had escalated. When Jonah tried to return to Venus Park, to revisit the scar left by his family's gift shop, the entire park had erupted in protest and violent riots. The Metasphere was a place he once loved, but since Granger's takeover it felt foreign to him. It no longer felt like home. Nowhere did.

On the third night of the voyage, Jonah and the others were invited to dine at the captain's table in a private room just below the bridge. Captain Teng arrived late, with news that there had been a major terrorist attack online. A virtual bank belonging to Matthew Granger had been virus-bombed. At least twenty avatars had been caught in the blast, corrupted or destroyed.

Dinner was sautéed fish, line-caught off the bow of the ship. The setting sun bathed the white steel room in an orange glow. Jonah devoured the authentic protein, and even braced himself to swallow down the grassy green tea. It was his first proper meal in a long, long time. But despite the fine food, there was a palpable tension in the air.

'Those Guardians have gone too far,' complained Captain Teng. 'They cannot continue to maim and kill and expect to be trusted.'

Jonah realised that Mr Chang had told him little about his four passengers, and none of them cared to enlighten him. The captain reminded Jonah of himself just days ago, in the classroom, deriding the Guardians and supporting the Millennials, without even knowing half of the truths behind either movement.

Jonah wasn't about to reveal his new loyalties, and none of his dinner companions did either. Instead, they ate politely and made awkward small talk with the captain.

Breakfast the next morning was the usual Pro-Meal pouches in the crewmen's mess hall. Jonah, Sam and Bradbury huddled around a corner table.

'Dad's already online,' said Sam. 'He said he couldn't sleep. I said I'd meet him in the Metasphere at nine and we could finish recruiting. You want to come?'

Bradbury answered for Jonah. 'The kid was thinking of visiting the Island of the Uploaded today – weren't you, kid?'

The implication was clear. Bradbury wanted Jonah to access his father's memories again, to find the other three Corners. He didn't know that Jonah already had that information.

I can't tell them yet, he thought. Jonah had decided to wait until the upcoming fight was over. He wanted to see what the Guardians did with one Corner before he told them about the others. He needed to be sure that telling them was the right thing to do.

He agreed to Bradbury's suggestion, anyway, to keep up appearances. Anyway, thought Jonah, a chat with his grandmother might be just what he needed – and he would ask her to help him meditate again. Maybe, just maybe, there was still something his dad's memories could tell him that would make sense of everything.

He returned to his cabin, and plugged himself in.

Jonah was prepared to swim.

He found himself back where he had started instead. Floundering, he fell out of his chair, hit the floor with a bump. He was still in the real world, in his real body, in the cabin. His connection had failed.

He waited for the walls to stop spinning about him, then picked himself up. He checked his Point of Origin co-ordinates. He had definitely entered the right numbers. He should have washed up on the shore of the Island, as usual.

Something was wrong. He was locked out.

The black Chang freighter chugged between two jutting land masses, into the sprawling Sydney Harbour. The skyline of the city stood against a stark, blue late-morning sky, still a good distance ahead. Jonah leaned on the metal railing of the starboard deck.

For him, this voyage couldn't be over soon enough.

He had tried twice more to get to the Island of the Uploaded. He had failed each time. He had waited for the others to come off-line, then asked Bradbury to take a look at his terminal. Sam had told him there was no need. They already knew what the problem was, and it was no simple hardware fault.

Access to the Island had been blocked by Matthew Granger.

Officially, it was a security measure. Granger was protecting the Uploaded from a potential terrorist threat, so he said. But the Guardians believed there was no such threat, and that Granger was deliberately holding the dead to ransom. He wanted the protests against his takeover of the Metasphere to stop – and, until they did, no one would be allowed to visit their deceased loved ones.

Every time Jonah thought about it, he burned with anger. His grandmother was the only family he had left – even if she was just a digital echo – and Granger wanted to take her from him too?

For the first time, he found himself in full agreement with the Guardians' objectives. He was beginning to understand their passion. Why *should* one man – a man like Granger – have so much power over his life? The sooner the Guardians seized the Southern Corner – the sooner they liberated that quarter of the Metasphere in which the Island of the

Uploaded was located – the happier Jonah would be.

He had been lost in thought, but looked up when he hear the sound of engines. A floatplane with twin pontoons was flying low above them. Jonah pointed it out to one of Teng's crew, whose blood drained from his face as he looked up.

'A spotter plane!' the crewman whispered before blowing furiously into his whistle.

Jonah hadn't noticed another ship in the harbour: a motorised yacht with billowing white sails. But suddenly, it was coming at the freighter's starboard side. A warning shout went up, and was echoed around the freighter by its crew.

The yacht was coming alongside. Jonah could see people on the deck. They were armed with machine guns, and one man hoisted a massive cylinder on his shoulder. *That can't be good*, Jonah thought.

'*Attention, crew of the Chang Corporation vessel.*' A woman on the yacht had raised a loudhailer to her mouth. '*You will cut your polluting engines and prepare to be boarded. Fail to comply, and we will open fire. There will be no second warning.*'

Jonah could hardly believe his eyes or ears.

They were under attack by pirates!

29

Jonah didn't have time to do more than gape.

He heard the pounding of booted footsteps, and suddenly the deck was filled with armed Chang Corp men. He didn't know where half of them had come from.

One of them shouted at him to get out of the way. The next instant, the air was filled with the harsh reports of gunfire. The Chang Corp men were shooting at the yacht, and the people on the yacht were firing back.

Jonah didn't need telling twice. He raced for cover. The door that led to the cabins, to safety, was just a few metres away from him.

He couldn't reach it. A bullet whistled by Jonah's ear, pinged off a bulkhead beside him, and he lost his nerve and threw himself down flat.

The freighter had slowed down to enter the harbour, but now he could feel it picking up speed, trying to shake off its attacker. Jonah didn't dare raise his head to see how it was doing. His sights were set on that door. There was a lull in the gunfire and he tensed, preparing himself to try for it again.

A fresh spray of bullets exploded above Jonah's head. Two Chang Corp men fell. One of them staggered backwards, and landed right next to Jonah. The man's eyes were staring sightlessly at the sky. He was dead.

And Jonah was pinned down.

He pressed himself against the cold metal deck and waited. To his relief, the fighting started to move away from him, along the deck towards the stern. He guessed that the freighter was outstripping the less powerful yacht – but the pirates weren't giving up, still firing after their hulking target.

Jonah scrambled for the door. It seemed to take him an age to reach it, to yank it open, to dive through it. He sagged against a bulkhead, his forehead drenched with sweat, his heart hammering.

He headed for Sam's cabin, and was relieved to see her coming out of it. She had been online most of the night and had slept in. Sam's green eyes were red-rimmed, her black coveralls rumpled as if she had slept in them.

She kept on going back the way Jonah had come, forcing him to follow.

'What's going on?' she asked.

Jonah grabbed her wrist, swinging her around to face him. 'You can't go up there, it's not safe!' He explained what he'd seen.

'Of all the stupid luck,' she muttered. 'A motor yacht, you said? Black and green stripes around the hull?'

'I'm not sure,' said Jonah. 'I think so, yeah.'

'*GuerreVert*,' said Sam. 'They patrol the harbour, attacking diesel ships. Delphine was boasting, back in France, about how many they'd sunk.'

'So, they… They're eco-terrorists, not pirates? They don't really want the cargo?'

Sam shook her head. 'They'd take it if they could, I'm sure, to fund their operations. But the cargo isn't their primary objective. They won't be happy until—'

They heard a whistling sound, followed by an explosion, almost right on top of them. Jonah leapt on top of Sam, trying to protect her. The boat shook with the force of the blast, and the pair of them ended up in a tangle on the floor.

'Rocket launchers!' Sam exclaimed as they picked themselves up. 'They're firing rocket launchers!'

'What were you going to say?' cried Jonah. '*GuerreVert* won't be happy until…? Until what?'

'Until they've sent this oil-guzzling boat to the bottom of the bay,' said Sam. Then she looked at Jonah, her face pale. 'Dad! Dad and Bradbury, they're probably in the Metasphere. They won't even know what's happening.'

Jonah understood. He nodded. 'We have to get them out of there,' he said, 'fast.'

They raced back down the corridor.

A second explosion rocked the boat as they reached Axel's cabin.

Jonah was still steadying himself when a third and larger blast stole his footing altogether. For the second time, he went down in a flail of limbs.

Sam had managed to keep herself upright. She tried the cabin door. It was locked. She hammered on it with her fists.

'Won't work,' said Jonah. 'If they haven't heard the racket outside, they're hardly likely to hear you knocking.'

Sam had already reached the same conclusion, and was trying to force the door open instead. Her first two attempts failed. Jonah tried as well, but only bruised his shoulder. Sam found a fire extinguisher, unhooked it from the wall. She attacked the door with it until the lock broke with a splintering crunch.

They squeezed into the cabin. Axel was lying on his bed, meta-tranced. Jonah thought he was alone, at first.

Then, Sam let out a gasp.

Bradbury had been hidden by the bed. But they could see him now, sprawled on the floor beside an upturned chair. An Ethernet cord snaked from a computer terminal. It was wound around the chair. The white adaptor on the end of it turned slowly in mid-air, and Jonah could see blood on it.

There was blood on Bradbury's exposed back, too.

'He's disconnected!' Sam knelt at Bradbury's side.

'Can't we just plug him back in?' asked Jonah, knowing full well that it wasn't that simple. Bradbury's disconnected avatar would need to be led back through his exit halo. And there wasn't enough time for either Jonah or Sam to risk logging on.

'Help me, Jonah. He's always watched out for my dad

and I, and if there's a chance—'

Jonah almost said, *Why? What's the point?* But he stopped himself in time. There was always the chance, however slim, that Bradbury's body could be rejoined with his avatar later, and his mind made whole. Until that happened, however, his body would remain in a vegetative state.

Sam was struggling to haul Bradbury to his feet, determined to save his body. Jonah rushed to her aid.

'You take his feet!' he shouted as he hoisted the comatose man by his underarms. Together, they dragged Bradbury to the doorway. There, Sam hesitated, looking back at Axel.

'I'll take him,' said Jonah. 'You should see to your dad.'

'Are you sure?' said Sam. 'Are you sure you can handle—?'

'I'm sure,' said Jonah.

Almost immediately, he wanted to revise that statement. Bradbury was a deadweight, totally unresponsive. Jonah had to half carry, half drag him down the corridor.

He had barely taken two steps, however, when the freighter was hit again.

The floor dropped out from beneath Jonah's feet. He tried to protect Bradbury, who couldn't protect himself. As a consequence, Jonah was slammed into a bulkhead. He was winded and had hit his head. He thought it might be bleeding.

Jonah blinked to clear his vision. He renewed his hold

on Bradbury and ploughed on. He smelled smoke and couldn't hear the freighter's engine any more. Adding to his troubles, the floor had tilted against him. They were starting to go down!

He dragged Bradbury up one flight of steel steps and stumbled out onto the deck, into a blur of running bodies and a cacophony of shouting voices. Jonah added his voice to the others, yelling for help. Two Chang Corp men saw his plight and took Bradbury from him.

No one was shooting any more, nor could Jonah see any sign of the *GuerreVert* yacht. Presumably it had withdrawn, its job well done.

The Chang Corp men hauled Bradbury into a red lifeboat. It was already full, but the other passengers squeezed aside to make room for him. A moment later the lifeboat was lowered onto the water. The next one along was already filling up.

Jonah felt a hand on his shoulder. Captain Teng. 'What are you still doing here, Jonah?' he cried. 'Did you not hear my instructions? Women and children first!'

'I'm not a—' Jonah began, but the captain pushed him firmly toward the second lifeboat, before dashing off to attend to someone else. 'Wait!' Jonah called after him. 'Sam! She's still in Axel's cabin. She...' No one was listening to him.

She'll be out in a second, thought Jonah. *She has to be. She was right behind me. She just had to wake Axel. They'll both be here!*

But, with each second that passed with no sign of his friends, he became less and less sure.

Water was pouring into the cabin.

Sam was up to her ankles in it. She shook Axel again, for all the good it would do her. She knew he wouldn't feel it. She had sent him a pop-up message – minutes ago, it felt like. What if he hadn't read it?

His terminal was fixed to the wall, low down, behind the bedhead. The water was already lapping around it. Sam had bundled up all the towels she could find, tried to protect the terminal with them, but it was no use. If it was damaged...

What was he *doing* in there?

Bradbury had left his trench coat slung over the dressing table. Sam rummaged through it, found a lead to connect her dad's terminal to the wall screen in the cabin. She unwound the lead, plugged it in. The screen came alive, with an image of a gryphon flying desperately between snow-topped mountain peaks.

The gryphon was dragging a Clydesdale horse along behind it.

'Sam!' Jonah had reappeared in the doorway. 'What's happening?'

'Jonah, what are you doing here? You shouldn't have come back! You—'

'I couldn't leave you. Where's Axel? Hasn't he—?'

'He's still in the Metasphere,' said Sam, helplessly.

239

'I should have known he'd do this. He won't leave Bradbury behind, even though he's disconnected. He's trying to get him back to his exit halo, but it's no use. He's just slowing Dad down.'

On the screen, Bradbury's avatar was hardly more responsive than his real-world body had been. He kept pulling away from Axel, trying to wander off on his own, confused, forcing the gryphon to stop for him.

Sam tapped at the screen, to bring up Axel's Point of Origin co-ordinates. Her heart sank. 'He's still too far away,' she said numbly. 'He won't make it.'

The boat lurched and tilted a little more. A fresh wave of water came slapping into the cabin. It was knee-deep now.

'We…we have to disconnect him too,' said Jonah.

'No,' protested Sam.

'We'll all die here if we don't,' argued Jonah.

The waterlogged terminal fizzed and sparked. The image on the screen flickered, blinked out, then returned at a lower resolution. Sam hurried back to Axel. 'I'm sorry, Dad,' she said, as she turned him over.

She wrapped her fingers around Axel's DI cord. She hesitated. She had to close her eyes, remind herself that she had no choice. If she didn't do this her father would die for sure. Sam gritted her teeth, and she did it.

She pulled Axel's plug.

The boat was listing wildly.

Jonah and Sam clung to the cold handrails to haul themselves up the sloping passageway, holding Axel's comatose body between them.

Jonah was just glad their cabins hadn't been on the port side; they would have been submerged by now. He was also relieved he had gone back for Sam. She could never have rescued Axel on her own. She would have died in the attempt.

But they weren't safe yet. The water was knee-high and rising fast.

'Hurry, Jonah!' shouted Sam. 'It's getting deeper.' Indeed, every step they took was steeper than the last. Jonah lost his footing, and Axel slipped out of his grasp.

'Dad!'

Jonah saw the look of abject horror on Sam's face as her father disappeared beneath the surface. In his current state, he wouldn't even think to hold his breath. He could drown in a second!

Jonah immediately drew a big breath and went under. He fished desperately for Axel, found him, dragged him back up. To his relief, he was still breathing.

There was nobody left on deck. The lifeboats had gone. A thick column of smoke rose from somewhere below the stern.

Casting around, Jonah saw a lifejacket by one of the lifeboat stations. Sam helped him wrestle it onto the lifeless Axel. There was no time to search for anything else. They both knew that, any second now, the ship could finally tip over and drag them underwater with it.

They jumped together, Axel between them. They cleared the stricken freighter, hitting the water with a smack. Jonah had been holding his breath, but the air was knocked out of him by the shock of impact.

He hadn't swum in real water before, hadn't swum with his awkward real-world body. The thought panicked him, and he found himself going under.

The water felt cold, and now it was in his nose and mouth. It tasted salty, unlike the oceans of the Metasphere, and it made his throat itch. His clothes dragged him down. He tried to kick off his shoes, but the laces were tied too tightly.

Axel had drifted away from Jonah. But Jonah could see that Sam had him. She was performing a confident backstroke, towing Axel with her, a hand under his chin to keep his head above water. Jonah was on his own. He tried to stay calm. He *could* swim, he just had to remind his arms and legs what to do.

He struck out after Sam. He could see that the shore wasn't too far away.

By the time Jonah reached it, his muscles were aching and his stomach heaving. He didn't think he had the strength to clamber onto dry land.

Then a hand reached out to him, and he took it.

Sam helped Jonah out of the water, up a steep, rocky slope, onto grassland. He collapsed there, gratefully. It was some time before he was strong enough to sit up.

Axel was lying beside him, on his back. He looked like he had in the cabin, like he was sleeping peacefully. Sam sat with her back to Jonah, her knees up to her chest, soaked and shivering despite the beating sun.

Jonah followed her gaze, out into the harbour, in time to see the prow of the Chang Corporation freighter sinking below the surface. Its passing was marked by a white froth of churning water, for a time, but then all was deathly still.

30

Jonah spotted the lifeboat and flagged it down.

Captain Teng must have done a headcount, realised they were missing, feared they might be in the water and sent someone back for them. Two crew members helped lift Axel aboard the small red vessel. Jonah and Sam were both weary and dispirited, but at least now they didn't have to trek all the way to Sydney. The city still looked a long way away across the bay.

Soon enough, however, they were sailing beneath the famous, arched Sydney Harbour Bridge, past the armadillo-shaped Opera House. It wasn't used for that purpose any more, of course. Jonah recalled from school that the iconic building had been pressed into service as a desalination plant.

Captain Teng was waiting for them at an old wharf, all apologetic for having left them behind – although he did remind Jonah that he had sent him to a lifeboat.

The captain noted Axel's condition with a sad shake of the head.

'Where can we get online?' asked Jonah. 'We need to find Axel's avatar – Bradbury's too – before they can wander too far from—'

'We don't have time,' said Sam. Her voice was quiet but firm. She turned to Captain Teng. 'Jonah and I have a plane to catch.'

'You're not serious!' cried Jonah.

Three times, he had seen schoolmates become accidentally disconnected. Each time, he had helped keep their lobotomised avatars from floating away. On the most recent occasion, he had helped Mr Peng and a couple of others take Kylie Ellis out into the schoolyard. They had waited for someone to find her real-world body and plug her in again so that her exit halo would reactivate. Then they had pushed her through it.

Axel's avatar hadn't been with friends when Sam had unplugged him – only with the equally befuddled Bradbury. Sam knew this. She knew that, the longer they delayed, the harder it would be to find the pair of them. Jonah had heard tales of disconnected avatars lost forever, wandering the Metasphere like ghosts while their real-world bodies were kept alive and fed through tubes.

'I know my dad,' said Sam, stubbornly, 'and he'd want us to go on. He wouldn't want us to compromise the mission for…for his sake.'

'Maybe so,' said Jonah, 'but *can* we even go on without him? Without Bradbury?'

'We've no choice,' said Sam. 'There are people relying on us. The *whole world* is relying on us to…' She glanced at Captain Teng and said no more.

'All the same, how can we—?'

'Please, Jonah!'

Jonah looked at Sam again. Her fists were balled, her whole body tensed as if to keep herself from breaking down. He could see how hard this was for her, leaving her father behind, but he could also see how determined she was. He had an idea.

'Captain Teng,' he said. 'Maybe you could…?'

Teng anticipated his request and nodded solemnly. 'I know nothing of your mission,' he said, 'and perhaps this is for the best. However, it is important to my employer, Mr Chang, else he would not have held up my sailing schedule to accommodate the four of you. So, I remain at your service.'

Captain Teng explained that he and his crew would be staying in a bunkhouse in Sydney, until another Chang Corp freighter could pick them up. He sounded resigned to this, as if he had lost boats in this way before. He probably had, thought Jonah.

'You mean it?' said Sam. 'We can leave Dad and Bradbury with you? You'll take care of them… Of their bodies?'

'My crewmen will have much time on their hands,' said Teng. 'I will have them search the Metasphere for your friends' missing avatars.'

Sam looked like she was about to cry with relief. She looked Jonah straight in the eyes and mouthed, *Thank you.* She bowed to the captain out of respect and gratitude. He offered her a datapad, on which she tapped in descriptions of Axel and Bradbury's avatars, and also their last-known co-ordinates.

Then she and Jonah took their leave, with Captain Teng wishing them the best of fortune. Jonah couldn't help but wonder if he would have been quite so solicitous had he known who they really were and where they were going.

Jonah didn't get to see much of Sydney. Sam led him on foot to an airstrip on the outskirts of the city where the name 'Kavanaugh' got them through security. Their plane, Sam explained, had been laid on by a wealthy Australian who wished to remain anonymous. There was just one problem. There was no pilot.

'It was Dad's contact,' said Sam. 'They must've planned for him to fly it.'

'I thought he taught you to fly?' said Jonah hopefully.

'A few basic lessons, and I've held the controls in mid-flight, but I'm no Axel.'

Jonah slammed his hand against the plane in frustration – and a sudden jolt of memories flooded his brain. He seized up. Jonah squinted shut his eyes, overwhelmed by the avalanche of images.

'Are you OK?' Sam asked. 'What's wrong?'

He remembered the meditation technique his grandmother had taught him. He gained control over the flashes and relaxed into them. Jonah ran his palm over the smooth fuselage as layer upon layer of memory guided his eyes. He checked for ill-fitting screws and inspected the pitot head.

He climbed into the plane and eased into the pilot's seat. Sam followed him into the cockpit. As he started the plane, he reviewed the instruments as if it were the most normal thing in the world. He looked at every gauge, watching closely as their needles bounced back to life from their slumber. The instrument panel felt more than familiar. It felt intuitive.

'I can do this,' he announced.

'What?'

'I can fly this plane,' he said.

Sam looked at Jonah like he had just declared he was a kangaroo.

'Jonah, you're scaring me.'

'Sam, it's all up here!' said Jonah, tapping his temple. 'In my dad's memories! I can access them, just like I accessed the location of the Southern Corner.'

The plane was an old twin-prop, not unlike the first one Jonah had flown in – the plane in which Hiram had carried the Guardians from France to Russia. This time, however, he was the one at the controls.

As Jonah taxied to the runway, he felt his father's memories become his own. He knew what to do based on instinct. He tested the rudder pedals, ensuring that the plane would yaw, and noted the wind direction, south-south-west, from the full red-and-white windsock.

Jonah revved the engines and hurtled the plane down the runway. The end of the runway was coming fast, and for a moment, he slipped back into conscious thought and was overwhelmed by the fact that he would have to take off or die.

You can do this.

He summoned his father's memories to the surface and they guided his arms as they gently pulled back on the steering column. The ground fell away beneath Jonah's feet.

I am doing this.

He held the plane at a steady angle but felt the steering column fighting against him. Jonah instinctively adjusted the trim of the aircraft, reducing the pressure and allowing him to control the plane with the lightest of touches.

When he levelled off, the steering column pulled and Jonah retrimmed the aeroplane to stabilise at seven thousand feet. His muscles had a memory of their own. His body knew what to do to keep the plane aloft.

I'm flying. In the real world!

He relaxed in his seat and looked out of the panoramic window at the city thinning out below him.

'You really did it,' said Sam.

'Thanks to my dad,' replied Jonah. 'It's his memories that guide me.'

But they were beginning to feel like Jonah's memories now. When he glanced at the altimeter, showing a steady seven thousand feet, it felt like he had done that routine check a million times before. A small, white puff of cloud shot by and Jonah was convinced that he himself had been an RAF pilot. He belonged in the cockpit.

Sam navigated, according to the plans she had made with Axel, and after fifteen minutes they had cleared the city. There was nothing beneath them now but desert sands. There was no other traffic up here. No turbulence, either: it was a clear, sunny day. And they were flying straight and level.

It was a perfect day for flying, except that Jonah was worried about Sam. She was staring straight ahead, glassy-eyed, lost in thought.

I shouldn't have mentioned my dad, thought Jonah.

'You did the right thing,' he reassured her. 'We'll get your dad back, I promise.'

'I just feel so helpless,' Sam replied. 'I mean, what kind of an aeroplane doesn't have a Metasphere connection?'

Jonah looked around the cockpit, but couldn't see a computer terminal.

'Captain Teng will find them,' said Jonah, wishing it to be true.

'I hope so,' whispered Sam. 'I'll log on when we reach Woomera.'

'You know, I've heard that some avatars, when they become disconnected, they just...float there. They don't move at all.'

Sam forced a smile. 'Not Axel. He's a wanderer. He's

been wandering off all my life. I feel like I've only just pinned him down, begun to get to know him. I never really knew my mum. I can't…I can't lose him too. He's my dad. I still need…' Sam trailed off. 'Jonah, I'm so sorry,' she said. 'I wasn't thinking.'

'It's OK,' said Jonah. He had been thinking about his own mum and dad, as Sam had guessed. It *was* OK, though. Hearing Sam talk like this, hearing her hopes and fears – so like his own – made him feel less alone.

'It's just that, you and Axel,' he said, 'you always seemed more like…well, friends. I forget, sometimes, that you're…'

Sam's smile, this time, was genuine, fond. 'I don't think Dad ever knew how to deal with a little girl. He tried his best, but for years it was like we were strangers. We made forced conversation at mealtimes, then plugged in and went our separate ways.'

'I remember Mum saying once,' said Jonah, 'that the world had changed so fast that my experience growing up was so different from hers. That she couldn't keep up.'

Sam nodded. 'It didn't help, of course, that Dad was spending so much time with the Guardians. We started missing each other at mealtimes, too.'

'When did he tell you about…all that?'

'On my eleventh birthday,' said Sam. 'I'd been asking awkward questions – like, how come Daddy spent so much time flying planes when all the planes had been grounded? Axel sat me down. He said I was old enough to understand now. He told me what he had really been doing – some of it, at least.

'I thought it was brilliant. My dad, the secret agent. I used to badger him with questions about it. He started teaching me mechanics, because I said I wanted to be a Guardian some day. Of course, he would still disappear – for days at a time – but when he was home, we had something to talk about. Something in common.'

'My dad never told me,' said Jonah, with a sigh. 'I wish he had. I wish we could have talked about it.'

Jonah didn't see the tiny, solitary village at first, nestled in a crook between two desert roads. Sam had to point it out to him.

They skimmed across the rooftops, found an airfield to the north-west of the village. Jonah oriented the plane with the single runway, began to ease its nose down.

The ground was coming up faster than he would have liked. This didn't feel right. Something in his head told him to pull up, try again. He had to trust that instinct.

Jonah circled the plane around. His earlier confidence was replaced by fear. Sam placed her hand on his. 'Take your time,' she said. 'You can do it.'

On his second attempt, Jonah guided the plane down on a smooth trajectory. He compensated for the high crosswinds and kept the wings level as the red dirt of the desert rose up to greet him.

The plane bounced twice on its landing wheels before

settling down onto the runway. It reminded Jonah of landing on his blades in the escape glider. He tried to push that horrible morning out of his head and focus on the fact that he had just flown, and landed, his first aeroplane. He pulled out the throttle, squeezed on the brakes, brought the plane to a slow and steady halt. He grinned at Sam in relief.

Sam grinned back.

Someone was running along the runway, coming to meet them: a short, wiry girl with dark skin and a thatch of black hair.

Jonah killed the engines, took a deep breath. He had flown the plane by channelling his father's memories, but now he had his own memories of flying. It was confusing to think where Jason's memories stopped and Jonah's began.

Sam grabbed his arm, shaking him out of his introspection. 'Well, Captain,' she said, 'are you ready for this?'

Jonah looked at her blankly. He honestly hadn't given much thought to what would happen once they had reached their destination. He was used to being told what to do, to just going along with whatever Axel and the others said.

'We've assembled an army here,' said Sam. 'They're just waiting for a leader. They're expecting my dad. We're going to have to persuade them that, as he can't make it, *we* can do the job instead.'

Jonah swallowed. 'Us? But we—'

'I went to all the same meetings as my dad,' said Sam. 'I know the plan back to front. I probably know it a lot better than he does, knowing him. I thought you understood, Jonah. I thought you knew that this… This is what we have to do.'

'I guess I thought there'd be someone else to lead…'

'There is no one else,' said Sam. 'There's just you and me. It's down to us, Jonah, the two of us. The attack on the Southern Corner is scheduled for tomorrow night. We have to lead it.'

31

The girl glared at Jonah and Sam suspiciously as they stepped out of their plane.

'Where is Axel Kavanaugh?' she asked in an accent Jonah had never heard before. She was young, younger than Jonah, and he guessed she was an Aboriginal Australian, descended from the earliest occupants of this continent.

'I'm Sam Kavanaugh, and this is Jonah Delacroix.'

'My name is Kala. But where is Axel?'

Sam explained that Axel wasn't coming and why.

'My people agreed to join Axel,' Kala said. 'Not two children.'

Jonah couldn't believe *she* was calling *them* children, but moreover, he thought she could have shown some sympathy for Sam's situation.

'The elders will reconsider the deal,' Kala grumbled as she led Jonah and Sam to two bizarre vehicles. Jonah had never seen anything like them before. They looked like hybrids of racing cars, boats and rockets. Their shiny metallic bodies were long and narrow, and low to the ground, reflecting the red dirt underneath. They each had four giant wheels and ten-metre-tall, fin-shaped sails rising from behind their cockpits.

A driver was waiting in one of the strange vehicles. Kala waved him away as she, Jonah and Sam climbed into the other.

A moment later they were gliding across the desert. Jonah was impressed by their speed, given that he could hear no engines.

'This is amazing,' he said. 'We're sailing on land!'

'A land yacht,' Sam added. 'No petrol to worry about. It's brilliant!'

'The wind is a great gift,' Kala explained cryptically.

They were seated one behind the other. From behind Jonah, Sam said, 'Kala's tribe has a fleet of these things. They're crucial to our plans.'

Two dozen people came to greet the land yacht as it sailed into the village. The majority of these were Aborigines too. Jonah guessed that few of the Guardians' supporters further away in the cities would have had the means to get here in time.

The crowd reacted with dismay, as Kala had, to find that their long-awaited allies were two teenagers. Jonah could hardly blame them. Sensing their discontent, and worried that they might abandon the mission, Sam stood on the bow of the land yacht and addressed them all.

'I apologise for my father's absence,' she said. 'I wish he could be with us too. But Jonah and I are here in Axel's place, and our objective has not changed.'

A murmur of doubt shot through the crowd, but

Sam continued undaunted.

'Thirty-six hours from now, we will cleanse Uluru. We will remove the men who occupy its heart and taint its soul.'

Jonah didn't know what she was talking about. What was 'Uluru'? He was impressed, however, at how confident Sam sounded, how in control.

Kala just scowled. 'We have heard these promises before,' she said.

'I know,' said Sam. 'I know you have, but—'

'You promised Uluru will be restored to its rightful owners. That is why my people agreed to join you in this fight.'

'And that is still our intention,' said Sam. 'My father told you that when we met in the virtual world. Although... Some things have changed, and it may now take a little longer than we thought before we can—'

The crowd didn't like that. Feeling he ought to help somehow, Jonah spoke up: 'Sam means what she says. You can trust her.'

'Uluru will be yours again,' said Sam. 'That hasn't changed, I swear to you.'

'We will trust you,' said Kala, speaking authoritatively. 'For now.'

The rest of the crowd followed her lead, and the crowd dispersed with only a few more grumbles of discontent. Kala and a few others stayed back, and took Jonah and Sam to see more of their land yachts, which were in the process of having odd, metal contraptions fitted to their backs. Jonah couldn't tell what they were, at first. It took him a moment to work out what they were.

'Sam, are those…catapults?'

'You didn't think we'd be going in through the front door, did you?'

Jonah realised he didn't know what the plan was.

Jonah had been glad to get inside, out of the desert sun.

Outside, he and Sam had seen boarded-up stores, squash courts, a police station. They had been taken by one of Kala's people past these and shown into a white, clapboard house. The house was unfurnished, but sheets and pillows had been left in each of its four rooms. One room each for Jonah and Sam. Two more for Axel and Bradbury.

'What is this place?' asked Jonah.

'It's called Woomera,' said Sam. 'They used to test rockets here, far away from any city. They built a village for the base's workers. But it's been abandoned for decades.'

'So, now Kala's people live here?' said Jonah.

'Some of them,' said Sam, distracted. 'Can you see a computer terminal?' She had been hunting around the downstairs room of the house as they talked.

'I have to get online. My dad—'

'I don't think there's any power,' said Jonah. 'I tried

turning on the air-conditioning in my room, but nothing happened. There's no water either.'

'I should have realised,' Sam muttered. 'Woomera would have been disconnected from the grid when they closed it down. They wouldn't even have fitted terminals here, so long ago.'

'Then how did Axel meet them online?' asked Jonah. 'They must have access, somewhere.'

She pushed past him, and ran out of the house.

Jonah followed her. The sun was going down, the shadows of the clapboard buildings growing longer. It took Jonah a moment to realise where Sam was heading – back to the land yachts. They were far, far newer than the village, and Jonah guessed, as Sam did, that they would have satellite uplinks.

Two mechanics were still working on the yachts, fixing the last of the catapults to them. When Sam explained what she wanted, they were happy to oblige her. But the first terminal she tried wouldn't boot up; apparently, its battery was charged by the rotation of the land yacht's wheels and had run flat.

Soon, however, Sam was seated inside a second cockpit, and plugged in.

Jonah watched over her slumped body as she meta-tranced, unsure of his surroundings and not knowing what else to do with himself. He hoped that no one would start asking him questions. He should have talked to Sam more in the plane, he thought, and found out some of the answers.

Sam was gone for almost an hour. Jonah didn't know if that was a good sign or a bad one. It was dark now, and he was still waiting when Kala came running out of the night. She looked irritated, although Jonah had come to see this as her default state.

'Everyone is waiting for you,' said Kala. Jonah looked at her blankly. 'The briefing,' she said, impatiently. It was the first he had heard of any such thing. 'Where is your girlfriend, the one who knows what she's doing?!' Kala demanded.

'She's not my—' Jonah began, before being cut off by Kala.

'Send her a pop-up message! My people are waiting.'

Jonah did not want Sam disturbed. 'She'll come out when she's ready,' he said.

The next few minutes seemed like hours to Jonah. Kala paced up and down, repeatedly glaring at Sam, in full meta-trance, and sighing in frustration. Jonah was almost ready to send that pop-up, after all, when Sam's eyelids began to flutter.

He helped Sam out of the land yacht as she readjusted to her real-world body. He could tell from her expression that the news wasn't good.

'There's no sign of them,' Sam reported. 'Either of them. Dad or Bradbury. Captain Teng has all his men working on it. They're widening the search area.'

'It took you a long time,' said Kala pointedly, 'to hear that.'

Jonah prickled at Kala's rudeness. He opened his mouth to say something, but Sam didn't rise to it. 'I met with some contacts,' she explained, 'in the Guardians. I brought them up to date on our situation. They're going to circulate descriptions of Dad and Bradbury's avatars. There'll be thousands of pairs of eyes watching out for them by this time tomorrow. I just hope...'

Kala tugged at Sam's sleeve, and set off determinedly in the expectation of being followed. 'Briefing,' she said firmly.

There were about sixty people waiting for them on an old squash court. Most of these were male, most of them young, and about two-thirds Aborigines. About half of them were seated on white collapsible chairs, the rest standing.

An open-topped jeep overtook Jonah, Sam and Kala as they approached. It screeched to a halt in front of them and disgorged four lean, white Australian men in combat fatigues who proceeded to unload a collection of assorted weapons.

People spilled out of the squash court and gathered around the jeep. The men were handing out guns to anyone who needed one, along with pointers on their operation.

Jonah and Sam's arrival went almost unnoticed.

A table with chairs behind it had been set up for them at one end of the court. As they took their places, Jonah eyed the activity around them. *So this is our army*, he thought. He felt deeply uncomfortable.

'You know,' he whispered to Sam, 'I still don't know what the plan is, exactly.'

'I'll do all the talking,' Sam promised. 'Just keep on backing me up.'

'What was Kala saying before? About some place called Uluru, and giving it back to its owners?'

'She means Ayers Rock,' said Sam. 'Uluru was its original name, the name the Aborigines gave it. It was – it still is – an important spiritual site to them.'

'Isn't it a solar power plant now?' said Jonah, keen to show that he wasn't entirely ignorant of real-world affairs.

Sam nodded. 'Uluru was bought by a small American power-generating company. No one knew, at the time, that that company was one of Matthew Granger's – but, of course, it must have been. The plant was just a front.'

'He bought Uluru – Ayers Rock – to build the Southern Corner inside it.'

'The Aborigines always claimed they were cheated out of their property,' said Sam. 'Knowing Granger, I'm sure they were.'

'Then the deal Axel made with Kala was…?'

'When the Guardians contacted Kala's people,' said Sam, 'we still thought the Chang Bridge was a back-up device. We thought, once we had taken the Southern Corner, we could transfer its operations to our own server farm within a month. The Aboriginal Australians could have done what they wanted with Uluru, then.'

'And now?' said Jonah.

There was no time for Sam to answer.

Kala had called for silence and now she introduced Jonah and Sam for the sake of those few who hadn't seen them already. Sam thanked her, and rose to her feet.

'We are going to take back Uluru by force,' she began. 'Anyone not ready for that should leave now.'

Nobody stirred, but Jonah felt a prickly dread in his stomach.

'As you all know, Uluru has been hollowed out and filled with thousands of computers. The access points to the facility are on the very top of the rock. That is its greatest defence. We can't climb up there on foot. We'd be sitting ducks for any Millennials standing above us. And that's why your land yachts have been rigged with catapults. We need to sail close enough to Uluru, through the security perimeter, to launch our attack from above.'

Sam continued to talk, about the electric fences that surrounded their target and the Millennial guards that would put up a fierce fight in its defence. She speculated on the most likely layout of the Southern Corner inside Ayers Rock, intelligence that was cobbled together from Millennial defectors and former construction crews.

Kala interjected a few times, to assign specific tasks

to specific groups of people – while Jonah just did as he had been told. He sat beside Sam and listened. He pretended he had heard all this before and was perfectly happy about it – which was no mean feat, as it happened.

The more Sam talked – the more Jonah heard about what was to happen tomorrow – the stronger his tingling sense of dread became.

32

Jonah didn't sleep much that night.

It wasn't just that the floor of his room was uncomfortable, although this didn't help. He was worried about the attack tomorrow.

He hadn't given it much thought before – until Sam had given her speech, until Jonah had learned exactly what was in store for him.

He told himself he had been in other risky situations – plenty of them, lately. It was just that, before now, he mostly hadn't seen them coming. There had hardly been time to think, to worry like this, only time to react.

This time, it was different. Jonah had looked at the weapons – ranging from spears to machine guns – that the Guardians had shared out between themselves. But he knew that the Millennials would have weapons too, and the advantage of fortification.

After Sam's speech was over, Kala had chipped in from the sidelines again. Her language had been blunter, more visceral, than Sam's had been. She had reminded her people of the cause they were fighting for – the return of their sacred place – and had made no bones about the fact that some of them would die for it.

Jonah remembered what Bradbury had said to him, on the Chang Corp freighter: *It's gonna get rough out there, and you ain't prepared.*

He knew now that Bradbury had been right. He had been right to tell Jonah he couldn't take part in the fighting. Evidently, however, he had said nothing about this to Sam. And how could Jonah bring up the subject now? What could he say that wouldn't look like he was letting her down, like he was a coward?

He wished he could see his grandmother. Not just for his own sake – because he knew she could make everything seem better – but for hers too. Who would visit her on the Island, Jonah asked himself, if something happened to him? In her confused state, would she even know she had been abandoned?

Perhaps, he thought, she would be happy with her memories. He hoped so.

And, suddenly, as Jonah lay there, alone in the darkness, an idea came to him.

They set off from Woomera at dawn: twenty converted land yachts sailing across the Australian Outback, sails fluttering behind them. The wind, fortunately, was good. Even so, it would take them all day to reach their destination.

Jonah was in the back of a three-seater cockpit, Sam in front of him. Their driver was an older Aboriginal man, with two white stripes painted on each cheek. Several of the Aborigines had put on face paint this morning, with some opting for more elaborate, colourful designs.

Jonah was still working on his idea in his mind. There was one big problem with it, a problem he couldn't find his way around.

He looked back over his shoulder, nervously, at the catapult mounted on the land yacht behind him. In a little under twelve hours' time, Jonah would be expected to climb into that catapult. He would be projected some three hundred and fifty metres into the air, sent hurtling towards a massive rock formation.

Oh, and there would be an enemy army on top of that rock, most likely trying to shoot him out of the sky before he could land. 'What could possibly go wrong?' he muttered to himself.

Jonah leaned forward, tapped Sam on the shoulder. 'This facility,' he said, 'the Southern Corner – you said it's entirely solar-powered?'

'That's right,' said Sam. 'Australia closed down the last of its fossil-fuel power stations a decade ago. What are you thinking?'

'We're arriving at Uluru at dusk,' said Jonah. 'So, if we could drain their solar batteries, they wouldn't be able to recharge them in a hurry.'

'I guess not,' said Sam.

'And that'd help us, yeah? Draining the batteries? It would mean the Millennials couldn't power their electric fences, or anything else they have prepared for us.'

'It could help,' agreed Sam. 'It could help us a lot. But how would we do it?'

'The Island of the Uploaded,' said Jonah. 'It's in the quarter of the Metasphere that the Southern Corner controls.'

'Right.'

'And all those people on the Island… They've Uploaded their minds, everything that made them who they were, and there are more arriving all the time. Too many. The Island doesn't have the processing power to cope with them all. Not all at once. That's why…that's one of the reasons why…they're always so confused.'

'Go on,' said Sam.

'Think what would happen,' said Jonah, 'if everyone on the Island, if they all tried to think at the same time. If they all *remembered*.'

Sam thought about it. 'It *could* work,' she said. 'It would certainly be a power drain. It'd spin every hard drive in the Southern Corner. The only problem is—'

'We can't get to the Island,' said Jonah, 'because of Granger's blockade. I know. I've been thinking about it all night, and I think I might be able to find a way. I have an idea I'd like to try, anyway. I just need to get back online.'

'All right,' said Sam, 'we have a Metasphere terminal. And I've already learned to stop underestimating you.'

*

Jonah appeared inside the Metasphere in mid-air.

He spread his enormous wings, and let the virtual wind catch them. He swooped low over a calm, sparkling blue ocean.

It felt like an age since he had done this, just flown. He closed his eyes, felt the sun on his face and the breeze in his nostrils. He lost himself in those joyous sensations, and almost forgot his worries.

It was over too soon. Jonah could see the Island, a dark silhouette against the horizon. His heart skipped a beat. He had expected the Island to be surrounded by a barrier. He hadn't really expected to be able to fly straight to it.

The Island was wreathed in mist. Jonah wasn't sure what that meant, but it couldn't be good. He kept on flying, anyway, and the mist closed in around him.

He couldn't see the Island any more. He knew it was straight ahead, though. If the purpose of the mist was to confuse him, disorient him, it wouldn't work.

The mist was cold, freezing cold. It sank into Jonah's leathery hide, numbed his bones. It was becoming thicker, too. It was almost opaque. He couldn't see past the end of his snout. He gritted his teeth, beat his wings, determined to keep going.

Then, suddenly, the mist lifted. The air was warm again, the sky and the sea blue.

And the Island of the Uploaded was nowhere to be seen.

Jonah stopped flying. He turned on the spot, confused. The Island was directly behind him. He could just make out its shape through the mist cloud that still clung to it. He must have flown right over it, he thought – but how could he have done? The Island was too big; he hadn't flown for long enough to cross it.

Jonah lowered his head, stubbornly, and struck out for the Island again.

Once again, the mist closed in around him, chilling him, blinding him. Once again, when it lifted, the Island of the Uploaded was behind him – so close, so achingly close, and yet apparently unreachable.

Jonah hovered at the edge of the mist cloud. Had it been a solid barrier, he could have tried to break through it. He could have used Harry's deconstruction virus. He considered doing it, anyway, spreading the virus into the mist. But he didn't know enough about what the mist was. What if he damaged the Island itself?

He didn't dare take that chance.

Fortunately, he had another option left to him. Just one more.

He could Upload himself.

33

Across the virtual sea from the Island of the Uploaded, the main ferry terminal was packed with avatars shouting and waving banners.

As Jonah flew closer, he saw they were protesting the blockade of the Island. He touched down in their midst and they closed in around him, jostling him. A mean-eyed vulture thrust its beak right up to Jonah's face and demanded to know if he was, 'Millennial or Guardian?'

'Matthew Granger killed my mother,' said Jonah, bitterly. 'What do you think?'

Clearly, this was the right answer. The avatars parted before him, and Jonah was able to reach the ferry terminal's sliding doors.

The atmosphere inside the terminal couldn't have been more different. As the doors slid together behind Jonah, they blocked out the sound of the protest completely. The air had a cool, almost sterile taste to it. There were plastic benches and electronic departure boards, the latter detailing the sailings of the day's 'death barges'. The next departure was in forty-five minutes.

There were several knots of people standing around the terminal: mourners gathered to say goodbye to cherished friends and family members. Some of them were weeping. Jonah could see the waiting death barge through the windows, and the sight of it made him shudder. It sat at the end of a long wooden jetty. It was sleek and black, and it flew a single flag: a white infinity symbol upon black.

As Jonah watched, a small group of mourners floated up to the barge. They took turns hugging and kissing an ancient, stooped blue frog, which finally turned away from them and half hopped, half shuffled up the boarding ramp. The mourners returned along the jetty and found a place at the waterside from which to wave loved ones away on their final voyage.

The man behind the blue frog avatar was probably lying on a comfortable couch in an Uploading centre. When the mourners returned to the real world, he would be gone, his corporeal body removed by the centre's undertakers. At least they would know that, in the virtual world, his avatar lived on.

As Jonah had guessed, Matthew Granger hadn't stopped the death barges from sailing, allowing the Island to collect more avatars and thus making his ownership of the Island all the more valuable. So he had left that single route to the Island open, confident in the knowledge that no one could survive the trip.

Jonah was gambling on the desperate hope that Granger was wrong.

He waited for another group to step outside, then tagged

along behind them. Jonah felt conspicuous in his huge red dragon avatar. He hoped no one would notice him and ask awkward questions.

He floated as far along the jetty, as close to the death barge as he dared. He waited impatiently as the mourners said their last farewells to an ageing pixie whose glow was dimming. He watched as the pixie climbed the boarding ramp, to be greeted by a red dialogue balloon at the top. He couldn't read what the pop-up said, but the pixie touched it with her finger, and it closed.

The pixie boarded the barge. Her mourners floated back along the jetty, passing by Jonah. He drew a few glances from them, as he had feared, but the mourners' eyes held nothing but sympathy for him. Of course, it must have seemed to them as if Jonah was preparing to Upload himself alone.

He could guess what the red pop-up had said. The pixie's avatar had been scanned and indexed, before she could set foot on board the barge. She had confirmed her agreement to the Uploading process, which would take place as she made her slow journey towards the Island. It couldn't be stopped now, for her.

Jonah went back into the terminal. He needed time to think. He watched through the windows as more avatars boarded the barge. Its deck was filling up.

He made a decision. He marched out through the sliding doors, pushed through the protesting avatars outside, ignoring their raucous chants. He slipped around the side of the terminal building. He found a place there, where he could reach the water without being seen. He lowered himself into it.

He hesitated before he let his head go under, remembering how he had almost drowned in Sydney Harbour. That had been in the real world, however. In the Metasphere, Jonah didn't have to breathe. Not if he didn't want to.

He used the dragon's wings to propel himself underwater. He kept the foundations of the ferry terminal to his right, following them around until he saw a wooden strut ahead of him. Peering upwards, Jonah saw the slats of the boarding jetty above his head. The water under his wings almost buoyed him to the surface; he had to will himself to remain submerged.

He followed the jetty to its end, where a long, narrow shadow fell over him. The flat, black bottom of the death barge. Jonah glided beneath it, then surfaced.

He was at the far side of the barge. As he had hoped, it completely blocked him from sight of the mourners – and any inquisitive officials – at the terminal.

Jonah floated upwards, until his eyes were level with the barge's flat deck. It was crowded with avatars by now, but most of them were looking back at the terminal, at the people and the places they were about to leave behind them. Jonah's heart soared. This was actually going to work! He started to climb aboard...

...and then a red dialogue balloon popped up in front of his snout.

WARNING, it said. YOU ARE ABOUT TO UPLOAD YOUR AVATAR TO THE METASPHERE. THIS PROCESS CANNOT BE UNDONE. DO YOU WISH TO PROCEED? Y/N.

Frustrated, Jonah stabbed at the No button. The pop-up disappeared, but Jonah was pushed back a metre or so as if by invisible hands. He was hovering above the water. He thrust himself at the barge again, but the pop-up reappeared, and that same invisible force brought him to a gentle but sudden halt.

He tried to fly around the pop-up. It was like pushing himself into a huge, invisible pillow. He couldn't make any headway.

He backed up a hundred metres, and the pop-up disappeared. Jonah lowered his head and flew at the barge with all the strength in his powerful wings. Once again, he was gently rebuffed; again, the dialogue balloon appeared in front of him, taunting him.

DO YOU WISH TO PROCEED? Y/N.

Jonah had known this might happen. He had had to

try, though. He had had to try, because the alternative terrified him.

He remembered what Mr Chang had told him, in his temple. *Yours is the only brain I have heard of that can store two avatars at once.* He remembered what had happened when Bradbury had tried to search his brain. The program had been unable to index both the avatars – Jonah's father's and his own – that were stored there right now. It had failed for that reason.

Jonah was counting on the belief that the Uploading program would only be able to latch onto one avatar.

Do you wish to proceed? Y/N.

They were taking up the boarding ramp. Jonah had to decide. Could he do this or not? Sam was counting on him to reach the Island, he thought. And the Guardians, and Kala's people... He thought about his dad, how Jason Delacroix had put his life on the line for the Guardians' cause. He felt he owed it to his dad to be as brave.

He reached out a trembling claw and brushed the Yes button. The dialogue in the pop-up changed. Indexing... it said, and there was a green progress bar.

Then the pop-up disappeared, along with the force that had been holding him back. And Jonah stepped aboard the barge, with a desperate prayer that in so doing he hadn't just committed suicide.

He didn't feel any different.

How would he know, he wondered, if he was being Uploaded, if his mind was being drawn out of his real-world body one memory at a time? He would start to feel confused, he supposed, like his grandmother.

Jonah tested himself. He picked a memory at random: a trip to the beach with his mum and dad, when he was a kid. A real-world beach. It had rained all day. The water had been filthy. They had sworn only to holiday in the Metasphere, after that. It all came back to Jonah, crystal clear. A special day. A memory of being loved.

He felt light-headed. He had to sit down on a bench. He had a sensation of metal fingers sifting through his brain. He told himself it was only his imagination.

Standing at the stern of the barge, a cloaked ferryman pushed off with a long pole.

The avatars on board exchanged final waves and blown kisses with those on land as the boat drifted slowly away from them. Soft music was playing from somewhere.

Jonah concentrated as hard as he could, tried to hold on to himself. His dizziness only worsened. It felt as if those fingers had stopped sifting now and had started to pull, squeeze, tear instead.

Pain lanced through Jonah's head, and he gasped and doubled over. There were tears in his eyes, a sick feeling in his stomach, and he feared he had made a dreadful mistake. He could feel information being ripped from his brain and he tried to hold onto his own thoughts, dreams and memories with a grip that made him weak.

At least he would be with his grandmother, he thought. They could live in their Uploaded memories and be confused together.

Just as Jonah was about to succumb, the pain suddenly disappeared.

Was that it? Is it over? he wondered. He opened one eye, tentatively. He saw a red pop-up, but his vision was too blurry to read it. He blinked twice and looked again.

UNKNOWN ERROR, said the pop-up.
AVATAR CODE SEQUENCE NOT RECOGNISED.
UPLOADING PROCESS DISCONTINUED.
PLEASE CONTACT A SYSTEM ADMINISTRATOR.

Relief flooded through Jonah's body. His dangerous gamble had paid off. He wiped his brow with the back of his hand, waved the pop-up away, pushed himself to his feet. He hesitated. He looked down at himself, at his two hands.

Hands, not claws.

He tried to flex his wing muscles, but couldn't feel them any more. He was a dragon no longer. Jonah was back in his old avatar, his humatar. He looked like himself again. *It must have been the Uploading program*, he realised. It had separated his dad's avatar from his own, taken the dragon but left the human-form behind.

Jonah searched his mind for his father's memories. He found only a distant echo of them, like a fingerprint on the back of his skull. He felt bereft. He had never wanted those memories in the first place, but now… Now he knew he would miss them.

A question occurred to him. If his dad's avatar wasn't inside him any more, then what had happened to it? Where was it? Then he heard a voice.

'Jonah? Son? Is that you?'

34

Jonah found the red dragon standing beside him, staring at him with its yellow eyes.

Unlike Jonah's first encounter in the secret cellar of the gift shop, this time the dragon avatar wasn't a recorded message. It was his father. Or at least, it was the digital echo of his dad.

'It *is* you,' said the dragon. 'You found me. I knew you'd find me. There's so much I have to tell you, so much you need to know. It's so good to see you, son.'

Jonah's heart was in his mouth.

'*Dad?*' he whispered. 'I can't believe you're here! I thought I'd never...'

He ran forward, threw his arms around the red dragon avatar – and, for a blissful few seconds, Jonah was a kid again, wrapped in his father's leathery wings, protected.

'You could have told me, Dad,' said Jonah, 'about the Guardians, and about the Four Corners. I would have understood.'

'You were always a bright kid,' said Jason Delacroix.

'I got into such a mess without you, but it's all right now.'

'We'll have to see what we can do about that school. The virtual one.'

'You're here now, Dad. I've got you back. You can tell me what to do.'

'You'd like to go to a Chang Academy, wouldn't you, son? The Metasphere, that's where the future is.'

Jonah broke out of the embrace. 'Dad, I... I'm a teenager now. You got me into that school, but it was years ago now.'

He could tell that his words weren't sinking in. His dad looked around him, as if noticing his surroundings for the first time. 'This is nice,' he said. 'Where are we?'

Of course. He was as confused as the other avatars aboard the barge, perhaps even more so. Jonah had seen it in their expressions, in the dulling of their eyes, as they had sailed ever further out to sea. The Uploading process was clouding their minds – and perhaps that was for the best, he thought. As for his father...

His father had been dead for a long time. He was like Jonah's grandmother now, living in his memories. Still, it was something.

'It's OK, Dad,' said Jonah, smiling. 'We're taking a little boat trip, that's all. The two of us, you and me. It's all good.'

'I knew you'd find me,' said Jason.

Their 'little boat trip' was taking for ever.

Jonah assumed, at first, that the Island of the Uploaded was simply further away than he had thought it to be. Another hour passed, however, with still nothing ahead but the distant horizon. At first he suspected that, in fact, the barge was trapped in a programming loop. It was crossing the same stretch of ocean over and over.

Was this Granger's doing? Jonah wondered. Or his own? Was it his presence aboard the barge – the only avatar with a conscious mind – that was holding it back? Even the cloaked ferryman, he had come to realise, was an Artificial Intelligence.

Would the Island simply not allow the living to approach it this way?

He told himself to calm down, to stop imagining the worst. There were at least thirty avatars on board, his own excepted. Of course it would take time for the servers of the Southern Corner to Upload them all, all that information. It made sense that the journey to the Island would take as long as it had to take.

In the meantime, his father was here.

Jonah had watched fondly as Dad had unfurled his wings, stretched his legs, thrown back his red dragon's head and breathed out a stream of fire.

'I feel like flying,' he had said. 'It seems like so long since I flew.'

He had taken to the air, and Jonah had felt a stab of panic. What if he flew right off the barge and was lost at sea?

Fortunately, the barge had its own invisible barrier – Jonah assumed it was to keep avatars onboard during the Uploading process – and his dad was gently returned to the deck.

He had tried to fly three more times since then, always with the same result, but he wasn't discouraged or downhearted. Each time Jonah's dad was grounded, he simply switched to a different train of thought and forgot his disappointment. It was never long, however, before the urge to spread his wings returned.

'There was something I had to tell you,' he said.

'It's all right, Dad,' said Jonah.

'It was something important.'

'I already know.'

'Shouldn't I be at work?' asked Dad.

'It's your day off.' The lie came easily to Jonah's lips. He was used to this with his grandmother: telling her whatever would ease her mind. Anything but the truth.

'No, no,' said Dad, shaking his head, 'that can't be right. Mr Granger needs me to fly him to…somewhere I can't say. No one else can do it. No one else knows—'

'You don't work for Granger, remember?'

Dad furrowed his brow, puzzled.

'I mean, you don't really work for him. You're a Guardian. You went undercover as Matthew Granger's pilot. That's what you wanted to tell me, Dad. You left a copy of your avatar in the gift shop, so I could find it and—'

Dad smiled. 'That's where the future is,' he said, 'in

the Metasphere. That gift shop, Jonah, that'll be your inheritance. One day—'

'You remember the Guardians, don't you?'

'Anarchists,' Dad spat. 'If we left it to them, there'd be a free-for-all. The Millennials have the right idea. Any world needs order. It needs—'

'No, Dad. I know that's not what you think. I'm not a kid any more. You don't have to pretend with me any more. You can tell me the truth.'

'I remember when you were born, Jonah. I was so afraid. I knew what kind of a world we were bringing you into, and I knew it could only get worse.'

'So, you decided to make it a better world. Axel! You must remember Axel!'

'I have to go to the Icarus tonight,' said Dad. 'Axel says he has something to tell me, and it's important. I'll meet you outside when I'm done.'

'I know what Axel has to tell you,' said Jonah. 'He's a Guardian, and he wants you to be a Guardian too. He wants you to take the pilot's job with Matthew Granger, as an undercover agent. He wants you to find out where—'

But Dad was no longer listening. He had that gleam in his eyes, the one that said he was about to attempt to fly again. He was looking around him, at the sky. Jonah sighed, and sank back down onto the bench. He felt he was getting nowhere.

Then, his dad looked at him and, instead of unfurling

his wings, he sat down on the bench beside him.

'I had to make a decision today,' said Dad.

'What decision?' asked Jonah.

'I can't tell you that, son. I just wanted you to know, it was tough. The toughest choice I've ever had to make.'

'Then…then how did you do it? How did you know…?'

'The right thing to do?' Dad smiled. 'I didn't. I still don't.'

'Then how—?'

'I did a lot of thinking, son, I can tell you that much. A lot of it was about you. I love you, Jonah. I can't bear the thought of ever leaving you – but this decision I've made, it means that one day I might have to.'

'Then don't do it,' whispered Jonah. 'Don't leave me!'

'I thought about the world we live in,' said Dad, 'and the future I wanted for that world – for you, son. I listened to the advice of friends. I even went to the Island and talked to my mother, your grandmother.'

'What did she say?'

'She didn't understand,' said Dad. 'I knew she wouldn't. I just thought it might help to talk to her, and it did. It made me realise something. I know what Mum would have said to me, if she could. I think I'd known it all along – because the part of her that isn't there on the Island, it's in here.' Dad pointed to his heart.

'So, what *would* Nan have said?' asked Jonah, eagerly. 'What would she have told you to do?'

'Nothing,' said Dad. 'That's the point. That's what I realised. She'd have told me what she thought, of course, about the Guardians and the Millennials. But then she'd have said it was my life, my choice. She didn't have all the answers, any more than I did. She'd have said I was old enough to make up my own mind – and that she trusted me to do what I thought was right.'

'I understand,' said Jonah, quietly.

'You were always a bright kid. It's so good to see you, son.' Dad had got to his feet again. He looked up at the sky and shook his wings. 'I feel like flying,' he said. 'It seems so long since I flew.'

'Soon,' said Jonah. 'You'll be able to fly again soon, Dad, I promise.'

A cold, damp cloud had descended upon the barge.

Some of the passengers were tutting, complaining. Jonah held his breath, waiting. He grinned as the tendrils of mist parted, as a familiar shape was revealed upon the calm, blue sea. The Island of the Uploaded. He felt like punching the air. He had made it.

Avatars were gathering on the beach – hundreds of them, thousands – to greet the newest arrivals. The barge came to a gentle rest, with its nose in the sand, and its passengers disembarked. They were laughing, flying, drinking in the sunlight. None of them appeared to recognise their surroundings. The majority of them must have visited the Island before, but they didn't remember. They were fully Uploaded.

Jonah's dad flew a circuit of the beach, his enormous wings spread wide to catch the virtual air currents. He swooped inland, and disappeared into a thick wooded area. Jonah found he didn't mind. He knew he would find him again.

In the meantime, he thought, he had a job to do – an important job – and, for the first time, he was harbouring no doubts, no second thoughts, about that prospect.

He took to the air himself and flew along the beach, headed for a familiar spot. She was right there, his grandmother, basking in the sand, apparently without a care in the world. She looked surprised as he landed beside her.

'Jonah,' she trumpeted. 'My little Jonah, all grown up!' She wrapped her elephant's trunk around him, pulled him into the crick of her neck.

'Nan,' said Jonah. 'I…I've so much to tell you. It's Dad. He's here! He's on the Island. We can talk to him again.'

Nan's eyes wrinkled with amusement. 'Well, of course we can, dear. I was talking to your father… Why, it can only have been a few days ago.'

'Of course you were,' said Jonah, grinning. 'Of course you were.'

'He was telling me all about Flight School. I worry about your father, you know, when he's away from home, flying his planes, but I know it makes him happy. Let me have a look at you, little Jonah. Why, you've changed so much!'

'Nan,' said Jonah, 'I need... I mean, *we* need, Dad and me... We need your help.'

'Anything,' said Nan. 'You know that.'

'We need you to gather up as many avatars as you can, and ask them to remember.'

'Remember what, dear?'

'Everything.'

35

Matthew Granger had barely closed his eyes when the internal phone by his bed chirruped. He snatched it up, barked angrily into the mouthpiece, 'What now?'

A nervous programmer apologised for disturbing his sleep. But, she went on to say, she was following Granger's own explicit orders.

By the time he put the phone down again, Granger was no longer angry.

He was smiling to himself as he reached for his cyber-kinetic legs, attached them to his stumps. This was finally it, he thought. The day he had been waiting for.

The Southern Corner's long-range sensors – brought back online by Granger only three days ago – had detected the approach of some twenty vehicles across the desert. The Guardians were coming.

He had expected them sooner. He had overestimated them. His enemies had given him plenty of time to prepare for them.

It was perfect, thought Granger. He would personally direct his Millennials into battle. The Guardians would be crushed, and news of their defeat would spread across the virtual world. That would set an example to the remaining dissidents. It would show them that Granger was not to be messed with. It would show everyone that his position, his power, was unassailable.

The sun was going down. It was almost time.

Ayers Rock had been visible, through the clear plastic canopy of the land yacht's cockpit, for some miles now. It had taken far longer than Sam had expected to reach it. She had underestimated its sheer size. Now, however, she could see the security fences that ringed the rock – and the facility within it.

She looked back at Jonah. He was still slumped in his seat, meta-tranced.

She looked down at the pistol she was cradling in her lap. Her dad's pistol. Sam had taken it from the comatose Axel's pocket. She would have to use it, soon.

For the past two days, since her dad had been lost, Sam had been putting on an act. She had had to affect a confidence she didn't feel. She had had to appear strong, or else the Guardians wouldn't have followed her.

The truth was, Sam had never fired a gun in anger before.

Oh, she knew what to do. Her dad had tutored her in the use of a variety of weapons. They had spent many hours on virtual shooting ranges and in combat simulations. Sam could have stripped down Axel's pistol, cleaned it and reassembled it in a matter of minutes. But to aim it at someone – a living, breathing human being, not a computer construct – and to squeeze that trigger…

She didn't know if she could do that.

There was only one way through the electric fences: a security checkpoint across the desert highway, manned by two figures in black fatigues. Sam could see more figures – just dots from this distance, like ants – swarming down the side of the rock.

She turned back to Jonah. 'If you're going to do something,' she muttered through clenched teeth, although she knew he couldn't hear her, 'now would be a good time.'

The sun still shone upon the Island of the Uploaded.

Jonah was painfully aware, however, of the passing of time in the real world. It was sunset in the Australian Northern Territories. He was almost out of time. He had done nowhere near enough.

The avatars of the dead were still coming to him. Jonah waited for them in a quiet forest clearing and they gathered around him, forty or fifty of them. It was something. It meant his grandmother was still spreading the word about him. She hadn't forgotten, as Jonah had feared she might.

They bombarded him with questions. 'Are you the little humatar with the story to tell?' asked a giant caterpillar.

'Are you the boy who can help us to remember?' asked a rhinoceros.

Jonah climbed up onto a tree stump and held out his hands for silence. Then he began to tell the Uploaded avatars a story, in terms he hoped they would understand. 'There is an evil spider that has spun a web around this island,' he told them. 'He is keeping your loved ones from coming here to see you, until they agree to serve him.'

The Uploaded avatars thought about this for a while, and agreed that none of them had had a visitor in a long, long time.

Jonah didn't name the villain of his story. He knew that a good proportion of his audience would have been supporters of Matthew Granger in life. Fortunately, the Uploaded, in their confused states, were more than willing to believe anyone who sounded as if he knew what he was talking about.

'I want you to help me break this evil spider's web,' said Jonah. 'All you have to do is close your eyes, take slow, deep breaths and listen to my voice...'

He was teaching them his grandmother's meditation trick.

'That's right, and now...now, I want you to think about someone you love. Someone you might have not seen in a long while. Think about a memory you shared with them. A good memory. A happy one.'

Some of the Uploaded were already losing interest, floating away, Jonah's story forgotten. The rest of them, however...

The rest were doing as Jonah had told them – and they were remembering. Not only that, but they were enjoying it; there were smiles on their faces, blissful sighs hanging in the humid forest air.

Jonah could leave now, and none of them would even notice. The Uploaded would remain in their meditative states long after he had gone, long after he had begun to tell his story to another audience in another clearing.

He desperately sought out groups of Uploaded avatars across the Island. He inspired them to remember before moving on to other groups.

The problem was, his audiences so far had been too few and far too small. Of the millions of avatars upon the Island, he had reached only a tiny fraction.

Jonah's plan was working – his story was spreading – but too slowly.

Sam's land yacht was in the lead, speeding towards Ayers Rock.

There were at least twenty guards now, between the two electric fences. They raised their guns, and the air was filled with their still-distant reports.

Sam's driver pulled a release handle, rolled back the cockpit canopy. Sam's eyes were stung by a gritty wind. She hadn't realised how fast they were going.

Before they reached the outer fence, the driver pulled his wheel around. The land yacht skidded on its tyres, made a ninety-degree turn to the right.

They were running parallel to the fences now. Sam hunkered down in front of her seat and poked her father's pistol over the land yacht's side. A bullet whistled over her head, almost parting her hair. There was sand in Sam's eyes and she couldn't see to aim properly, but the Guardians were waiting on her next move.

The Millennials had opened fire first, she told herself.

She squeezed her trigger four, five, six times – every time she saw a dark-clad shape in her sights. Most of Sam's bullets ricocheted off the outer fence, in showers of blue sparks, before they could reach their targets. There was still current running through those wires. Jonah had failed in his quest to drain the Southern Corner's power.

But then, thought Sam, why hadn't he come back?

The other land yachts had followed the lead of Sam's. They were fanning out around the electric fences: twenty low-riding, fast-moving targets. They were strafing the fences with gunfire, much of it from bigger and nastier weapons than Sam's pistol.

She heard the chatter of machine guns, and the whistle and crump of a Guardian rocket launcher. A cloud of dust and sand was blasted up from the desert floor, a stretch of the outer fence mangled. The Millennials behind it scattered and took cover, as much they could, behind other fence posts, still firing.

Sam's land yacht came around again for a second

strafing run. As it did, Sam saw the front tyre of another yacht blown out by a machine-gun bullet, sending it into an uncontrolled skid. Her eyes widened when she spotted a Millennial hoist a rocket launcher onto his shoulder.

The disabled land yacht is a sitting duck, she thought.

'Get out of there!' she shouted.

The land yacht's three occupants leapt out of the cockpit and raced to get clear, as their vehicle was blown apart. Sam was showered with debris.

She loosed off a second volley of six shots. The fourth struck a Millennial in the chest, sending him flying in a spray of blood. Sam's first kill – or a serious wound at the very least. She tried not to think about it. Her victim would have done the same to her in a heartbeat, she told herself.

She was loading a fresh clip into her pistol when she realised something. The fence. It hadn't sparked, this time, as her bullets had pinged off it. Sam didn't know if that was because of the damage it had sustained, or because of something Jonah had done. Either way, it meant only one thing.

She switched the cockpit radio to a general channel, snatched up her handset. 'The electric fences are down!' she announced. 'I repeat, the electric fences are down!'

The Guardians knew what to do.

The remaining nineteen land yachts – Sam's included – broke off their attack. They sped back out into the desert as if in retreat, but then they circled around to approach the fence head-on. Sam's driver closed their cockpit canopy and put his foot down hard.

The land yachts barrelled towards the dead fences, relying no longer on wind but on their built-up battery power, using the distance they had gained to pick up speed. Many of the Millennials, when they saw them coming, ran for it. A few stayed, and peppered the approaching vehicles with bullets, to little avail. The canopy over Sam's head was cracked but not holed.

She heard an explosion to her left. Another Millennial rocket. She didn't have time to wait for the dust to settle, to assess the damage that might have been done.

The nose of Sam's land yacht hit the first of the fences.

Jonah heard his own voice slurring.

He wasn't sure what was happening to him. Tiredness, perhaps?

He was in another clearing, addressing another audience of Uploaded avatars. He felt it was hopeless. The attack on the Southern Corner must have begun by now. He had to keep trying, anyway.

He was urging the Uploaded to remember – not just sights and sounds, but smells, tastes and textures. He told them they had to build as vivid a picture of the past as they could in their minds. Jonah raised his hand, to rub his weary eyes, but the movement of his arm was slow, sluggish.

He looked closely at his fingers. He wiggled them. There was a noticeable lag between his deciding what to do and his avatar responding to his brain's command.

A shadow fell over him. Jonah looked up and saw a familiar avatar coming in to land beside him. A sleek and powerful red dragon. Dad.

'Jonah? Son? Is that you?'

Jonah smiled. 'It's me, Dad.'

'You found me. I knew you'd find me.'

'Actually, Dad, it was you who found me this time.' Jonah's words were coming back to his ears a half-second after he spoke them. It was weird.

'I spoke to your grandmother,' said Dad.

'I'd love to talk,' said Jonah, 'I really would. But I'm in the middle of something right now, and I think… I think it might just be starting to work.'

'I've been doing what I can,' said Dad.

'I don't know why it should,' said Jonah. 'I didn't think I'd reached enough of the Uploaded. But it is. We're putting too great a demand on the Southern Corner's servers. They're starting to slow down. They're… What did you just say?'

'I've been spreading this story of yours,' said Dad. 'I can't say I understand it, but you're old enough now, Jonah. I trust you to do what you think is right.'

'Nan told you the story? I didn't think she'd remember it. I didn't think *you'd* remember it, at least not for long enough to—'

'She said the story was important to you, son. So, it's important to us too.'

'I don't know what to say,' said Jonah. 'Yes. Yes, it's important. It—'

'I can handle things here from now on, son.'

'Are you sure? Some of the Uploaded, they must be starting to come out of their meditations already. We need to tell more, keep up the pressure on the—'

'We'll keep spreading the story, your grandmother and I,' Dad promised. 'We'll keep telling them to remember.'

Jonah nodded. 'Thank you,' he said. 'Thanks, Dad. I *could* do with... I don't know what's been happening in the real world, with Sam and the others. I could do with getting back there. They might need my help.'

36

Sam braced herself, half expecting to feel a lethal electric jolt.

Of course, it didn't come.

The fence buckled with the impact of her vehicle, strands of wire snapping, but it didn't quite give. The land yacht's engines strained against the obdurate barrier, wheels spinning in the sand, failing to find traction.

A second land yacht hit the fence, then a third and a fourth, ten more. More wires were severed, pillars torn up from the sand. The fence collapsed. The last of the Millennial guards dived for cover.

The second fence was only a hundred metres behind the first. Sam's vehicle had lost much of its momentum, but the same wasn't true of the rest of the fleet. The land yachts hit the second fence, shredded it and surged forward in triumph.

There was nothing between the Guardians and their objective now. Nothing but three miles of desert sands. They were leaving the Millennial guards, stunned, behind them. Just a handful of them had recovered their wits enough to climb to their feet, to fire their weapons after their receding foes.

The other land yachts fell back, allowing Sam's to retake the lead.

She shouted instructions to her Aboriginal driver. He stepped on the accelerator again. They approached the looming red shape of Ayers Rock, but veered off to follow the line of its broad southern face to its western tip. They had gained two miles on the Millennial guards, and were concealed from them by the rock.

It was time to put the next stage of their plan into operation.

The land yachts came to a halt. Their occupants disembarked. All but one.

Jonah was still meta-tranced in his seat. Sam sent him a pop-up message, then turned to their driver. 'I need you to stay with him,' she said. 'If he hasn't come back by the time the Millennials get here—'

The older Aborigine nodded. 'I will protect him,' he promised.

Sam looked around at the other land yachts. She counted seventeen, all told. They must have lost two more to the Millennials' rocket launchers as they had rushed the outer fence. It could have been a lot worse.

The Guardians knew what to do. They had parked their vehicles facing Ayers Rock, and had begun to calibrate the catapults on their backs. Sam looked nervously at the catapult attached to her own vehicle.

Her driver produced a laser rangefinder. He sighted through it at the rock, calculating its distance away and height at this point. He clicked his tongue thoughtfully, as he knelt by the catapult and adjusted it according to his readings.

Sam didn't dare speak, she didn't want to risk distracting him.

The moment she had been dreading came at last. She pulled on her parachute harness. It wasn't a full chute, but it would slow her descent a little.

The driver turned to her. 'It is ready,' he said.

Sam's heart was pounding as she stepped up onto the back of the land yacht and lowered herself into the catapult seat. She was tilted backwards, so all she could see was the dark sky, freckled with more stars than she had ever seen before.

There were still more adjustments to make for Sam's size and weight. As she waited, she heard the first catapults being sprung. Several human shapes soared through the air above her. From this angle, she couldn't tell if her fellow Guardians had landed safely or not. She heard gunfire from atop Ayers Rock, which suggested that at least some of them had made it.

Then, her driver straightened up, told her to brace herself, and Sam's throat dried. It was her turn.

Sam didn't feel the moment she was shot up into the air. It happened too fast.

Suddenly, she was flying. It felt like being in the Metasphere – only she was in her real-world form. And she appeared to have left her stomach on the ground.

Sam had to remind herself that this *was* the real world. She didn't have her unicorn's wings here, couldn't use them to control her flight. She was at the mercy of such real-world forces as momentum and gravity.

She closed her eyes, bit her lip, remembered what she had been told. She had to suppress the natural urge to struggle, had to straighten her body, keep it limp.

Her chute operated automatically, just as the momentum given her by the catapult wore off and gravity seized hold of her. Her driver's calculations had been near-flawless. Sam was still going to hit hard – but she had expected as much. That was why she had padded herself this morning.

She had the briefest of impressions of figures fighting on top of Uluru as she hurtled towards them.

Before she could think of anything else, Sam was rolling in red dust, so far and so fast that she thought she might just roll right off the far side of the rock.

She rolled, skidded, bumped to a halt, lying on her back, bruised, breathless.

But there was no time to indulge her aches and pains. She hardly felt them, anyway, over her jubilation at having made it up here intact. She pushed herself to her feet, decoupled her chute, drew her pistol.

And Sam raced to join the battle.

*

The Millennials were taken by surprise.

The last thing they had expected was for their enemies to reach them so quickly. Only nine or ten of them were waiting on the vast, flat top of Ayers Rock – and their immediate brief, Sam imagined, had just been to keep an eye on events below.

Suddenly, there were Guardians hurtling towards the Millennials – and, within a few seconds, those Guardians were upon them, and had outnumbered them.

By the time Sam arrived, both sides were shooting at each other. There was little cover up here – just a raised hatchway leading down into the rock – so the air was thick with bullets. One whizzed by Sam's left ear, close enough that she could feel the heat from its casing. She chalked her survival up to nothing more than luck.

The Guardians had the edge in numbers, but the Millennials were better armed. The Guardians had expected this, though. They closed with their foes, challenging them hand-to-hand, making full use of their knives and spears and sticks and whatever else they had been able to lay their hands on back in Woomera.

An older Millennial woman crouched behind the raised hatchway, her rifle readied, looking for a target in the ever-expanding scrum. Sam charged her, knocked her to the ground, and they rolled in the dust together.

The Millennial lost her weapon, and made the mistake of scrambling after it. Sam leapt on her from behind, got her in a chokehold. She held it until the Millennial's face turned red, until she was on the verge of passing out.

Sam hadn't intended to kill her. There was no need. However, her enemy stiffened in her grip as a bullet thudded into her chest. It had come from the gun of another Millennial: a stocky kid, who recoiled in horror and dropped his weapon as he realised he had just shot an ally. Evidently, he had been aiming at Sam.

A moment later, the kid disappeared beneath a seething mass of Guardians.

Numbers were winning the day. The last of the Millennials broke free from the melee and raced for the hatchway. He was cut down by a hail of bullets in mid-dive.

The Guardians had suffered just four fatalities – although a similar number again had broken their own bones in awkward landings.

'*Uluru!*' The shout came from the Aboriginal girl, Kala. She lifted her painted face to the night sky, and fired her pistol above her head in victory. Without waiting for Sam, she ordered her people onwards. They dropped through the entrance hatch, one by one, baying for more Millennial blood.

Sam clambered through the hatchway, her foot finding the first rung of a ladder beneath it. She dropped into a large, open space, which was littered with wooden packing crates – some sort of unloading area.

She saw a row of three lifts and could hear gears grinding, unoiled chains squealing. One of the lifts was active, doubtless bringing up Millennial reinforcements.

She didn't have to warn the others. Kala was already lining them up in ambush, at least the ones with guns. The lift doors parted to reveal six Millennials. Like their fellows above, they were taken aback at how far their foes had got.

They didn't get off a single shot between them.

Kala leaned into the metal cage lift, hit the controls and dodged out again as the doors slid shut. The lift shuddered, groaned and began its downwards journey with six dead passengers – an unmistakable message for whoever had sent them.

Kala let out her war cry again, and the other Aborigines joined in.

There was a stairwell in the corner and Kala led the way towards it, unstoppable now. Sam called after her, 'Be careful, please!' This war wasn't won yet. She doubted, however, that the girl had even heard her.

The rest of the Guardians were dropping through the hatchway, hurrying past Sam, following their allies downstairs. Sam made for the lifts, intending to disable them so that no more Millennials could use them to get up here.

Then, suddenly, the unloading area began to fill with gas.

It hissed out of tiny nozzles in the walls around Sam, tinting the air green. As she drew breath, she felt the gas, stinging, in her throat. It clawed at her eyes, drawing out tears. She made for the ladder, but there were too many people in her way. They were coughing, crying out in panic, stampeding each other in their rush for fresh air.

More Guardians came up behind Sam, returning from the stairs, finding them impassable. But there was no sign of Kala, or her followers. They must have pressed on.

'Get down!' spluttered Sam. 'On the floor. The gas is lighter than air!'

She threw herself onto her stomach, searched her coverall pockets for a handkerchief. She found one, pressed it over her nose and mouth, breathed through it. It helped, but not much. The stinging gas was in Sam's lungs. She had swallowed a mouthful of it too. Her stomach was convulsing. Beside her, a sun-bronzed, blond-haired man with bandoliers slung over his rippling muscles was sick on the floor.

Behind Sam, an Aboriginal woman lost her grip on the exit ladder and fell.

In front of her, through a green haze, she could see the indicator lights of the three lifts. Two of them – the two not occupied by Millennial corpses – were rising.

37

It had taken Jonah an age to fly back to his exit halo. He felt much slower in his regained humatar than he had in his father's dragon form.

At last, however, he saw it before him, its glow reflected in the sea below.

Jonah took one last look over his shoulder, but could no longer see the Island of the Uploaded through the mist that had closed back in around it. He dived through his exit halo, and his mind began the process of readjustment to the real world.

In those few dreamlike seconds, he thought he could hear gunfire.

It came as a shock to him to realise the sounds were real.

The two lifts pinged, almost in unison. They had reached this floor.

The other Guardians – those still conscious – were struggling on hands and knees, crawling behind wooden crates for cover. Sam took a final breath, held it, discarded her handkerchief and raised her pistol.

Millennials swarmed out of each of the lifts. They were wearing gas masks.

Mindful of the fate of those who had come before them, they were already firing. Their bullets sprayed across the room, ricocheting off the walls, punching holes through the crates.

The Guardians had one advantage. The haze of green gas helped to conceal them – but they knew where the Millennials were. As a handful of Guardians found the strength to fire back, the Millennials scattered.

In his haste, one of them stumbled over Sam. Sam tugged at his ankle, brought him down beside her. She wrenched the gas mask from his face, jammed it over her own, but had no time to don it properly. She gulped in two breaths of sweet, filtered air, then dropped the mask as the Millennial wrestled with her.

He was trying to bring his rifle to bear. Sam took hold of the barrel, wrenched it upwards. The Millennial, choking on the gas, fired into the ceiling. Almost by chance, his flailing boot kicked Sam in the stomach, forcing the clean air from her lungs.

The two of them lunged for the gas mask at once.

Sam was the first to reach it, to snatch it up. Her elbow caught the Millennial in the face and he doubled up, retching. By the time Sam had fastened the mask's straps around her head, the gas had rendered her opponent unconscious.

Sam straightened up, her pistol in her hand. Her eyes were streaming. She could hardly see a thing. She realised too late that a Millennial had come up behind her. She spun around to face him. The Millennial lowered his shotgun, made a gesture of apology. He had made out Sam's gas mask through the haze and assumed her to be an ally.

She couldn't count on being so lucky again.

The rest of the Guardians had fallen, unconscious or worse. The Millennials were climbing the exit ladder, going after the escapees. A couple of them were starting to look at Sam, suspiciously. She couldn't possibly fight all of them.

She edged away from the Millennials. Her hands searched behind her back, and found the button that called the lift. She pressed it.

Every one of the Millennials turned towards Sam now, alerted by the sound of doors rumbling open. Before they could work out what was happening, Sam had leapt into the lift, flattened herself against the wall and was stabbing at the controls.

The doors began to close, too slowly. The Millennials fired through the narrowing gap between them. Sam dropped into the corner, making herself as small a target as she could as bullets bounced around the confined space. She breathed a sigh of relief as the doors came together and the lift began to descend.

Sam had no way of knowing what she would find when those doors opened again. She didn't know how many Guardians had made it through the gas. She didn't know how many Millennials would be waiting at the bottom of the stairs for them. She only knew that the battle above her was lost.

She was pinning her hopes now on the battle below.

Matthew Granger was in the control room.

He was watching numbers careering across a monitor. He was typing at two datapads simultaneously – but, for once in his life, he couldn't make the numbers do as he instructed them. There was sweat on his brow.

He couldn't quite believe what was happening. He wasn't sure what *was* happening – only that, for some reason, his servers were being taxed to their limits.

There ought to have been back-up systems in place. There had been, once. Before the real-world governments and their cost-cutting measures.

The best Granger could do for now was improvise a series of software workarounds and take as much pressure as he could off the failing hardware. It was a losing battle. And the Guardians were almost here. He could hear them fighting with his own Millennial followers, almost at his door already.

They had been clever, Granger had to grant them that. Whatever the Guardians had done to cause the server overload, it had drained the Southern Corner's power, shut down its defences. It had also been extremely reckless.

One-quarter of the virtual world was controlled from

here, from these servers. If they should crash, then that quarter of the Metasphere would be erased.

And if Matthew Granger – the smartest man in the world – couldn't stop it, if he couldn't prevent that disaster, then who could?

Jonah ducked. At least, he tried to. He didn't yet have full control of his real-world body. He was still in the back of the land yacht's cockpit. He slid off his seat to land with a bump, yanking out his DI lead.

The first thing Jonah saw, as his vision cleared, was the monolithic silhouette of Ayers Rock against the bright night sky. The other land yachts were parked in the scrub around him, abandoned. An older Aboriginal man was crouching behind one of them. He had his back to Jonah.

He was under attack from a younger man – a Millennial – with a pistol, sniping around the rock itself. The Aboriginal Guardian appeared to be unarmed. As Jonah looked again, however, he saw a second Millennial sprawled at the feet of the first, a spear through his throat, dead.

The survivor was taking no chances. He was staying under cover. He had his foe pinned down, even so.

As Jonah watched, the Millennial's gun clicked dry. He ducked out of sight, presumably to reload – but his enemy had been waiting for this chance. The Aborigine sprang into action. He vaulted over the land yacht and disappeared too. Jonah made to follow him, thinking he ought to help somehow.

He heard a gunshot.

He dropped between the land yachts. He waited.

A figure emerged from behind the rock. It was the Aborigine. Jonah saw his white-striped face, and recognised him as his former driver.

'What...what did I miss?' asked Jonah, standing. 'Is the plan...?'

'The others are up there,' said the driver, nodding towards the top of the rock. 'I stayed behind to look after your body as you dreamed.'

'But the fences... Did it work? Did the fences go down?'

'They did.' The driver placed his foot on the first dead Millennial's chest. He gripped his spear with both hands and yanked it from the corpse's throat. It was caked in blood. He returned to his land yacht, and climbed into the catapult seat.

'Wait,' said Jonah. 'Where are you...? You can't leave me here!'

'You are no longer dreaming. You can protect yourself.'

'But what if more Millennials come? I don't have any weapons. I can't...'

'They were the last,' said the driver, 'from the gates. The rest are climbing Uluru, to aid their allies at the top. We must do the same for ours.'

And, with that, he released a catch by his side and was flung into the air before Jonah could start to voice another protest. He craned his neck to follow the old man's arc but was unable to see, from this angle, whether he landed safely or not. For all Jonah knew, he could have overshot the rock, or been dashed into its side.

We must do the same, the old man had said. *We...* As if he had expected Jonah to follow him. Jonah looked at the catapult and swallowed nervously.

Suddenly, he felt very alone.

Sam's lift went only a few floors down, then stopped.

The lift's datapad demanded a special code to travel any further down, so Sam stepped out into a dusty workstation. Through a window, she could see rows of giant solar batteries. She was in the power station, the public face of the Ayers Rock installation.

Sam searched for the staircase.

A security bulkhead had been half-lowered across the stairs. Sam guessed it had run out of power before it could fully close. She ducked under it. Wisps of green gas still clung to her, so she kept her gas mask on. Despite the uncertainty of the situation, she felt a little thrill at the thought that she was inside the Southern Corner now, a place she had dreamed about all her life.

Sam could hear fighting below her. That was good,

she told herself. It meant there were Guardians down there, still standing.

As she rounded a staircase corner, she saw the full truth of it.

The Guardians and the Millennials were brawling four flights below her. The Millennials, Sam guessed, must have tried to hold the line here. They had been overrun.

The Guardians were winning, trampling on their fallen foes and forcing the remainder back, back into what appeared to be a lobby area behind them.

A Millennial broke free from the scrum, climbed a couple of steps, then turned back with his gun raised. Sam ran up behind him, sent him sprawling with a punch to his neck. He fell between two Guardians, who beat him to the ground.

The Guardians made a concerted push forward, and suddenly the staircase was clear but for the fallen. Sam removed her mask and picked her way between the bodies, making to follow. After all the planning, all the worry, this was it. *We're almost there!*

She stumbled over a body. She glanced down, and immediately her euphoria was drained from her. She was looking at Kala. The Aboriginal girl's eyes were wide open, staring sightlessly, and there was a bullet hole in her forehead.

'Sir, we can't hold them back. The Guardians are—'

'—didn't employ the gas in time, sir. They—'

'—still fighting on top of the rock, but—'

'—sent too many men out, sir. We didn't expect them to—'

'—out of here. Mr Granger, did you hear me? We have to get you out of here!'

Matthew Granger wasn't listening.

He knew how bad the situation was. He knew it only too well. He didn't need a cacophony of well-meaning voices to remind him of the facts.

'I can't,' he said quietly. 'I can't leave here. Not now.' His eyes were rooted to his monitor, his fingers a blur over his datapads.

'Sir, you have no choice.' Granger recognised the giant Kiwi who had helped escort him into Ayers Rock, a week ago. He placed a hand on Granger's shoulder.

Granger brushed it away. 'How could you understand?' he snapped. 'My world! They're destroying my world!' The demand on the clapped-out servers was only increasing. He had traced the fault to the Island of the Uploaded, but he couldn't find the cause of it, couldn't stop the fault from spreading.

'The Guardians will be inside this room within seconds,' said the mercenary. 'If they find you here, they'll—'

'Just one more minute.' Granger kept on typing.

The mercenary gripped his seat, spun it around to face him. 'You don't have that minute, sir. The Guardians are inside, advancing. And, whatever the problem is, there's nothing you can—'

'One quarter of the virtual world! Do you even comprehend what that—?'

'There's nothing you can do about that if you're dead!'

Granger glared up at the towering figure in front of him. The Kiwi glared back.

For the first time in his life, Granger was the first to blink.

'You're right,' he said. 'I can't afford to be captured, whatever the cost. I'm the only man who can put things right.'

The Kiwi led Granger out of the control room, back towards the service corridor that led to the secret cave entrance. They heard gunfire ahead of them, however, and Granger turned back and made off in the opposite direction.

'I've a better way out,' he said.

The mercenary remained at Granger's heels, to ensure that no one tried to follow him. Soon enough, in a quiet corner out of earshot of the melee, Granger found what he was looking for: a small cargo elevator built for hoisting computer servers, not people, but large enough for one small man to squeeze into.

The Guardians would never even know he had been here.

Granger pulled the lift door shut behind him, leaving

the Kiwi mercenary to return to the battle. The lift rocketed skywards.

This was only a temporary setback, he told himself.

So, Granger had lost the Southern Corner. Within the hour, there would *be* no more Southern Corner – and his enemies would bear the blame for that.

They had caused this disaster – and Granger would make sure everyone knew it too. Everyone would see, at last, the consequences of the Guardians' brand of anarchy. It would be the end of their movement.

Oh yes, thought Granger, *this might well turn out to be a good day, after all.*

38

At the foot of Ayers Rock, Jonah paced up and down between the Guardians' land yachts. He looked at the catapults on their backs.

He climbed into the seat of the catapult on the yacht that had brought him here. He was wearing his parachute harness. He had reset the spring and set the catapult for his build and weight. He wasn't sure he had done it right.

Jonah found the release catch by his left side, closed his fingers around it.

He couldn't bring himself to pull it.

He jumped out of the catapult seat. He could still hear gunfire from the top of the rock, though less persistent than it had been. What could he do up there anyway, without a weapon? Hadn't he done enough?

But what if Sam was in trouble?

He could climb the rock, he thought. It would take him some time, but at least he would get there, and in one piece. At least he would be doing something.

His mind was made up. Jonah set off, away from the land yachts, around the rock. He had barely gone two steps when a voice sounded behind him:

'Jonah? Jonah? Are you there? Can you hear me? Come in, Jonah.'

This ought to have been a day of celebration.

The Guardians had taken one of the Four Corners. Sam had led the way into the control room herself. In her worst nightmares, she could never have predicted what she had found there.

'Sam? Is that you?'

'Jonah!' Sam had found a comms program on the system and entered the frequency of the land yachts' cockpit radios. 'Listen, I'm in the control room, but we have a big problem here.'

The control room lights were flickering as the power supply dwindled.

'The control room?' echoed Jonah. *'You mean you—?'*

'Yes, Jonah, we did it. A few of the Millennials are still fighting in the corridors, but we did it. We won. But, listen, what you did on the Island—'

'It worked, Sam. The plan worked. I got the Uploaded to remember, and they—'

'I know it worked, Jonah. It worked too well. The servers here are in a worse state even than we thought they were. They're failing!'

'Failing? But… Won't that mean…?'

'It means that a quarter of the Metasphere is about to crash. Hard. It means that every avatar logged in to that quarter will be lost. For ever.'

'What… What can we do?'

'You have to get back there,' said Sam.

I can't. I wish I could, Sam, but—'

'You have to stop the Uploaded from remembering, before they—'

'It would kill me, Sam. The way I used to get to the Island – it would kill me to try it a second time.'

'It's their only chance, Jonah. We can evacuate the living, most of them, but the dead…the dead can't leave the Island. They're stuck there!'

'The mistwall!' said Jonah. *'Granger's barrier. Now you have access to his systems, maybe you could—?'*

'I'll see what I can do,' said Sam. She cut off the connection.

The control room was in turmoil. Twenty Guardians hovered helplessly over the monitors and datapads. Twenty more were panicking loudly. Of course, the people Sam had led here had mostly been fighters. She needed programmers, technicians. She needed a leader.

Sam needed her dad.

A monitor in front of her was outputting a stream of figures. Their prognosis wasn't good. Even if she could get Jonah to the Island of the Uploaded and if he could stop the server drain, Sam feared it might only be delaying the inevitable.

The damage had already been done.

*

For some time after Sam had broken off contact, Jonah sat frozen, one thought ringing in his head: *This is all my fault.*

He had climbed into a land yacht to use its cockpit radio. He climbed out now, and began to pace again. Each time he passed a yacht, Jonah glared into it, at its radio, as if he could will Sam's voice to sound again, tell him everything was OK after all.

How long had it been already?

Jonah didn't know how to contact Sam inside the rock, and didn't want to disturb her. But he had to know what was happening.

He searched the land yachts until he found a handheld monitor. He plugged it into a Metasphere terminal. He inputted co-ordinates for a zone close to the Island.

On the monitor, he saw desperate avatars flying in slow motion, jerkily, as Jonah had on the Island, flying for their lives through the virtual streets.

They were panicking and shrieking, unable to understand why they couldn't move faster. Some of them were lost and screaming for help.

Warning messages were scrolling across every available surface: across walls, along roads, in the sky itself. Avatars were being told to flee to another quarter of the Metasphere, or out of it altogether, whichever option was the quickest. Sam had been as good as her word. She must have organised this.

The avatars were sluggish and fighting against

the failing servers that betrayed them. Still, they were reaching their exit halos, many of them, diving through to safety.

All Jonah could think of, however, was what Sam had said: *The dead can't leave... They're stuck...*

He had been so proud of himself, thought he'd been so clever, convincing the Uploaded to tax the Southern Corner's servers. He had even left his dad to keep spreading the word... If only he could contact him and tell him to stop!

Jonah typed the co-ordinates of the Island of the Uploaded. The picture on the monitor changed. Now, it showed only grey mist.

A lump formed in Jonah's throat. He was about to lose his grandmother – and his father, all over again – and that was only the tip of the iceberg. Everyone knew someone, had someone they loved, on the Island. Everyone would lose someone, if the Island crashed. All those avatars, those remnants of lives once lived, they would all be destroyed for ever – and Jonah would be the one to blame.

He smacked the handheld monitor against the land yacht's instrument panel, as if he could clear the grey haze from its screen. It broke.

Why hadn't Sam been back in touch? Why hadn't she lowered the mistwall yet? They were running out of time.

*

'Why should I help you? Guardian scum!'

The Millennial prisoner lay on his bed, facing the wall stubbornly. Two Guardians marched into the bunkroom and hauled him to his feet. One of them put a gun to his head, but Sam told him to lower it.

The Millennial's name was Warren. He was just a teenager, blond-haired and twitchy. He had been captured in the control room.

'You wouldn't be doing this to help the Guardians,' said Sam, reasonably. 'You'd be doing it to help the whole world. You know the servers are crashing. We need—'

'And whose fault is that?'

'That…that doesn't matter now. We need those access codes, so we can—'

'—lower the mistwall around the Island. So you said. But why should I believe you? This sounds like a trick to me, to get your hands on—'

'Why would I?' cried Sam in frustration. 'Why would anyone want to destroy the Island of the Uploaded?'

'Like the Guardians care about human life? You're terrorists, killers! For all I know, you could be plotting to destroy the whole of the—'

'Don't you have someone on the Island? A parent or a grandparent, or a brother or a sister or a best friend?'

Warren stared down at his shoes. Sam had struck a nerve. She sat down on the bed beside him and gently asked, 'Who is it?'

'My brother. He had terminal leukaemia. We Uploaded him just in time. That's why I joined the Millennials – to protect him, to let him live forever.'

'Then you know why I need those codes,' Sam begged. 'What harm could it do to give them to me now? And maybe we can save your brother together.'

'But I don't have them,' said Warren, sullenly. 'I don't have the access codes. Only Mr Granger has them.'

'Then I'll take you to the control room. You must have some way of contacting Granger… Don't you? You could ask him to lower the mistwall himself.'

The prisoner shook his head. 'He won't do it!'

'He has to,' insisted Sam. 'Once he knows what's at stake…'

'Don't you think he knows already?'

'So, you're saying he won't help us,' said Sam, angrily, 'is that it? He'd rather see the Southern Corner crash, sacrifice all those lives?'

Warren looked up, glaring at Sam with renewed defiance. 'Mr Granger did all he could to save those lives,' he snarled. 'He stayed at his datapad for as long as he could, longer than was safe for him. If it hadn't been for you Guardians—'

'Wait,' said Sam. 'You're saying he was…?'

'Matthew Granger is the smartest man in the world, but even he couldn't stop the server crash that you started. What hope do you think you have?'

'*Granger was here?*' cried Sam.

Warren closed his mouth and blinked nervously, as he realised he had said too much. 'Matthew Granger was right here?' repeated Sam. 'In this facility?'

Jonah couldn't bear the waiting any longer.

He still hadn't heard back from Sam. *What if something else had gone wrong?* he thought. *What if she had other problems to deal with?*

If so, then everything was down to him. Jonah had to do something, fix the problem he had created – but how?

What if I did *board the death barge again?* he asked himself. It was a desperate notion, but Jonah was feeling desperate. *It would get me through the mistwall, like it did last time… But with only one avatar left in my brain, it would kill me!*

Maybe it'd be worth it to save the Island. To save the dead.

There had to be another way.

Jonah thrust his hands deep into his pockets, his head aching with thought. His left hand brushed against something cold and metal. He didn't know what it was.

Then he remembered.

Jonah's heart leapt as he pulled out the Chang Bridge device, inspected it in the bright moonlight.

It will create a bridge between the Metasphere and a new virtual world. That was what Mr Chang had said about his invention. And what else? He had talked about his new world's increased processing power. And wasn't that just what the Uploaded needed?

Had Jonah really been holding the device that could save them, all along?

He remembered Mr Chang's instructions: *The Chang Bridge must be physically interfaced with the servers of any of the Four Corners. Once this has been achieved, the rest is automatic.*

He had to get inside Ayers Rock.

Jonah ran to the land yacht in which he had travelled, the one whose catapult he had set for himself. He leapt into the catapult seat and didn't hesitate this time.

He pulled the release catch.

39

Jonah thought he might have screamed as he was catapulted into the sky. He wasn't sure. Any sound he might have made had been whipped away by the stinging wind before it could reach his ears.

When the Aboriginal driver had done this, he had made it look easy. He had been in perfect control of his body, as if he was flying. This was nothing like flying.

Jonah couldn't control his arms or legs. They were flailing about, making things even worse. He could see the top of the rock below him.

Jonah was too high, coming in too fast. He didn't stand a chance.

The lift had carried Granger up to the loading area. There, he had picked up an executive escape glider before climbing the ladder to the top of Ayers Rock. Four clusters of solar panels marred the top of Uluru. Granger looked underneath the panels, between their supporting steel girders, and scanned across the flat planes of the sun collectors.

He couldn't see anyone up here, at least no one still standing. He couldn't take any chances, though. Some of the bodies that were sprawled in the sand might still be clinging to life, and might raise the alarm if they saw him.

Granger ducked beneath an array of solar panels. He crouched down in the diffused moonlight beneath them, and pulled the glider harness onto his shoulders.

A shadow fell over him. Granger looked up, saw a dark shape in the sky between the translucent panels and the moon. A flock of cockatoos, he thought at first.

But, no, this shape was coming closer... It was plummeting towards him...

Granger flung himself aside as the solar panels exploded inwards.

He hadn't moved quite fast enough. He was struck by something soft, warm and heavy. A body, he realised. A human body. The breath was knocked out of Granger as he landed on his stomach, and the intruder landed on his back.

He threw up his hands to protect his head from a shower of glass shards.

Jonah had tried to get his feet under him. Instead, he had sent himself into a spin. The last thing he had managed to do before impact was curl up into a ball.

He had been lucky. Instead of hitting an unyielding rock surface, Jonah had crashed into and through a grid of fragile solar panels. He should still have hit the rock beneath the glass panels hard, but something had cushioned his fall.

He tested each of his limbs in turn, wiggling toes and fingers. He was smarting all over, but nothing appeared to be broken. He hoped the same could be said of the Chang Bridge device in his pocket.

Jonah heard a sickly groan. He leapt to his feet, alarmed. 'Are you OK?' he asked.

His 'cushion' was alive, doubled over in pain and cupping a hand over his face to conceal his features. As the man rose to his feet, however, Jonah caught a glint of moonlight off the man's shiny, metallic legs.

'Oh no,' Jonah gasped. 'It…it's *you*, isn't it?'

Matthew Granger sighed. There were some drawbacks to fame.

He dropped his hand from his face, to look closely at the kid who had landed on him. The Guardians were recruiting them young these days, he thought.

The kid didn't look like much: too scrawny to pose any real physical threat.

He pounced while the kid was still reeling in surprise. He grabbed hold of him, spun him around, clamped a hand to his mouth and forced him to his knees. 'I don't want to have to hurt you,' Granger hissed in the kid's ear. 'I just want to get out of here. But make the slightest sound, and I'll snap your neck!'

*

Jonah heard footsteps. Two pairs of footsteps. Then, a voice, a man's voice:

'Is anyone there?' it called. The accent was Aboriginal.

Guardians, then. They must have seen Jonah plunging through the panels. He wanted to yell out to them, but Granger's threat was still ringing in his ears.

He heard the Guardians muttering to each other. He prayed they would keep searching for him. His stomach sank as, instead, they moved away. He heard them descend the metal stairs of the access hatch.

'Very good,' whispered Granger. 'Now, all you have to do is stay still and keep quiet for another few seconds, and we'll be out of each other's hair for good.'

Granger let go of Jonah, who saw for the first time the escape glider on his captor's back. He was walking away from Jonah, his metal feet crunching on broken glass, about to fly out of here – and Jonah's first impulse was to let him go.

Another lucky break, he thought. After all the times Granger had tried to kill him…and yet, when he had had Jonah right there in his grasp, he hadn't recognised him.

But then, another sensation built inside Jonah's chest: a white-hot anger.

Why should Granger escape? Why should he fly free, live to fight another day, when so many others haven't?

Granger was approaching the edge of the rock. In

another few seconds, he'd be gone.

Not if Jonah could help it.

Granger turned around. The kid came hurtling at him, a spitting, screaming ball of fury.

He tackled Granger around the artificial legs, and for the second time the two of them fell in a tangle of limbs.

Granger wasn't a man used to fighting with his fists, but he was bigger, heavier than his opponent. He soon gained the advantage. He managed to get on top of the kid, put a titanium knee to his chest and pin his arms to the floor. 'Listen, kid,' he said, 'I meant what I said. Let me go on my way, and no one has to get—'

'No!' The kid was struggling hard. It was like trying to hold on to an octopus.

'What is it with you, anyway? What makes a kid like you join a terrorist group like the Guardians? Why would you—?'

'You,' the kid spat. 'I joined the Guardians because of you, to get back at you. You... I used to worship you. And then you took everything from me. My father. My home. *You killed my mum!*'

Jonah had fought all he could.

His outburst against Granger had drained him. His brief adrenalin rush had worked its way through his system, left him sweating and shaking.

Granger let go of Jonah's arms and stood up. He

made no move towards the edge of the rock, however. He looked down at Jonah, frowning, and Jonah wondered why he had called off his attack. Jonah pushed himself up with his feet into a sitting position. He leaned back against a girder, breathing hard, fighting back tears.

'I'm sorry,' said Granger.

Jonah was completely taken aback. 'What?'

'I said I was sorry. About your mother.'

'You didn't even know her!'

'I know that, sometimes, my desire to build a better world can lead to people getting hurt. I wish it didn't have to be that way, but—'

'It doesn't!'

'I mean what I say,' said Granger. 'I never wanted this war between the Guardians and the Millennials.'

'My mum wasn't a Guardian,' said Jonah. 'She was just…just someone who got in your way. You didn't even know her name!'

'Tell me her name,' said Granger.

And Jonah knew he shouldn't do it, should keep his mouth shut, but he couldn't help himself. All he could feel was anger and pain, and he needed to release it somehow. He wanted Granger to know, to know what he had done.

'Her name was Miriam,' he said. 'My mum was Miriam Delacroix.'

Now, it was Granger's turn to look astonished. 'Delacroix?' he repeated. 'You mean you… You're Jason's son? Did you come here with him? Is Jason here?'

Jonah shook his head. 'My dad's dead,' he said. 'He died three years ago.'

Granger just stared at Jonah, for a very long time.

Then he did the last thing Jonah would ever have expected.

Granger threw back his head and he laughed out loud.

40

Jonah scowled at Granger. 'I don't see what's so funny,' he said.

Granger wiped his eyes on his sleeve. 'A child,' he said. 'All this time, I've been chasing a *child* around the world?'

'I'm not a child,' said Jonah.

'No,' said Granger, 'of course you aren't. A child could never have come this far. You filtered your father's avatar, I assume?'

A soft night breeze played around Jonah's shoulders. The world was silent but for his own breathing and Matthew Granger's voice. They were perfectly alone up here, on the top of Ayers Rock, beneath the shattered solar panels.

'More than just his avatar, though,' said Granger. 'For you to have found this place, the Southern Corner, you must have accessed Jason's knowledge too.'

Jonah didn't say anything. He was nervous and exhausted, and beginning to fear he had said too much already.

'So,' said Granger, 'it was you who wore your father's avatar to the Icarus, with the City Tower in London as your RWL. It was you who met the Guardians in Dover.'

'I've told them everything,' Jonah lied. 'The Guardians know where all the Four Corners are, so killing me won't do you any good.'

'I don't intend to kill you, Jonah,' said Granger. 'It is Jonah, isn't it? Little Jonah Delacroix... Jason used to talk about you all the time. He was so proud.'

'Don't talk about him like that,' snapped Jonah. 'As if you were friends.'

'As far as I knew,' said Granger, 'we *were* friends.'

'Dad worked for you, that's all, and only because—'

'Because the Guardians asked him to. Yes, Jonah, I am aware of that fact now. At the time, however, your father played his part well. Perhaps too well.'

'What do you mean?'

'Jason was my pilot for almost a decade,' said Granger. 'I trusted him – I had to trust him – and, believe me, Jonah, my trust cannot be bought cheaply.'

'So?'

'So, I had your father investigated, quite thoroughly.'

'Yeah. I bet you did.'

'I sent agents into that new gift shop of his, and the Icarus – even, on occasion, into your family home. For ten years, Jason hardly took a step that I didn't know about.'

'He still managed to fool you.'

'Yes,' said Granger. 'Yes, Jonah, he did. Jason fooled us both. It must have come as a great shock to you too, to finally learn the truth about him.'

'I don't know what you—'

'I had agents in your schools too. You never gave the slightest hint of your father's true sympathies. Your loyalty towards me was quite…inspiring.'

'That…that was because…'

'It's all right, Jonah.' Granger smiled. 'I understand.'

'My dad wouldn't have… I know he wouldn't have lied to me unless…'

'I believe you,' said Granger. 'One thing I do know about your father, one thing I still trust, is that he was a good man. He did what he thought was right.'

Jonah couldn't quite believe he was having this conversation. This was the man who killed his mother, and who had tried, repeatedly, to kill him.

Many times, since his mother's death, he had imagined confronting her killer. It had never been like this. In Jonah's daydreams, Granger had been a ranting monster, boastful and unrepentant. Not calm like this.

Not thoughtful. Not reasonable. Not quite so… *persuasive…*

Jonah would have felt more comfortable with the monster.

'Your father saved my life,' said Granger. 'Did you know that?'

Jonah shook his head.

'It was on that day, that terrible day. We had landed at Heathrow. I was walking across the tarmac. Jason called me back to the plane. He said he needed my thumbprint on a requisition form. We were thrown off our feet by the first explosion.'

'He was with you when…?'

'Jason ran into the airport,' said Granger. 'He saw people trapped inside and didn't think twice. I wish I could have been as brave.'

'I wish he had been *less* brave,' Jonah muttered.

'I understand your hating me, I really do,' said Granger. 'I knew your mother. I met Miriam several times. I liked her. May I ask how she…?'

'The City Tower,' said Jonah. 'She worked in the City Tower.'

Granger nodded, gravely. 'I didn't know,' he said. 'Even if I had… Like your father, I believed I was doing what I had to do. That's on my conscience.'

Jonah turned away, biting his lip. He didn't want to hear excuses.

'What I don't understand,' said Granger, 'is your alliance with the Guardians. They bombed the airports that day, after all. They were to blame for Jason's death.'

'Not the ones I'm working with,' said Jonah.

'Is that what they told you?'

'It's the truth.'

'I suppose that is an advantage of a group without leaders. No one can ever be held responsible. The buck can always be passed.'

'They're fighting for what they believe in,' said Jonah.

'As are we all,' Granger countered, 'but tell me, Jonah – you've spent some time with Axel Kavanaugh's Guardian cell now.'

'I suppose.'

'Can you honestly say you have no doubts about their methods?'

Jonah thought about *GuerreVert* and the Russian pirates. He thought about Mr Chang.

'The Metasphere should be free,' he said, 'and the Guardians will make it free.' But he didn't sound convincing, even to himself.

'And you'll fight for that cause?' asked Granger.

'Yes.'

'You'll risk your life for it?'

'I will.'

'Kill for it?'

Jonah's throat dried.

'You might not have fired a gun yourself,' said Granger, 'but people have died tonight – Guardians and Millennials both – and you have played your part in that.'

'We...we had to do something,' stammered Jonah. 'We had to stop you from...from taking over the Metasphere.'

'And you really believe that?' asked Granger. 'You believe that the virtual world needs no organisation, no leadership? No one with a vision for its future?'

'It doesn't need you. You just want to...to tax people and tell them what to do.'

'You've seen the real world, Jonah,' said Granger. 'You've seen what happens when structures and institutions fail. People lose hope. And when that happens, it's a downward spiral with no end. Is that what you want for the Metasphere?'

'I…I don't…'

'I built the Metasphere for all of us who had lost faith in the real world. My Metasphere is a world where we can have hope again. And I think, and deep down I know you agree with me, Jonah, that it's worth fighting for.'

'Worth killing for?' Jonah whispered.

'Be careful who you judge, Jonah. In many ways, we're quite alike. We have both borne the tragic loss of our parents. We can both be single-minded, focused, even ruthless when we have to be. I'm just asking you to think again about some of your choices. I want you to be sure that every death today was worth it.'

There was a long, uneasy silence.

Matthew Granger stood, looking down at Jonah. Jonah sat with his back to the cold, hard steel girder and stared at his own hands.

Granger made the first move. He started towards the edge of the rock, and Jonah leapt to his feet with a small wail of protest.

'I can't stay here,' said Granger. 'You know that, Jonah.'

'I can't… I won't let you escape. I…I'll shout for the others.'

'If that's what you want. But think about it first, Jonah. You know they'll kill me if they catch me. The Guardians will kill me.'

Jonah wanted to scream.

'And then you'd have my death on your conscience too, Jonah,' Granger continued. 'Ask yourself, haven't we both seen enough bloodshed for one day?'

He had thought he had everything worked out, after his talk with his dad. He had known which side he was on. Now, instead, he was more confused than ever.

Jonah needed time to think, but he had to make a choice right now. He had to let his worst enemy go or be responsible for his death – because Granger was right about that much, the Guardians *would* kill him if they could. Not Sam, maybe, but the others…

'You know,' said Granger, 'there is one thing I am curious about.'

'What?' asked Jonah.

'When Jason saved my life,' said Granger, 'at Heathrow that day – did he know what he was doing? Did he know those bombs were about to go off?'

'No,' said Jonah. 'He couldn't have—'

'Of course, he wouldn't have been involved,' said Granger. 'But when the bombers targeted me, they endangered his life too. Your father was extremely important to the Guardians. Surely they would have thought to warn him about their plans?'

'You're saying... You think...?'

'I really don't know what to think,' said Granger. 'Was it just by chance that Jason called me back to my plane when he did?'

'But why...why would he...?'

'...save my life? I told you, Jonah, Jason was my pilot for a long time. I trusted him. I thought we had become friends. And, perhaps—'

'No.'

'Perhaps he had begun to feel the same way about—'

'*No!*'

'Your father died,' said Granger, 'saving the victims of Guardian bombs. That is hardly the act of a loyal follower, is it? It seems to me that, on that day, when those bombs went off...that was when Jason Delacroix thought again about *his* choices.'

Jonah could hear voices, from the direction of the entrance hatch.

'And now,' said Granger, 'I really do have to go. But we will meet again, Jonah. Until that day, I want you to think about something for me, think about it very hard. I want you to think about joining my movement.'

'What? You want me to...?'

'You are Millennial material, Jonah. Leadership material. We would make an excellent team, the two of us. We could save the world together!'

And with that, Matthew Granger turned and was gone, slipping through the maze of girders that held up

341

the solar panels like a fleeting shadow, leaving Jonah alone with a whirlwind of thoughts.

He wasn't alone for long.

Sam found him. She came running up to him, two gun-toting Guardians at her heels. 'Jonah? Jonah, is that you? Were you just talking to someone? I thought I heard…'

'He was here,' said Jonah quietly.

'Who?' asked Sam. 'Who was here?'

Jonah just looked at her. Sam frowned. Then, her eyes widened. 'Matthew Granger!' she cried.

The other two Guardians were already in motion. They raced out from under the solar panels, to the edge of the rock. Jonah heard a few gunshots. Then, the first of the Guardians returned, shaking his head. 'We were too late,' he reported. 'Granger had an escape glider. He was out of range before we could shoot him down.'

Sam rounded on Jonah. 'Why didn't you say something? Why didn't you shout for help when you heard us coming?'

Jonah shrugged helplessly. He really didn't know the answers to those questions.

'Was Granger holding you hostage?' asked Sam. 'Did he threaten you? Of course he did. I should have realised.' She sighed. 'Granger was our last hope. We needed his access codes to lower the mistwall around the Island. Without them…'

Jonah started guiltily as Sam's words reminded him what he had come here to do. He had been so caught up in his conversation with Granger, so confused, that he had almost forgotten. He reached into his pocket, pulled out the Chang Bridge.

'I had another idea,' he said. He just hoped it wasn't too late.

41

The atmosphere inside the control room was tense.

Jonah paced up and down, playing anxiously with his hands. No one had spoken in minutes. There was nothing they could do now. Nothing but wait and hope.

The Chang Bridge had been easy enough to install, as Mr Chang had promised. Jonah had opened a server panel and simply clicked the device into an available slot. Immediately, the LEDs on its front edge had begun to flash green in sequence.

Seated at a computer monitor, Sam had reported on the device's progress. 'It's building the bridge now... I'm rewriting the entrance co-ordinates...'

Sam had been reluctant to do this. She had reminded Jonah of what Axel had said, in Shanghai: *We install that device over my dead body.* Jonah had persuaded her that they had no choice. This was their only hope of saving the Uploaded. There would be time enough later to worry about the consequences.

'It's done,' said Sam. 'The bridge is complete!'

'So, what happens now?' asked Jonah.

'I wish I knew,' said Sam. 'But the Chang Bridge has penetrated the mistwall. It built itself in the sky above the Island.'

'So, the Uploaded have their escape route,' said Jonah, relieved.

Sam nodded. 'I just hope they realise it.'

'We're losing another row of servers!' someone cried, from across the room.

The Guardians all crowded around. On another screen, they could see an aerial view of a quarter of the Metasphere. Its Southern Corner. As they watched, to Jonah's dismay, the lights of a whole cluster of zones flickered and went out.

A grey stain was spreading across the virtual world. Jonah remembered the Recyclers' attacks upon the Icarus and his family's gift shop, and he knew what that grey stain was. It was destruction. It was the void.

'Do you think…?' breathed someone. 'Do you think everyone made it out?'

'They should have done,' said Sam. 'We gave them plenty of warning. I'm not worried about the living. They can take care of themselves. But the dead…'

'We have to keep the Island of the Uploaded running,' another Guardian agreed.

'For as long as possible,' said Sam. 'Whatever else we have to sacrifice. We have to give the Uploaded as much time as we can to find the bridge and get out of there.'

Jonah wandered away from the others. He had a terrible feeling of foreboding in his stomach. He sat down at a monitor, pulled up a datapad. He entered the co-ordinates of the Island of the Uploaded, of his grandmother's beach. He saw only grey mist, as before. He had expected no more than this, but still he could have wept.

Then, to Jonah's amazement, the mist cleared. Only for a second – but, in that second, he saw blue sky and yellow sand and green trees.

He leapt to his feet. 'The mistwall!' he cried. 'Of course! The mistwall is controlled by these servers too, and it's failing! We might be able to get through it! Sam…'

'Jonah, I don't know…' Sam hurried over, looked at Jonah's monitor. It was grey again. 'Even if we could… Jonah, you can't mean to go back in there.'

'I have to! You said it yourself, Sam, you know how confused the Uploaded get.'

Sam nodded. 'Of course. But—'

'And they're so used to being on the Island… They don't even think about leaving it. It's in their programming. We might have given them a way out, Sam, but I don't think they'll use it. Not unless we can tell them, show them what to do…'

'Jonah, no! The whole system could collapse while you're in there.'

'It's the only way, Sam.'

'But it's suicide!'

'Someone has to do this,' Jonah said. 'And it should be me. I caused this problem. And hey, I've beaten suicide once already.'

Sam looked at Jonah for a long time. Then, she sighed and nodded.

'OK,' she said. 'I suppose I can't talk you out of this, can I? But you're not doing it alone. No, don't argue with me, Jonah, there's no time for that. I've made up my mind too. I'm coming to the Island with you.'

They appeared in the sky, just a short way from the Island.

Sam reacted to Jonah's humatar with surprise. Of course, she hadn't seen it before; she had only seen him as the dragon. She could hardly have mistaken him for anyone else, though. Jonah looked too similar to his real-world self.

He began to explain, but Sam gave a wave of her unicorn's hoof, telling him it could wait. She beat her wings, heading for the Island, and Jonah followed her.

The cold, grey mist enveloped him as it had done before. He could barely even make out Sam, mere metres ahead of him. This wasn't going to work, he thought. The barrier was still too strong. And indeed, a moment later, he and Sam flew out of the mist cloud and the Island was behind them.

Jonah railed against this latest failure, but Sam laid a hoof on his shoulder, calming him down. She suggested they wait.

Jonah heard an ominous rumble, like thunder, and the sea beneath him trembled.

The mistwall parted, and suddenly the Island was right there in front of him, basking in the sunshine. 'Now!' Sam cried – and they dived for the shore together.

They were moving in slow motion, affected by the failing servers. Jonah thought they wouldn't make it. He expected the mist to close in, to frustrate him again.

He was elated as he touched down, kicking up sand with his heels. The beach was as crowded as always. Thousands of avatars milled about, oblivious to their peril. Some of them recognised Jonah and gathered around him. 'Are you the little humatar with the story to tell?' they asked him. 'Are you the boy who can help us to remember?'

'No,' said Jonah. 'I mean, yes. Yes, I am, but... You have to stop remembering now. Please. Listen to me. You're in danger.'

Sam tugged at Jonah's sleeve. She was floating beside him, staring upwards. Jonah followed her gaze and caught his breath.

There was a window of light in the sky.

The light was pure, white and brilliant, and Jonah had to shield his eyes against it. He could see the silhouettes of a hundred avatars. They were floating around the light, peering into it, like moths dancing around a flame. So, this was the Chang Bridge, he thought. This was how it appeared in the virtual world.

'You were right, Jonah,' said Sam. 'The Uploaded are curious about the bridge, but they aren't crossing it.'

'Listen,' Jonah addressed the avatars that were pressing in around him. 'Listen, please, all of you. You have to leave the Island. You have to—'

'Leave?'

It began as a whisper, rippling through the crowd.

'Leave the Island?'

'How can we…?'

'…can't remember the last time I…'

'…never heard such…'

The avatars of the Uploaded were looking at each other, incredulous, exchanging shrugs. Some of them were already floating away, shaking their heads.

Jonah raised his voice, desperate to get through to them. 'I know you're confused,' he said. 'Some of you have been here for a very long time. But I know you've been remembering…other places, other worlds than this one.'

He had got their attention, some of them.

'Do you know,' said a purple porcupine, 'I don't remember how long I've been here. I have quite lost track of time. Isn't that strange?'

'Strange,' a blue orb agreed.

'But quite a wonderful holiday,' chirped a yellow canary.

Jonah heard another rumble, and this time he could feel the Island shaking beneath his feet. The sky had darkened around the circle of white light, and there was a chill in the air. The Uploaded were disconcerted by the change in the weather, grumbling to each other as they drifted slowly inland in search of shelter.

They seemed to have forgotten about Jonah altogether.

'The thing is,' Sam spoke up, 'you can't stay here. You can feel what's happening, can't you? Earthquakes and storms. They're only going to get worse!'

'I know you've had a great time here,' added Jonah. 'It's been a wonderful long summer. But the summer's over now. Time to go…' He had been about to say *home*. He stopped himself. Home was the last place these avatars could go.

'Do you see that light up there?' said Sam. 'There's a whole new world on the other side of that light. A bigger, brighter world. Let us take you to it!'

She took to the air, beckoning to the Uploaded to follow her. A handful did, but hesitantly, looking back at their fellows on the ground and faltering, some of them turning back. Jonah thought the rest would turn back too, but then there came another earth tremor, stronger than the last. The sea itself reared up and sent a waist-high wave crashing towards the shore. Its tip reached Jonah, and soaked his feet.

A narrow fissure crazed its way across the beach. A bottomless, grey fissure.

The Uploaded were more than disconcerted now. Many of them had floated up into the sky, thinking it safer up there. 'That's right,' shouted Jonah, taking full advantage of their uncertainty, 'follow Sam. Head into the light!'

Slowly, painfully slowly, it was beginning to work. The avatars of the Uploaded were beginning to obey him. Sam gathered as large a flock as she could, then she led it towards the Chang Bridge. Jonah followed at the rear, chivvying along the stragglers. And, as they flew, something wonderful happened. More and more Uploaded avatars streamed towards them and swelled their ranks.

Jonah heard some of them talking. 'What's happening?' they asked.

'Where are we going?'

But no one could answer those questions. Everyone was just following somebody else, caught up in the flock's sense of purpose.

Sam had reached the Chang Bridge now. Jonah couldn't look at her without being dazzled by the circle of light behind her. She floated in that light, and ushered the Uploaded past her. For a moment, Jonah feared they wouldn't go. But, one by one, they were swallowed up by the light, and disappeared. And the more avatars went into the light, the more eager the rest were to follow them.

They were coming from all over now, from the beaches and the forests and the valleys, like millions of iron filings being drawn towards a powerful magnet. It was working. For the first time ever, the Uploaded were leaving the Island.

But there were two more people Jonah still had to save.

42

Jonah found his father's avatar inland, in the forest, close to where he had left him.

'You found me,' said Jason Delacroix. 'I knew you'd find me.'

'What are you still doing here, Dad?'

'It's so good to see you, son.'

'We've got to get you out of here. The Island is collapsing and—'

'I've been doing what I can. I've been spreading this story of yours.'

'I know,' said Jonah. 'I know you have, Dad. And you did really well. But you have to stop now. I need you to follow the others out of here.'

'I've been telling them to remember.'

'I know. Please, Dad...'

'But the earthquakes... It's so hard to concentrate with all these earthquakes. I've been trying to remember... There was something I had to tell you.'

'And there are things I need to ask you too, but they can wait.'

The sky had turned pitch-black. The Island had begun to shake constantly. Grey fault lines were spreading everywhere, disintegrating chunks of ground where they crisscrossed. Jonah had to be careful not to touch them, in case the damage spread to him. He saw a tree beginning to depixelate by his shoulder, and he leapt away from it.

Sam flew up behind Jonah. She eyed the red dragon avatar in front of him. 'You found him,' she said. 'I'm glad. But, Jonah…'

'I know,' said Jonah. 'Dad, I need you to do something for me. Something else.'

'Of course, son. If I can.'

'That white light in the sky. I need you to fly into it, Dad. Like the others. Follow the other avatars.'

'Can't I just stay here with you, Jonah?'

'I'll find you again, Dad, I promise. I'll find you on the other side, where it's safe and we can be together.'

'Just like old times,' said Jason Delacroix.

'Just like old times,' repeated Jonah, wishing it was true, wishing he didn't have to lie. He knew that nothing would ever be like it was. But this version of his father, this confused Uploaded avatar, was better than having no dad at all. 'Now go. Fly!'

Jason spread his dragon's wings and flew off, towards the light. Towards the bridge. Jonah watched him go, until he felt Sam tugging at his arm with her teeth.

'We have to go now too,' she said.

'Not yet,' said Jonah. 'I still have to find Nan.'

'There isn't time!'

But Jonah was already flying headlong through the

forest, towards the shore, towards the part of the Island he knew best. His grandmother's beach.

'She'll have left already,' insisted Sam, at his heels. 'Almost everyone has left.'

'But what if she hasn't? What if she's confused? What if Nan is still looking for people to help remember, like Dad was? What if...?'

The beach was just ahead of them. Jonah could hear the sea, lapping against the shore, but there was something odd about the sound. It was on a loop, he realised, repeating itself endlessly. He flew out from between the trees, but came up short.

There *was* no sea, and no shore. There was nothing at all in front of him. Nothing but the void. And he had almost flown right into it.

Sam screamed his name. She tackled Jonah, pushing him with her horn. Another section of the Island crumbled underneath him, and around him. The void had taken a great bite out of the forest now, too. Jonah saw grey pixels spreading up his arm, and cried out in alarm. Fortunately, his terminal, back in the Southern Corner, was able to refresh his avatar. This time.

'We have to go,' said Sam, and this time Jonah didn't argue with her.

They flew straight up. The air was icy cold now. The sun had gone. Without the bright white light from the Chang Bridge opening, they would have been lost.

Jonah watched numbly as, bathed in that light, the Island of the Uploaded sank at last into the sea. Within seconds, it was gone completely, with barely a ripple to show where it had once stood. Then, the sea itself began to disintegrate.

Jonah spotted a final few avatars escaping the destruction, fleeing towards the light. He strained to make out their shapes, hoping to see an elephant among them.

Sam prodded him with her horn again, and ushered him away from there.

They flew as hard and as fast as they could. Jonah had never missed the red dragon avatar and its powerful wings more. Sam was faster than he was, but she kept slowing down for him, concerned about leaving him behind.

The greyness was spreading across the dark sky, like storm clouds gathering, only these storm clouds were without any depth or texture. They were clouds of nothingness, and they were closing in rapidly around Jonah and Sam.

Sam's movements had become slow, jerky. She turned her head towards Jonah, and left a temporary frozen image of her forward-facing self behind. Her voice was time-delayed and slurred: 'We arennnnn't going to mmmmmake it-it-it-it-it!'

There were flecks of grey in Sam's white hide and her red mane.

Jonah tried to shout to her, '*Leave me behind. Save yourself!*' All that came out was the first syllable, stuttered over and over. It was too late, anyway.

They could see the pinprick lights of their exit halos, hovering in mid-air in the distance, too far away. They watched in horror as the grey clouds engulfed them.

They looked at each other helplessly. Their exit halos, their gateways back to the real world, were gone. They were trapped here now, trapped in this doomed quarter of the Metasphere. Unless...

Jonah commanded his inventory space to open. It took an age to respond, but at last it did. He reached in, frantically, felt for one particular item. Mr Peng's cat statuette. It had snapped shut, and Jonah had to try to remember how his teacher had opened it. His questing fingers found tiny pressure plates in the cat's neck and shoulders, and he prodded and pushed at these until the two-faced head popped open.

Sam looked at Jonah, quizzically. Jonah tried to explain, tried to tell Sam to hold on to the statuette with him, but he couldn't speak at all now. He took hold of one of her hooves and dragged it slowly – maddeningly slowly – to the button in the cat's neck. He just prayed this would work with two of them.

He placed his hand on top of Sam's hoof, and they pressed the button together.

They appeared in the mountain temple.

Jonah took a deep breath, closed his eyes and rode out the expected wave of nausea. It took Sam a little longer to pull herself together, which at least gave Jonah a moment to look over both himself and Sam and confirm that their avatars were intact.

'Where are we?' asked Sam.

'I don't know exactly,' said Jonah. 'This is where I met Mr Chang.'

'Oh,' said Sam. She seemed uncomfortable to be here.

'Coming here, it was the only way I could think of to—'

'I know.' Sam smiled. 'That was good thinking, Jonah. You saved our lives.'

'Did you see, though?' said Jonah. 'Our exit halos…'

'I saw. We'll have to get a message to the control room at Ayers Rock. Someone there will have to hack into our terminals and create new halos for us. But, Jonah?'

'Yeah?'

'There's no door,' said Sam, starting to panic. 'No exit from this room.'

Jonah nodded. 'Behind that tapestry over there.'

'Right. You had me worried there.'

'You, worried?' laughed Jonah. 'The girl who just took on the Millennials and won?'

Sam started towards the tapestry, but Jonah hung back.

'You want to wait for Mr Chang?' Sam guessed.

'I thought we should at least explain to him what

we're doing in his temple.'

'How did you contact him last time?'

'I didn't,' said Jonah. 'He just… I think the statuette must tell him when it brings someone here.' He looked behind the bamboo screen from which Mr Chang's coiled dragon avatar had appeared before. There was nothing there.

'Perhaps he's busy,' said Jonah.

'Could be,' agreed Sam. 'Or perhaps…'

'What? Perhaps what?'

'We did what Mr Chang wanted. We installed his device in the Southern Corner. There's a permanent bridge now between the Metasphere and this new virtual world of his, the Changsphere. Mr Chang doesn't need us any more.'

Jonah said nothing. He was weary of trying to second-guess people's motives, of trying to work out who he could trust and who was lying to him.

He took one last look around the mountain temple, until he was satisfied that – for whatever reason – Mr Chang wasn't coming. Then he turned and, with a sigh, he followed Sam through the tapestry and out of that place.

43

It was the biggest news story in years:

ONE QUARTER OF THE METASPHERE LOST.
HUNDREDS OF AVATARS MISSING, PRESUMED DELETED.
MATTHEW GRANGER BLAMES GUARDIANS FOR
METASPHERE CRASH.

Granger was, in fact, appearing on countless news programmes, ensuring that his version of events reached the widest possible audience.

A different story emerged from Mr Chang, however – or rather, from his spokespeople; as the young entrepreneur remained hidden in the shadows as usual.

Chang Corp's take on the crash was that it proved the folly of giving one man too much power. They said it was Matthew Granger's hubris that had led to this disaster. Chang Corp claimed the credit for the saving of the Uploaded, and invited everyone to join them in their new and more efficient Changsphere.

Granger was furious, of course. He accused Mr Chang of stealing his proprietary software, and of wanting nothing less than total power for himself.

Meanwhile, reports of casualties were still coming in. Fortunately, they were few in number, thanks to Sam's evacuation of the affected zones. Still, a lot of people had lost a lot of meta-dollars in the crash. They wanted compensation from someone.

Some were saying they were afraid to go back into the Metasphere now. What if more servers failed, they asked? What if there was no warning next time?

Many took up Chang Corp on their offer. Settlers began to move their families, their businesses, their whole online lives to the Changsphere.

At the edge of the Metasphere – its new edge – there was an aching grey void. But, in the heart of that void, visible for miles around, a window of pure white light shone. In increasing numbers, avatars were flying across the void, into that light. They were seeking a new world of safety and security. And the Changsphere was ready to accommodate them.

Jonah followed these events on a monitor, in his bunkroom, inside Ayers Rock. Sometimes, he had to pinch himself to be sure he wasn't dreaming.

Everyone was talking about what he had done. Oh, sure, they hadn't mentioned him by name. They didn't know what he looked like.

But Jonah knew. He knew the part he had played in recent events.

When he had filtered his father's avatar, those few

short weeks ago in the gift shop cellar, he couldn't have imagined it would lead to this.

Jonah was just a poor nobody from a Clapham Common bus-flat. He had just been trying to stay alive – and yet somehow, in the process, he had changed the world.

It was a very odd feeling.

Three days after the taking of the Southern Corner, amid the clean up at Uluru, Sam got a lead from a Guardian contact, and she and Jonah plugged themselves into the Metasphere to visit a virtual fairground.

The fairground boasted re-creations of the world's greatest rollercoasters. It all seemed a little old hat to Jonah, who was used to greater thrills. Still, the rides were popular with the older generation.

At the end of a long pier, beside a candyfloss stand, they found two familiar avatars: a gryphon and a Clydesdale horse.

'There they are,' said Sam.

Axel and Bradbury were hovering aimlessly, mindlessly, gazing out to sea. Sam ran up to her father, threw her front legs around him in relief. He looked right through her.

'Dad, it's me, Sam,' she said. Jonah could sense the tears behind her trembling voice. 'We found you.'

They led the disconnected avatars away from the pier. Axel and Bradbury came willingly, but Jonah and Sam had to keep a close eye on them to keep them from forgetting where they were and wandering off again.

They flew all day, Sam dragging her father and Jonah pushing Bradbury. Jonah grew tired – mentally tired – and worried that his real-world body hadn't eaten, but Sam wouldn't hear of them taking a break for any reason.

At last, they reached the virtual city of Neo Tokyo, where their charges had entered the Metasphere three days ago.

Jonah and Sam searched the skies above the neon streets until two exit halos glowed, beckoning Axel and Bradbury back to the real world. Sam nudged her father towards his halo.

'Please wake up, Dad,' she said, and she kissed Axel softly on his forehead before she pushed him through the ring of light. The halo swallowed him and disappeared. Jonah then gave Bradbury an almighty shove into his halo, leaving Sam and Jonah hovering in the sky together, waiting for news from the real world.

'Thank you, Jonah,' she said.

'For what?' asked Jonah. He felt he was just doing what anyone would do for a best friend.

'For never giving up. Ever.'

The news came, at last, in the form of a pop-up addressed to Sam. Jonah couldn't see the private message, but he saw Sam's reaction as she read it. He put his arms around the unicorn avatar's neck and hugged her tightly as she cried with relief.

'They're all right!' she said, regaining her composure. 'Captain Teng says they woke up in his bunkhouse a few minutes ago, confused and hungry but with no brain damage.'

Jonah was delighted for her. For the past few days, Sam had looked as if she was carrying a great weight around on her shoulders. Now, she was smiling again. He had missed seeing her smile.

'They're on their way from Sydney in a land yacht,' said Sam. 'They should be with us in two days.' She darted forward and, before Jonah knew what she was doing, she had planted a quick kiss on his cheek. He wasn't sure, but he thought that maybe his avatar was blushing.

Axel and Bradbury weren't the only Guardians en route to Ayers Rock.

They arrived in dribs and drabs over the next few days, from all over Australia and in some cases from beyond. Some of them were fighters, pledged to defend the Southern Corner from any Millennial attempt to recapture it. Others were technicians and engineers, who set about repairing the damaged servers.

Axel and Bradbury joined them, as scheduled, on the evening of the second day. Sam raced across the red sand to greet her father, who jumped out of his land yacht and ran to meet her. Axel picked up Sam and swung her around.

'I'm sorry I got lost, kiddo,' he said.

'But we found you,' said Sam.

Axel was like a kid at Christmas, too excited to keep still. He insisted on touring the facility inside Uluru, and on hearing the story of its capture three or four times.

'The Southern Corner,' he kept saying to himself, with a broad grin on his face. 'I'm inside the Southern Corner. I can't believe it!'

One time, he even ruffled Jonah's hair and said, 'And it's all down to our secret weapon here. Jason's little boy. Who'd have thought it?'

Jonah didn't want to take any credit. Granger's words still played on his conscience: *I'm just asking you to think again about some of your choices… We would make an excellent team, the two of us.*

'It was Sam who led the attack,' he mumbled.

'And a brilliant job she did of it too,' said Axel, with a wink in his daughter's direction. 'Well done, kiddo. A real chip off the old block!'

Bradbury was less effusive with his praise. He reminded Axel that not everything had gone according to plan. Granger still controlled the three other corners.

'And what exactly did happen on the Island?' he challenged. 'Why was the Chang Bridge installed at all?'

The answers made him scowl, and Jonah felt as if

Bradbury was blaming him personally for everything that had gone wrong.

Axel, however, was not to be disheartened. 'So, Mr Chang has his new world up and running,' he said. 'Who cares? The Changsphere might be flavour of the month right now, but people will soon see it's just the same old same old.'

'Maybe,' said Bradbury, doubtfully.

'Definitely,' said Axel. 'Once they have a choice, between another dictatorship and a Metasphere that's free and open...'

'We're a long way from that,' Sam reminded him.

'We're a quarter of the way there,' said Axel, 'and we still have our secret weapon.' He turned to Jonah, slapped him on the back. 'How about it, kid? You found us one of the Four Corners. You reckon you can find us the other three?'

They rebooted the Southern Corner the next morning.

The control room was packed with Guardians, poised with baited breath over rows of blank monitor screens. At Axel's nod, Sam flicked the switch, and Jonah felt vibrations from the servers beneath him thrumming through the floor.

Five seconds passed, ten, and then the monitors began to light up one by one.

At first, only white lines appeared on them, snaking across grey backgrounds, but then those white lines intersected and began to form the skeletons of shapes, and those shapes were filled with colours and after that textures.

Soon enough, Jonah was looking at cities and forests and oceans and deserts, and his ears were ringing with the cheers of his Guardian allies.

They hadn't been able to bring everything back. Some of the data on the hard drives was badly corrupted. Still, about ninety-eight per cent of the Southern Corner's lost infrastructure had been restored – and it was safely out of Granger's control.

Jonah's gaze lingered on one particular screen, at the familiar image of the Island of the Uploaded. With the sun shining upon it and the sea lapping its shores, it looked like the paradise it had always been. But the Island was empty now, of course.

In the sky above the Island, white light still streamed from the opening to the Changsphere. Bradbury thought he might be able to close that opening, using Mr Chang's device, but Axel talked him down.

'I don't like it any more than you do,' he said, 'but right now the Chang Bridge isn't just a way out of the Metasphere, it's also the path back. We have to keep it open.'

Axel had brought something with him from Sydney: a bottle of sparkling wine. Jonah couldn't imagine how he might have come by it without spending a fortune. Axel handed paper cups around the room, and poured a splash of wine into each of them until the bottle ran dry. Then he lifted his own cup and proposed a toast.

'To the Guardians,' said Axel. 'To victory. To freedom!'

'*Freedom!*' the assembled Guardians chorused.

Jonah didn't enjoy his wine. It had a bitter aftertaste to it, and the fizz went up his nose. Anyway, he wasn't sure he had much cause for celebration.

He had helped the Guardians seize control of the Southern Corner. Without him, they would still be searching for it.

In the process, he had caused the biggest disaster the Metasphere had ever seen. He had almost wiped out the Uploaded, and had stood by as scores of people had died in the real world.

And he had lost his home, and his mum.

And this was only the beginning of the metawars.

I'm just asking you to think again about some of your choices.

Granger had been so sure of himself, convinced he was right. He had presented his case not emotionally but with cold, hard logic. And, when faced with those logical arguments, Jonah had been unable to counter them. He still couldn't.

What Granger had said – about the Metasphere needing structure, organisation and vision – that was what Jonah had believed for most of his life. But then, he believed in freedom too. He believed in Sam and in Axel, and in what they stood for.

Yes, Jonah Delacroix had changed the world.

He only wished he knew if he had changed it for the better or for the worse.

Epilogue

On a mountaintop in the Changsphere, a family reunion was taking place.

The air up here was cold, crisp and clean. The scenery was spectacular, so many colours and textures. Rivers chuckled through the valleys between the mountains, towards the gleaming spires of great cities on the horizon. The elephant avatar unfurled her great trunk and trumpeted for joy.

The red dragon avatar kissed the elephant on her wrinkled forehead. Then he wrapped his wings around the wiry humatar with the freckles and the tuft of dark hair, and the humatar laughed and told the dragon and the elephant that he loved them.

They didn't notice the storm clouds gathering in the sky.

The three avatars were being watched, being stalked, by a kestrel called Joshua.

Hovering behind a threatening grey cloud, the kestrel avatar glared at them, with hunger burnin in his heart. A hunger for life.

The bird of prey could sense life and began to remember... Events from before the Island.

He remembered the doctor standing over his bed, so sombre, and the smell of the hospital ward. Another building: austere on the outside but comfortable inside, with leather couches and organ music playing. There had been some forms to thumbprint, and then...then, he had lain down on one of the couches and plugged himself in, and the pain in his bones had gone away.

Joshua remembered a sea journey taken alone, and thinking how unfair it was that this day had come so soon, before he could find someone to share it with him.

He wanted more than this, more than the half-life he had been living.

And that was what the humatar had, Joshua realised. He had what had been cruelly taken from the kestrel, and from all who had resided on the Island of the Uploaded.

The humatar was *alive*. And the kestrel wanted – no, he *hungered* for – that life.

And he was going to take it.

1

Jonah Delacroix loved to fly.

He spread his arms wide and pushed his toes together. He swooped low over the sprawling new digital city of Changhai. The warm wind against his face was virtual, but the thrill in his stomach was real.

In the bustling streets below him, buildings pixelated into existence and throngs of avatars populated this brave new world. Behind each avatar was a real person whose brain interfaced directly with the internet, generating a digital representation of the user.

Jonah lived most of his waking life inside the virtual world called the Metasphere. In this, he wasn't unusual. Most people had gone *meta*.

But now, the Metasphere had a rival.

This fast-growing new world that Jonah soared above was called the Changsphere, and it was drawing avatars from the Metasphere with its higher-resolution graphics, faster servers and infectious sense of optimism. To Jonah, the Metasphere – with its rich 3D rendering and sharp, lifelike recreation of all five senses – had always seemed more real than the crumbling real world. Inside the Changsphere, however, everything seemed richer and sharper still.

One of the things Jonah loved about the virtual world was the sheer diversity of avatars. They took all shapes and sizes, from the familiar to the ridiculous. As he soared, he saw a cat riding an elephant. On the city streets below him, he spotted a chimpanzee selling apps to a raptor, and a shark strolling on two legs. He noticed two translucent triangles (one isosceles and one equilateral) pulsing as they bickered, and a mallard duck parading three ducklings behind it.

Suddenly, an unsettling thought occurred to Jonah. He wasn't sure if those avatars below did, in fact, have a real person behind them. They could, for all he knew, be dead.

In the Metasphere of old, some users chose to Upload themselves, digitising all of their memories and storing them in their avatar. They would live on in the virtual world, in a state of ignorant bliss, confined to a specific island, the Island of the Uploaded. The uploading process, however, killed the user; every Uploaded avatar had committed suicide to get there. But in return they were immortal. Immortal, but not indestructible.

The server farm that stored their memories had almost crashed, and in the nick of time, Jonah had led the millions of Uploaded avatars into the light of the new Changsphere world, where they were now roaming free among the living. For Jonah it was a miracle that the dead could come back to life – or at least a digital life.

Jonah had opened the portal between the worlds two months ago. Looking down, it was hard to believe that back then Changhai had been nothing but a digital grid, zoned for development. In fact, this entire world had only recently come into existence.

Jonah wasn't alone in the sky. He flew past a silver, five-pointed star and nodded his head. 'Good morning.'

'It certainly is in here,' the star replied.

Jonah caught a glimpse of his avatar in the star's reflection. He looked just like his real-world self, gangly with an unruly tuft of dark hair. But what struck Jonah more than anything was how lifelike he looked. The graphics here were so sharp that he could have sworn he was looking into a mirror in the real world, and not at a digital reflection.

Thousands of new settlers were arriving in the Changsphere every day. They were buying up virtual plots of virtual land, building homes and businesses and moving their entire online lives here. Jonah shared the optimism of these virtual pioneers as they explored their new surroundings. But to Jonah, the Changsphere represented more than a second chance. It was the one place where his father was still alive.

But not everyone was happy.

Below Jonah, a demonstration was taking place in Changhai Square. He hovered high above to see what the commotion was about. *Why would anyone be unhappy here?* he wondered.

About a hundred avatars had gathered and their angry voices drifted up to him:

'Boycott the Changsphere!'

'Don't support terrorism!'

'Hand back the Southern Corner!'

Jonah felt a surge of anger. *They don't know what they're talking about!* he thought. Part of him wanted to fly down there and argue with them, but he was outnumbered a hundred to one and he knew his voice would be drowned out. Besides, he was on his way to see his Uploaded father.

'Hand back the Southern Corner! Don't support terrorism!'

David Foster grinned to himself. This was going well.

He had started with just a few hardcore Millennials – his own people – but the flash mob he had whipped up had soon gone viral and attracted more supporters through the main portal.

A mangy blue hyena flew into the air and cackled, *'Death to the Guardians! Down with Mr Chang!'*

David waddled through the crowd, urging the protestors to get angrier, to shout louder. In the virtual worlds, David took the form of an emperor penguin. He would rather have been a more imposing avatar like a bird of prey, but it was a cruel quirk of Direct Interface, the method of connecting the brain to the virtual world, that the user did not choose his avatar. The subconscious mind generated the avatar, and the conscious mind just had to live with it.

With a little more prodding, he thought, *I can get these dupes to riot, and perhaps Mr Granger will finally promote me out of Anti-Virus.*

'That's right,' he yelled, 'let 'em know what we think of their Changsphere!'

But something was wrong. The crowd was actually growing *quieter*. Some of the demonstrators had clammed up completely and were staring at the sky. It was difficult for David, as a penguin, to look up, but he strained to follow their gazes.

Another group of avatars had arrived, about twenty of them. They were hovering above the demonstrators' heads, and they didn't look like they had come to join in. One of the newcomers, a zebra with neon green and black stripes, looked down at David and spat, 'If you don't like it here, then waddle back to the Metasphere.'

A few of his demonstrators floated up to the newcomers' level, but David remained warily on the ground. He had lit the spark of protest and wanted to see how fast his fire would spread.

The hyena squared up to the zebra. 'We'll leave,' it hissed, 'as soon as Mr Chang gives back the quarter of the Metasphere his Guardian friends stole!'

'You'll leave now,' said the zebra, 'or we'll make you sorry!'

'Oh, yeah? There are more of us than there are of

you. Who are you, anyway? I'll bet you're Guardians yourselves.'

'Guardian terrorist scum!' cried David, and five more protesters took up the shout and lifted off to square up to the newcomers.

'The Guardians saved us,' said the zebra. 'They led us into the Changsphere when our Island was destroyed. So, we won't let you—'

The hyena suddenly turned from affronted to afraid. 'You're…Uploaded?'

It cowered away from the zebra as a whisper of fear wove through the demonstrators: *'Uploaded!'*

David felt a shiver too. He thought it was unnatural, unholy. The dead shouldn't be allowed to roam among the living. *I can't even tell them apart from us*, he thought.

He knew he had to do something. His flash mob was on the verge of dissipating, losing its nerve. He yelled up at the newcomers, 'These are matters for the living, not the dead! You have no say! You have no rights!'

He wasn't sure who had struck the first blow, but the standoff exploded into a brawl. The blue hyena shrieked and clawed at the zebra. A giant, fat leech – an Uploaded – sprang onto a protesting minotaur's head with an audible slurp.

This is golden, David told himself. *This'll get us on the big video blogs for sure, maybe even onto Bryony's vlog—*

A gasp went up from all around him. Half the Uploaded avatars had broken away from the others and were dive-bombing the people on the ground.

A vampire bat swooped down on a slow-moving cow and sank its claws into its shoulders. At first, the cow was more irritated than afraid, but it kicked and thrashed as it was lifted into the air. It succeeded in breaking free, but only for a second. The bat was on the cow's back before it could fly away, and its mouth opened wide… and *kept* on opening…

David stared in horror at the bat. Its mouth was now as wide as its prey was big – even wider – and in a swift, angry motion, it jabbed its little head forward and gulped the startled cow down whole. The bovine avatar disappeared completely into the Uploaded bat.

David couldn't believe what he was seeing. It was impossible. He watched helplessly as his protesters scattered half blindly. The Uploaded stalked them with their mouths gaping open. David didn't wait to see if any more were caught and devoured.

He had to get out of here before the Uploaded came after him!

He turned and flew along the street. He beat his flippers as hard as he could, gaining height until he could see the shiny new shopping mall, where inside he had parked his exit halo. It wasn't far away. He was going to make it. But then David Foster made one fatal mistake.

He looked back.

A quick glance over his shoulder. It was enough.

A hulking green caterpillar slammed into him, sending him reeling into the claws of a waiting kestrel that snatched him and dropped him onto a nearby rooftop. As David struggled in the bird's fierce grip, three more Uploaded landed around him: the caterpillar, the leech he had seen before and their leader, the zebra.

'Where are you waddling off to, little penguin-man?' the zebra sneered. 'We're just getting started.'

'Let me have him, Suki,' the leech pleaded in a sucking, slurping voice. 'I'm so hungry.'

'Please, leave me alone,' David cried. 'I was just passing by.'

'You're their ringleader,' said the zebra in an accusing tone.

'No, I'm not,' wailed David. 'I swear, I'm not. I was just—'

'You were right, what you said,' said the zebra. 'We are dead, but you, you have life.'

'Let me have him, Suki.' The leech was straining forward, saliva drooling from its mouth. 'I wouldn't waste his life like he has.'

The zebra shook its head. 'No.'

Thank God, thought David. 'Th-thank you,' he stammered. 'Thank you. I—'

'Joshua caught him,' said the zebra. 'He should have him.'

'No!' cried David. 'No, please, you can't! No, *please*!'

The kestrel had let go of him, but the Uploaded

avatars had David surrounded. There was nothing he could do. Nothing but tremble as the bird of prey hovered over him, its beady eyes fixed upon him. It flexed its little sharp beak and with a crack of bone, dislodged its jaw and opened its beak.

'I'm so hungry,' said the kestrel in an old man's voice.

David could feel the kestrel's hot breath on his face.

The kestrel lunged at him. David screamed as it opened its ever-expanding beak around him, and he found himself plunging into a deep, dark abyss.

High above the fray, Jonah looked down in confusion. An Uploaded bat had ingested a cow and then a kestrel had swallowed a penguin. He didn't understand what was happening. Where did they go?

The only way out of the virtual world was through a user's unique exit halo. *Perhaps the bat has also swallowed the cow's halo*, Jonah thought, hopefully. So far, none of the brawling avatars had taken any notice of him hovering high in the sky, but he knew he shouldn't stay, just in case things escalated.

As he flew on, he was torn about what to do. He knew he should reveal to the Guardians and Mr Chang what he had seen, but he didn't fully understand it himself. If the Uploaded were turning violent, Jonah worried that all of them could be banished. He couldn't take that risk. He'd just got his father back.

He would do anything not to lose him again.